Praise for the works of Lori

#CassiNova

Lori G. Matthews had me laughing in public—exactly what I needed in these stressful times. She completely sucked me in! The characters were almost familiar, like friends I already have. The romance felt real, and I never doubted the motives behind Sam and Alex's actions. I spent many years so hungry for representation that I'd read anything you threw at me, but I'm happy to say this book set the bar so much higher for me. A flirty, fun romp through Hollywood.

-MJ's Reviews, *Bookshop Santa Cruz*

#CassiNova is such a fun read. I pictured this title making its way into my beach bag for a fun, upbeat read in the sunshine. The language is trendy and at times edgy, giving the book a youthful, modern Hollywood vibe. The slow burn romance is tempered with humor that keeps the pace until the romance peaks. Keeping with great timing, there are also well written genuine and sincere moments. *#CassiNova* is a cute, funny, light read. I'd recommend it for any of my friends looking for a sweet, easygoing RomCom.

-*The Lesbian Review*

Delightfully funny. I read this with a grin and outright laughter. I will look for future books from the author.

-Kaye C., *NetGalley*

Omg, this was an amazing, funny and sweet book. You will laugh and cry and laugh some more. The main characters are meant for each other from the first meet. They are both goofy, with ideas out of this world. They make their relationship hot, and happy and don't stop playing around. It looks so easy when you read this one and you root for their happy ending. Excellent book in my opinion.

-Kat W., *NetGalley*

I Dare You to Love Me

Other Bella Books by Lori G. Matthews

#CassiNova

About the Author

Lori G. Matthews lives outside of Philadelphia with her wife and two cats. Her first brush with literary fame came at the age of thirteen when her composition, an amusing tale told from the perspective of a soccer ball, was the only one read aloud by her teacher. To this day, she still loves to write lighthearted comedies because laughter truly is the best medicine. When she's not writing, Lori plays ice hockey, hikes, bikes, and bird-watches. But her favorite place to be is on the golf course, where she's proudly earned the nickname Long and Wrong.

I Dare You to Love Me

Lori G. Matthews

BELLA
B O O K S
2022

Bella Books, Inc.
P.O. Box 10543
Tallahassee, FL 32302

Printed in the United States of America on acid-free paper.

First Edition - 2022

Editor: Heather Flournoy
Cover Designer: Heather Honeywell

ISBN: 978-1-64247-389-6

PUBLISHER'S NOTE

Acknowledgments

I'd first like to thank Bella Books for all their support and for believing in me and this story. Also, thanks to my editor Heather Flournoy. On our first zoomie, Heather said, "I laughed—" Upon hearing "laughed," I immediately zoned out, thinking, "Yes! I made my editor laugh!" I have no clue what she said after that. She might've said, "I laughed at my cats this morning before reading your manuscript and it put me in a good mood, thank God, because you added an "s" to every forward, backward, and afterward and I must've corrected it a thousand times." Thank you, Heather!

To my buddy Elizabeth in Seattle, thank you E. She had been working at a doggie daycare, and always had a funny story about the dogs. One day we were texting, and I said, "I should write a story about this." The rest, as they say, is history.

Thanks to Lisa M, my wingman, who would read a chapter and throw out a funny idea, saying, "Run with it." Thank you to my biggest supporter, Ana W. She's always propping up my fragile writing ego, which must be exhausting. Thank you to my beta readers, fellow GCLS Writing Academy alums Nan Campbell and Cade Haddock Strong. Thank you to McGee Mathews for providing sensitivity reading. Thank you to my buddy Rita Potter, who provided and still provides much inspiration. She'll email me and say, "My goal is to write 30k words this weekend!" I'm like, "My goal is to not shank my golf ball into the woods this weekend." Hm. Priorities?

Another big shout out to Connie from Ireland. Connie had reached out to me via Twitter after reading my first novel #Cassinova, and we became Twitter mates. She literally came up with the title for this book, because book titling is not my strong suit. She probably was also responsible for jacking up my #Cassinova sales for a few months with all her re-tweets. Thank you, Connie!

To all my instructors at the GCLS Writing Academy, I know your dedication and encouragement made this story better.

Thank you. One of the greatest things about the academy is getting a mentor at the end of the year who will take the time to read your manuscript and offer insights and helpful advice. Mentors are current sapphic authors with loads of experience. My mentor was Susan X. Meagher, author of over forty novels. I would call that experience, wouldn't you? We spoke on the phone several times, and she gave me some wonderful suggestions.

Much love to my wife, Tara, who has been putting up with me for well over twenty years. Bless her heart, poor thing. And lastly, thank you to my cats, Jasper and Andre, for allowing me to live in their house, rent free. Well, maybe not rent free. They do demand Fancy Feast. And all empty Amazon boxes must be left on the living room floor for months and months, because "cats dig boxes." Thank you, boys!

CHAPTER ONE

A growl. A hiss. A swat.

The house on Edgehill Street near downtown Seattle had been quiet, but now the dog and cat moved around the room like gladiators, poking and prodding, each looking for a weakness in the other. When the orange, long-haired tabby jumped to higher ground, the golden retriever grew frustrated and grabbed a pillow from the chair, shaking it back and forth. When that wasn't good enough, he placed both of his paws on it and ripped at the fabric with his mouth. And continued ripping until stuffing floated around the room like snowflakes.

"Oh my God." Danielle Clark shot up from her seat at the dining room table and made a grab for what was left of the pillow. "No, no. Let me have it." After a minute of scuffling around the room with their new addition to the family, Dani held up tattered remnants of the pillow to Jinx the cat. "Well. Another one bites the dust. That's two in the last three hours. How can something so cute be so...destructive?"

Jinx appeared equally flummoxed and did what any self-respecting cat would do when faced with such an existential question. He licked his butt.

Dani collapsed back into the chair. *I'm so not ready for a dog.* With a deep breath to calm her fraying nerves, she continued typing patient notes into her laptop.

Will had brought the dog home last night. Someone at his office had rescued it from the Seattle Animal Shelter but couldn't keep it. After a lively discussion on whether they should adopt the dog, and against her better judgment, Dani had relented.

Jinx took a flying leap onto the dining room table and stretched out, willing to supervise Dani now that his annoying adversary was digging at some imaginary spot on the carpet. From time to time, his meaty kitty paw would punch the keyboard and a series of letters would scroll across the screen.

"I don't think Mrs. Duncan will agree with your diagnosis."

He gave a soft mewl and rolled onto his back, placing both paws on the screen.

Dani scratched him under the chin. "Don't you have someplace to be? Aren't there birds to stalk?"

She squeezed her eyes shut as loud barking echoed around the room. The dog had grown bored with the carpet and was now busy chasing Jinx's twitching tail that dangled from the table.

With teeth bared, Jinx voiced his displeasure.

The family fun was interrupted by the buzz of Dani's phone. It was her bestie. "Hey, Zoe."

"Jesus Christ, turn your TV down. What are you watching, *101 Dalmatians*?"

"That's not the TV. It's our dog."

"A dog? When did you get a dog?"

Dani sighed. "Last night. Will brought him home."

"What's his name?"

"We haven't decided. Will's trying to come up with the perfect name."

"You don't sound happy."

Dani rubbed her temples. "I have no idea how we're gonna take care of a dog with our schedules."

"Tell him it's you or the dog."

In jest, Dani said, "He'd probably choose the dog."

"Good."

Dani frowned, regretting her quip because Zoey had never approved of the match. It was a battle they waged every so often, Zoey begging Dani to wait for true love to sweep her off her feet, and Dani defending her decisions. "We're engaged, maybe you should accept it."

"You've been engaged for three years."

"It's hard to find time to have a wedding."

"Or…you don't want to marry him. Maybe you know deep down that you're settling. You're only thirty-three, you've—"

Dani groaned. "I'm not settling. Listen. Not everyone can have what you and Jen have. You two are lucky." Already on edge with the cat and dog fiasco, she tried to rush Zoey off the phone. "I gotta go, I'll see you later."

"Wait! Come to the bar with us tonight. Jen, tell her to come with us."

Jen's perky voice pleaded through the phone. "C'mon, Dani. You need a night with the girls."

"I'm swamped with paperwork."

"It's Saturday night," Zoey said. "Maybe you'll meet Miss Right."

Dani rolled her eyes. "Will you *stop*."

"All right…"

Dani's shoulders sagged with relief, because today she'd won the battle.

"…how about I find Miss Right for you?"

So much for winning. "Hello? Ring on my finger." She absently raised her hand and quickly put it back down. The ring was not where it should be. It was still on the shelf in the bathroom.

"Leave her alone," Jen said in the background. "Dani, ignore her. Just come out and have a drink with us."

Zoey refused to get down from her soapbox. "You know I'm a master matchmaker. I did introduce you to Suzanne in college."

The mention of her college sweetheart caused a twitch of pain near her heart. It was one of those regrets you learned to live with. One of those decisions you wished you could go back and change.

The dog's growl disrupted any further thoughts. Something had piqued his interest. His hind end was in the air and his head was under the couch. "I gotta go." She disconnected the call while Zoey was in midsentence.

Dani hustled over to see what had him so enthralled. It was her hospital badge. *Shit. How did it get under there?* Grabbing it, she wiped off the slobber and tucked it into her briefcase, which she then placed on top of the oak china cabinet. With a glance down at the dog and back to the bag, she calculated his jump radius. It should be out of reach. Hopefully. Dogs couldn't jump as high as cats, right?

Jinx continued to hiss from his perch on the table. "I know, Jinxy. Blame your daddy."

Dani plopped onto the couch, sinking into the soft leather cushions. She pushed a wayward strand of hair from her face. It was too short to stay in a ponytail, but long enough to fall into her eyes. A haircut was in order, but who had time for that?

She jammed a fist into her lower back and rubbed at the knot above her hip bone. Fourteen-hour days were the norm, however this past week she'd worked three eighteen-hour shifts. But it was worth it. The lower back aches. The limited sleep. All of it. Her surgical residency would be over in a year, and she would have her pick of jobs at UWMC or any other hospital in the city.

Her phone vibrated again with a text from Will.

Sorry babe will be late tonight. Don't wait up. Love you!

Good. Maybe she could get all these notes done tonight. But as soon as she opened the next file, Zoey's voice rattled around her brain and her fingers hovered over the laptop. *Am I settling?* Was there something more out there? Or someone?

Stop it. Will was great. He was kind, and caring, and fun. They'd known each other for years, came from similar backgrounds, and both wanted to be doctors. What more could she ask for? They were perfect together.

Aren't we?

A tinge of doubt nibbled at her psyche.

Dani was afraid to answer.

* * *

Kara Britton leaned against the bar. She loved to people-watch here. She also loved the divey feel of The Rose, with its five-dollar microbrews, Taco Tuesdays, and themed dance parties. It was a welcoming space that packed them in on a Saturday night.

Her friend Val Pisecki finished her beer and pushed the empty bottle away. "I'll get the next round." She waved a twenty-dollar bill at the bartender and ordered a couple of local IPAs.

Someone tapped Kara on the shoulder, and she spun around.

"Are you Kara Britton?" a petite woman asked.

Kara didn't recognize her. "Yeah?"

"I'm Jen Rowe."

Kara bit her bottom lip and searched through her memory banks for a woman with warm brown eyes and a blond, curly, pixie haircut, but she drew a blank.

"We went to high school together. I was a couple years behind you. We both played basketball..."

"Oh, Jen, yes, now I remember. I'm sorry I didn't recognize you. How are you?"

"I'm good. How about you?"

Another woman stood close by and nudged Jen's shoulder.

"Oh. This is my girlfriend, Zoey. Zoe, this is Kara," Jen said. "She was the star of the team back in the day. She made 'The Shot.'" Jen used air quotes. "Her buzzer-beater won us the state championship that year."

Zoey, a couple of inches taller than Jen, had a mod messy 'do and crooked smile. With great fanfare, she extended a hand. "Howdy!"

Kara liked her instantly. "Nice to meet you, Zoey. This is my friend Val."

"So do you play professional basketball now?" Jen asked.

Kara grinned at the question. It wasn't the first time she'd heard it. Usually when she ran into old high school buddies, it was the first thing they asked. Most people assumed that being good on one's high school team automatically translated into a pro basketball career. "No. I don't play professionally."

"Why not? You were so good. I heard you got a free ride to the University of Oregon."

"I did get a scholarship. But I tore my knee up senior year and missed the entire season."

"Oh damn, that must've sucked."

Kara briefly flashed back to that moment in time, the late nights in the gym, the countless hours of physical therapy. Pushing through the pain to try and get back to the team before the end of the season, only to come up short and then questioning if it had all been worth it. "It sucked when it happened. But after rehabbing…" She shrugged. "I found out I didn't love it anymore. To play pro, you gotta love it."

"Yeah, I guess so."

"It turned out okay. I may not be on the Seattle Storm, but I got my business degree."

Val patted her on the back. "And now she owns her own business, Emily's Tails for Trails Pet Resort!" She raised her glass. "The best dog kennel and day care in the city."

Kara gave them a wry smile. "Val's my second-in-command, so her opinion is a bit biased."

"Who's Emily?" Zoey asked.

"My mom," Kara replied. "She passed away eight years ago. When I bought the kennel, I named it after her."

"Oh, damn, sorry about your mom," Zoey said.

"Thank you."

A waitress arrived to let Kara know their table was ready.

"Why don't you guys join us?" Val asked.

They sat down and ordered some appetizers.

"Explain to me the day care thing because we have two monsters at home," Zoey said. "I told Jen we could get one, but she insisted on two."

"They were brothers," Jen explained. "I couldn't separate them."

"Well, now it's double the work and double the shit in the backyard. And there's no room on the couch or the bed."

"They're not that bad," Jen said.

Zoey's eyes widened and her lip curled up at the corner. "Not that bad? Roscoe literally kicked me out of bed the other night. I was barely hanging on as it was, and he stretched and I ended up on the floor. Here, look." She rolled up her sleeve, revealing a nasty bruise near her elbow.

"Ouch," Kara said.

"And what about last night? The two of them decided to run a track meet from the den to the front door. For half an hour."

After a pause, Jen asked, "How does day care work?"

"You can either drop them off or we come and get them," Kara said.

Zoey gasped. "You actually come and pick them up?"

"Yep."

"And then what?" Zoey asked. "You bring them back? Or do you keep them? You can keep them."

Jen playfully punched her. "Hey."

"Ow." Zoey continued, "I know, you pick them up and keep them, and bring back, like a cat, or a kitten."

Jen giggled. "Stop it. You'll have to forgive her; she's a cat person."

Kara made a show of rolling her eyes. "Ah. A cat person! Say no more. Why don't we do this? I'll pick your dogs up Monday, and you can see if you like it."

"Done!" Zoey said.

The group ordered another round of drinks. "What do you guys do?" Val asked.

"I work at Amazon," Zoey said. "Been writing code since I was in diapers."

"And I work as a nanny for this couple over on Mercer Island," Jen said. "Pays good until I figure some things out."

"How old are the kids?" Kara asked.

"Five, two, and three months."

"Wow, they're young."

"Yeah, don't be surprised if she orders you a juice box from the bar," Zoey said. "Sometimes she forgets she's with adults."

"I do not."

"Yeah, you do. Last night you told me it was beddie-bye time and to put my jam-jams on. You're losing your adult vocabulary."

"I am not!"

Kara smiled at their banter. They sounded like an old married couple. "How long have you guys been together?"

"Five years," Jen said.

"That's great." Kara felt a pang of loneliness. *Will I have that someday?*

"What about you two? Are you together?" Jen asked.

Kara shook her head. "No, just friends. Val has a girlfriend."

Zoey pointed at Kara. "Not you?"

"Nope. Single right now."

"Who can we set her up with?" Jen tapped a finger to her chin.

Kara held up a hand. "I don't need to be set up. I'm on a self-imposed hiatus from women right now."

"Why?" Zoey asked.

"Let's just say, my last breakup was a little messy. I need a breather."

"How long ago was that?" Zoey asked.

Kara did the math in her head. "About seven or eight months."

"You need to get back on the wagon. I know a redhead I can set you up with," Zoey said.

Jen's eyes narrowed. "Stop it."

Zoey waved a hand dismissively. "She's five foot six, shoulder-length hair, and blue eyes. She's a doctor and—"

"Zoey…" Jen warned. "Kara, ignore her please." Jen rested her chin in her hand.

"There's gotta be someone we know."

Kara groaned. "Seriously ladies, I'm fine being single right now. If that changes, I'll let you know."

CHAPTER TWO

Dani leaned on the counter at the nurse's station and picked up the chart for tomorrow's surgery.

"There's my favorite doctor."

She recognized the voice and spun around with a smile on her face. "And here's my favorite EMT. Don't tell me you brought in some horrific accident victim who needs surgery."

Ethan Rowe, Jen's burly big brother, gave her a hug. "No, just a broken leg. I haven't seen you in a while. How've you been?"

"Busy as usual."

"How's Will?"

"He's great."

"Tell him I expect an invite to the hospital golf outing again this year."

After exchanging some small talk, she hugged Ethan goodbye and headed into the room across from the nurse's station. "Hey, Mrs. Mitchell, how are you today?" She pulled up a chair next to her patient.

The older woman gave her a wavering smile, and her frail hand clutched at the thin hospital blanket. "I'm doing okay."

"Good. We're going to be running tests today to make sure everything else is fine for your surgery tomorrow. How's your pain level?"

"It's manageable."

She nodded and made some notes on the chart. "Do you have any other concerns about the surgery? Any questions?"

"I'm nervous."

Dani rested her hand on Mrs. Mitchell's arm. "I know it's scary. But I promise, I'll take good care of you."

"I wish all my doctors were as sweet as you, dear. You know, my son will be in later today, and I told him he had to meet my beautiful doctor. Now, what time are you done?"

Dani's lips twitched in amusement. Her older patients always tried to set her up with their sons. "Well, that's nice, but I'm engaged."

"Engaged? Where's your ring?"

She chuckled. "It's an occupational hazard to wear it here."

"Listen, if it doesn't work out with your man, you call me. My Thomas is handsome and fun."

"I will. Now you get some rest, and I'll check back on you later today."

Dani walked into the hallway and checked her text messages. One was from Zoey. It was a picture of a van with a dog logo on it and something about Trails for Tails. Typical Zoey, vague with no explanation. She swiped to the next and sighed. Her mom wanted to meet for coffee in fifteen minutes. Already privy to what the conversation would be about, she groaned.

When she arrived at the hospital cafeteria, her mom waved from a table in the corner. Dani weaved through the mostly empty tables and bent down to place a kiss on her mom's cheek. "Hey, Mom."

"You've got dark circles under your eyes. Aren't you getting enough sleep? You have to manage your schedule better or your work will suffer."

Dani rubbed at the offending orbs. "It's been hectic. And the dog started barking at three a.m. and woke me up."

"When did you get a dog?"

A young intern interrupted their conversation. "Dr. Clark, may I bother you for a quick second?"

Her mom nodded and engaged with the young woman while Dani enjoyed a few seconds of welcomed peace, thankful that she wasn't the Dr. Clark the woman sought.

The intern left and the inquisition continued.

"So when did you get a dog?" her mom asked.

"Will got one the other day."

"That's wonderful."

Dani tilted her head to the side. "We don't have time for a dog right now. We're both working late hours."

"I'm sure it'll be fine." Her mom brought out her phone and pulled up the calendar. "Have you settled on a date yet?"

As usual, there was no recognition of the strain Dani was under. She tossed out the first month that came into her brain. "September."

Her mom's eyes widened. "Hooray! At least we have a month picked out."

"I don't have time to even plan it."

"Don't worry. I'll plan it. Six months will be almost impossible to pull off, but I'll manage. Any particular day? Or should I guess?"

"I'll…get back to you on that."

"What about your dress?"

"Uh, I don't know."

"There's not enough time for something custom. You'll wear something simple. I'll call Margaret at Bellevue Bridal; she owes me a favor."

"Okay." A dull pain began to throb in Dani's temples.

"We'll need to book a date at the church." She grimaced. "At this late date, I hope we can get something. I'll probably have to call in another favor. Of course, Reverend Monahan will do the service."

"Of course." Dani checked her watch and decided she'd had enough mom talk. "Crap, I have to go. I'll talk to you later." She gave her mom another peck on the cheek and hustled away.

CHAPTER THREE

"Yeah?" Dani rested the phone between her chin and shoulder as she rushed around trying to get out the door the next morning.

"Why hello to you too, bestie. Why so pleasant?" Zoey asked.

"I'm in a foul mood. I've barely slept. It's my day to walk the dog, so I'm running behind schedule, and one of my patients had a reaction to some meds, and what the hell else is new in my life?"

"I think you secretly love the chaos."

"I think you're secretly a pain in my ass." Dani pulled on her shoes, hopping toward the front door.

"I solved your dog problem."

"My *dog problem*? More like a dog apocalypse. It's been a few days and most of our furniture is destroyed. He ate the ottoman."

"That ottoman was ugly."

Dani blew out a frustrated breath. "Tell me how you solved my dog problem."

"Did you get my text?"

"I don't remember."

"Well, we met some chick at the bar on Saturday, someone Jen knew in high school. Next thing you know, they've Facebooked, Instagrammed, and Tweeted—"

"I assume this is leading somewhere?"

"This chick owns a kennel and doggie day care service."

"When do I have time to drive a dog to doggie day care?"

"They *pick up* your dog, take them away for the day, and deliver them back to the house later."

Intrigued, Dani stared at the dog. He was chewing on Will's favorite slipper. "Keep talking."

"That's it, she'll be there in five minutes."

"What? Wait…today? I can't!"

"Yes, you can. Get your pooch ready."

"Jesus, I don't have time for this. I'm late already."

"She'll be there any second. For God's sake, it won't kill you to be a couple of minutes late. Well, it might kill your patient. But it won't kill you."

"Okay, okay. I'll wait." She ran a hand through her hair. It felt disheveled. *Did I brush it?*

"Good. She's been taking our two maniacs the last few days and they come home all tired and shit. It's a beautiful thing."

"How much does this doggie chauffeur service cost?"

"Just give her your credit card. You can afford it."

"All right, I have to go. The hospital's on the other line."

"Oh, Dans!"

"What?"

"She's cute."

"Why do I need to know she's cute?"

"Bye!"

* * *

Kara hopped from the white cargo van. The windows stayed open to allow air flow for the three dogs that waited not so patiently in the back. The two large ones barked their annoyance at stopping while the other one low-key whined. "Be good, boys."

She studied the house in front of her. *Stately* came to mind. It was a huge three-story brick home with black shutters and white trim around the windows.

The landscaping had a professional feel, with tightly coiffed evergreen shrubs and strategically placed clusters of lavender and catmint, interspersed with glossy elephant ears and showy daylilies the color of buttercream. The oyster-shaped concrete birdbath was getting some action as two cardinals dunked and fluttered and flitted.

When she rang the doorbell, a woman with a phone stuck to her ear threw open the door and glanced at the van in the driveway. "You here for the dog?"

Kara nodded. "Yeah, Jen and Zoey told me to come over and get him."

The woman waved her in. She was shorter than Kara by an inch or two, and her wavy reddish hair fell even with her shoulders. It was thick. Or matted. Kara couldn't tell. She passed a large, hairy, orange cat sitting on the arm of the couch and flinched when it gleefully took a swipe at her. *Ugh, cats.*

The phone conversation ended, but the woman still didn't turn around as she made her way to the back of the house. "He's around here somewhere, chewing on something, I'm sure."

She wore light-blue scrubs. Was she a doctor? If so, it would explain the big house. Or they were pajamas. Maybe she was a bored housewife who had just rolled out of bed. Kara hustled to keep pace. "What's his name?"

The woman turned and her brows creased into a deep V. "Uh…hmm. Good question." Her phone rang. "Sorry. I have to take this."

Kara was dumbfounded. Good question? It was a simple question. She didn't ask about the theory of relativity. Or the space-time continuum. Or her thoughts on global warming. She'd merely asked for the dog's name. *How the hell doesn't she know the dog's name?*

Snapping fingers interrupted her introspection. The redhead pointed under the dining room table.

Ambling over, she peered under. The dog in question rolled onto its back. White stuffing hung like drool from his mouth. He looked like a golden retriever, though not particularly large, probably around forty-five pounds, but he had the typical retriever coat, long, wavy, and strawberry blond.

Kara waved to get the woman's attention and mouthed, "Do you have a leash?" She was rewarded with another point. Kara followed the point into the kitchen. She walked in and stopped short as she glanced around with appreciation. It was a beautiful, open space, with top-of-the-line stainless steel appliances, creamy-colored granite countertops, and an island with a sink and barstools. A breakfast nook was off to the left and flanked with windows on three sides, making it the perfect space to have a cup of morning coffee. It was the kind of kitchen to drool over. Kara's mom used to page through design magazines while in line at the supermarket and clutch at her chest with a dreamy expression in her eyes. *Someday. Someday we'll have a kitchen like this.* Kara would smile, indulging her mom's fantasy, knowing they barely had enough money for food, let alone a kitchen renovation.

The leash and collar dangled from a hook by the back door. Grabbing both, she approached the dog. The aroma of the beef jerky treat in her hand was too enticing to ignore, and he loped over. At least he was food motivated. He gulped it down doggie style, with a slurp and a swallow, no chewing necessary, then pushed his nose into her hand looking for more. She slipped the collar on and attached the leash. Clearing her throat, she asked in a low voice, "How do you want to pay for this? We take credit cards, check, cash."

The woman continued her phone conversation while digging into a briefcase. Medical mumbo jumbo fell from her lips. In a flash, she yanked out a check, signed it, and handed it over.

Kara cocked a brow. What kind of person hands some stranger a blank check? She was either stupidly trusting, or so rich it didn't matter. Kara went with the latter. "I'll bring"—she checked the dog's collar—"Oliver back around five. Is that good?" Kara received a nod and figured she was dismissed when the woman turned away. She led the dog back toward the front door, mumbling, "Nice to meet you too. I'm Kara, by the way."

Once Oliver was safe in the van with the other dogs, Kara headed back to the farm. When she arrived, Val greeted her. "Hey, did they say when they're dropping off the food delivery? The Hammonds need a bag."

"This afternoon."

Val grabbed one of the dogs and took him over to the play area. "Incoming!" When she came back, she pointed to Oliver. "Who's this?"

"New client."

"What's his name?"

"Oliver. Get this, the chick who owns him didn't even know his name."

"How do you not know your dog's name?"

"Right? She's some sort of doctor. Big house on Edgehill." She shouted to one of the women in the yard, "Ellie, new dog, keep your eye on him."

Oliver shot into the enclosure and joined the other dogs as they ran around a large ten-acre space filled with trees and kiddie pools. Several employees, the "wranglers" as they liked to call themselves, moved through the yard keeping order and breaking up any scuffles.

Kara's chest swelled with pride as she watched the dogs romp around. Right after college, she'd gotten a job at the kennel as assistant manager. After a few years of hard work, she became manager. The previous owners, looking to retire, were only too happy to sell the business to their favorite employee. She was able to marry her business degree with her love for dogs. She'd renovated the house, converting it to a store, and moved into the small cottage behind the farmhouse. It was the perfect situation.

Val removed her baseball hat and wiped the perspiration from her forehead. She was tall in stature, her ash-blond hair buzzed close, giving her a more masculine look. "What's the doctor's name?"

Kara glanced at the blank check. "Ah…Danielle Clark." As she read the name aloud, she experienced a feeling of déjà vu.

The name tried to trigger a memory, and she searched but came up empty.

"Why's the check blank?"

It took a moment for Kara to process the question. "Um... she was too busy to fill it out."

"Busy doing what?"

"She was on the phone, talking doctor stuff. She kind of ignored me."

"Ignored you?"

"Yeah."

"Was she cute?"

"She had a nice ass."

Val pretended to be appalled. "You meet a new customer and that's the only thing you came away with?"

Kara laughed. "Her back was to me most of the time."

* * *

Oliver was delivered home promptly at five p.m. by the same brunette who had picked him up earlier. Now that Dani wasn't so rushed, she had time to check her out. Zoey was right. The woman was attractive. Her hair hung below her shoulders and had a natural wave, and her slim body moved with the grace of an athlete. Dark brows and lashes created the perfect frame for her green eyes.

The dog calmly walked in the door. The woman took a treat from her pocket and made the dog sit while the leash was removed. He stayed put until told "Okay," and then staggered over to his bed. Dani wasn't sure she'd ever seen him lie down before, and she had to begrudgingly admit she was a bit impressed with the sit-stay.

The brunette took the blank check from her pocket. "I brought this back since we didn't talk about costs. I'm Kara, by the way, and your dog's name is Oliver."

Dani, who had another hellacious day, noted the tone in Kara's voice. She was being judged for not knowing the dog's name earlier. And it rankled her. "We just rescued him and didn't name him yet."

"We?"

"My fiancé and I."

"Oh. Where's your ring?"

Dani was taken aback at the boldness of the question. "I don't wear it to work. I'm a surgeon, and I don't need to be losing it inside a patient." She hoped her voice dripped with the proper amount of condescension.

Kara smirked.

Dani had half a mind to tell her to go pound sand, but then she glanced over at the exhausted dog. "He seems pretty tired."

"It's called exercise. All dogs need it."

Dani glared and tried to convey her annoyance. In her head, she weighed the pros and cons of having to deal with this woman on a regular basis: getting judged every day vs. tired dog sleeping all night, getting aggravated by the brunette vs. not pulling things out of the dog's mouth. "How much we talking here?"

"The cost for pickup and day care is sixty-five dollars a day."

"Jesus Christ, is child day care that much?"

"It's a half hour ride to get him, and a half hour back to the farm."

"Yeah, but you're already at Zoey and Jen's, which is fifteen minutes away."

"Look, it is what it is." Kara slipped the blank check onto the table in the foyer and opened the front door.

Suddenly Dani had visions of chewed shoes, shredded pillows, and stuffing fluff all over the house. "Wait!" She grabbed the check. "How about I try it again tomorrow, and we'll see how it goes."

Kara took the blank check. "Do you want to fill it out?"

Dani called a truce in her head and tried to be nice. "No, you can fill it out, thanks."

"Your dog is food motivated, so he's easy to train. If you take the time."

And…the truce was off! "I don't have time to train a dog. I'm a little busy, what with doctoring and all." *The nerve of this woman.* First the name thing, now the shaming for not training.

"Oliver. His name's Oliver. Maybe you should start with that." She headed toward the van.

"Very funny, Karen. I'll see you tomorrow." With a huff, Dani slammed the door shut.

CHAPTER FOUR

The next day, Kara pulled into the Clarks' driveway. With a chuckle, she recounted the banter from yesterday, and the way Dani's eyes blazed with defiance when she questioned the cost of day care. Kara was never combative with customers, but Dani stimulated her. And it wasn't unpleasant.

She walked to the door and rang the bell. When Dani answered, she again had the phone glued to her ear.

"Hold on a sec, Kyle." She pulled the phone away from her mouth. "Hey. C'mon in. I, ah, lost track of him about a half hour ago."

Kara's brows rose. Why couldn't this woman keep track of her dog? "Where did you last see him?"

Dani pursed her lips in thought. "In the sunroom. I was working in there and the phone rang, and I walked into the kitchen, and, shit, my briefcase! He's already chewed my hospital badge once." She took off running.

Kara followed, giving a wide berth to the hissing, spitting, orange furball perched on the back of the couch. Upon entering the sunroom, she found Dani on her knees.

"Kyle, I gotta call you back in a few." Dani sifted through her briefcase. "Well, here's the badge, that's safe, but I feel slobber, so I know he was in here." She directed a questioning glance in Kara's direction. "Maybe you could help look. I refuse to be late for work again today. I'm never late. But this whole dog thing has me stressed out." She continued to poke around the bag. "Oh, it's my wallet. No!"

Dani's face drooped, and Kara swore her bottom lip wobbled. She almost felt bad. Almost. "Are you gonna cry?"

"No, I'm not gonna cry." She sat back on her heels. "I love that wallet. I've had it for fifteen years."

"Wow, fifteen years? Don't you ever open it?"

Dani narrowed her baby blues. "Are you suggesting I'm cheap? Is this because I said you charge too much for picking up a dog?"

"If the shoe fits," Kara mumbled as she left the sunroom.

"I heard that!"

Kara walked to the bottom of the staircase. Credit cards littered the steps like breadcrumbs. "I think he's upstairs."

In an instant, Dani joined her at the bottom of the steps. "Crap, there's my Visa." She raised it in the air victoriously. "Not chewed!"

"Congrats on the Visa, but Mister MasterCard has seen better days." Kara picked up the mangled card.

"I don't use that one much." Dani brushed past and ran upstairs.

Kara sighed and checked her watch. She was already late for the next pickup.

"Found him! Karen, in here!" Dani hollered.

Kara rolled her eyes at the Karen thing. She walked into an oversized bedroom. Which happened to be bigger than her living room.

Dani was on her knees peering under the bed, ass sticking in the air. "Come here, buddy. Please. Bring Mommy the wallet. C'mon. Be a good boy."

Kara got down on the floor and glanced under the bed. Oliver was having a time of it with the wallet. She grabbed Dani's driver's license, which must have fallen out before he snuggled against the back wall. It was none the worse for wear. She waved it at Dani, who was hyperfocused on the slowly disintegrating wallet. "Here."

"Thank you." Dani stretched out and was now flat on her stomach, head in hand. She gazed back at Kara. "Welp, my wallet is pretty much fucked."

Kara mimicked Dani's position. "Seems that way." Dani's eyes were the color of the sky on a bright clear day. Her tousled hair was streaked with natural gold highlights, and Kara resisted the urge to run fingers through it. A light smattering of freckles peppered her cheeks and nose. Had they met under different circumstances, Kara was sure she'd be intrigued.

A burp from under the bed broke the spell. Oliver had sufficiently softened the wallet enough to swallow half of it.

Dani sighed. "Guess I'll see that in the yard later. C'mon, buddy, bring Mommy the other half of the wallet. Please."

The name thing was driving her nuts. "His name is Oliver. Say it with me, Ol-i-ver."

Dani's eyes narrowed. "I don't like your tone."

For some reason, Kara got a kick out of antagonizing her. She used sign language, fingerspelling the name. "O-L-I-V-E-R. Do you need me to write it down for you?"

Dani raised one half of her lip and huffed. "We're giving him a new name!"

"He responds pretty well to Oliver. You should just keep it." Kara figured she'd tortured the good doctor enough for one morning. Pulling a treat from her pocket, she cooed at Oliver, who immediately left the tasteless leather for a piece of chicken jerky. She gently pulled him from under the bed.

Dani rolled onto her side. "Did you have treats the whole time?"

Kara nodded.

"So, you could've gotten him out of there before he swallowed my wallet?"

"Yeah, I guess."

"Thanks a lot."

Kara chuckled. "As much as I'm enjoying this little adventure of ours, I'm late."

Dani bounced up and followed Kara down the hallway. "You're late? I have surgery in a few hours."

Kara started down the steps with Oliver in hot pursuit. "We all have schedules, Miss Clark. Or do you prefer Dr. Clark? Or world-renowned surgeon Danielle Clark."

"I'm just saying, you had treats. You could have ended all this ten minutes ago, and my wallet would be in one piece, not half under the bed and half buried in dog crap later. And neither of us would be late."

"It's not my fault your dog likes to chew things." Kara wandered into the kitchen to get Oliver's leash. "Probably take two days for the wallet to make its way into your backyard." She walked toward the front door. "Be back at five?"

"I might not be here."

"Oh darn. Just when we were having so much fun. How do I get Oliver back in the house?"

"My fiancé, Will, should be home."

"Okay. Goodbye, Dr. Danielle Clark." Kara walked toward the van.

"Goodbye...Karen." Dani slammed the front door.

Kara chuckled. Maybe she should wear a name tag around the good doctor, although it hadn't worked for Oliver.

* * *

On the drive to the hospital, Dani let her annoyance get the better of her and she blew a red light. She peeked in the rearview mirror. No sirens or flashing lights. *Phew.*

As if she didn't have enough on her plate without being chastised for not knowing Oliver's name. She couldn't help it if her mind was preoccupied with other things. Like her unrelenting schedule at the hospital. Like her upcoming nuptials. Like how green the woman's eyes were. *Wait. Where did that come from? Huh.* Well, she did have a thing for green eyes. Ever since she was young and met a girl at the hospital with big, green eyes and long, dark lashes.

Her thoughts circled back to Kara. How did she know sign language? Was there more to her than being a pompous ass? Probably not. But she had killer hands. Elegant, long fingers. Nice, neat nails. Green eyes and sexy hands. A deadly combination.

When she arrived at the OR, Dr. Kyle Montgomery greeted her. Today, they would both be scrubbing in for the same surgery.

"Hey, Dani." He glanced at the clock on the wall. "You don't usually cut it this close."

"I'm gonna have to adjust my routine for our dog." She rinsed her arms and hands.

"When did you get a dog?"

"I'll tell you all about it later."

The surgery was completed in three hours, and both relaxed in the surgeon's lounge afterward.

"Did you guys set a date yet?" Kyle took off his surgical cap and rubbed at his short, dark afro.

"September." Dani poured a cup of coffee and collapsed onto the couch next to him. With a slouch, she rested her head on the back cushion.

"You don't sound very excited. What's up?"

Dani sighed before answering. Kyle was a good friend. They were completing the same rotations and had spent many a night in the surgeon's lounge commiserating about the long hours and low pay, so she knew he could be trusted with her innermost thoughts. "I don't know. Sometimes...I'm not sure I wanna get married."

"Shit. When did this happen?"

"I don't know. Lately I feel like I'm suffocating. Sometimes I'm not sure I wanna be with him forever. But then the next day I think, just get married. You get along with him, you like him, you can talk to him."

"You love him, right?"

Dani hesitated. "I've always loved him. We've been best friends forever."

"Nobody says you have to marry your best friend. Are you *in love* with him?"

There it was. That torturous question. "I don't know. Maybe that's the problem. Shouldn't I know?" Dani stared ahead for a few moments with eyes focused but not seeing. "Ugh. How the hell did I get here?" As she stood to leave, the tension began to pound behind her eyes. "I'm gonna grab a bite to eat, you wanna join me?"

"Can't, buddy. I'm behind in my paperwork."

"Okay, well, thanks for the counseling session."

"I don't think I helped, but you're welcome. And, Dani?"

She turned.

"Nobody can force you to get married."

"Ha! You'd be surprised."

On the walk to the cafeteria, she imagined what would happen if she broke things off with Will. Her dad would freak out. Her mom would disown her. Well, okay, she wouldn't disown her, but she would give her that look, the look that said, "Why are you making the biggest mistake of your life?" Dani had been on the receiving end of that look many times.

Why don't I just stand up to them?

Because it was easier to go along with what they wanted. So much energy was wasted when she was younger trying to buck the Clark system. It wasn't worth it. Besides, true love, the all-encompassing kind, was something that existed only in the movies. It wasn't real life. It wasn't how things really were. If you found someone you could get along with, if you found someone who had the same goals in life, who treated you well, then you should feel lucky. Get married. Have children. Make the perfect family. There, decision made. *Stop being an idiot.*

CHAPTER FIVE

Dani finally had a Saturday off and was having a celebratory lunch with Zoey, who had just arrived, deli order in hand. "Where's Jen?"

"She had to stop at Ethan's. She'll be here later. I got your fave, pastrami on rye, with Thousand Island dressing," Zoey said.

"You are simply the best."

She held up a second paper bag. "And…for dessert I stopped at Pike's Market and got some doughnuts at you-know-where."

Dani's mouth watered just thinking about the sugary sweetness of mini fried dough from Daily Dozen Doughnuts. "What kind?" She held her breath.

"Cinnamon."

"Oh. I love you."

"Of course you do."

They both sat at the counter in Dani's kitchen.

"Where's Jinx?" Zoey asked. "I have tuna fish. Jinxy! Come here, handsome!" The large kitty sashayed in to greet his favorite aunt, and she sprinkled some tuna fish on the floor, smiling with satisfaction as he inhaled it. "And where's the dog?" She took a big bite of her sandwich.

"He was here a minute ago. Probably chewing a door or something. We're gonna have to redo the entire house."

The dog made his way down the steps and greeted Zoey.

"Hey, boy. What's his name?"

"Oliver."

"Congrats on finally naming him."

Dani frowned. "You sound like the day care woman. She was really put off because I didn't know his name that first day."

"Well. It did take a while."

Dani huffed. "It was like, one day."

Zoey stared at Oliver. "What's he doing?"

Oliver sniffed the stool next to Zoey.

"I don't know. Sniffing?"

"He's gonna pee...oh, there goes the leg."

"Shit, Oliver, no!" Dani tried to stop him but was too late. He peed, but instead of a straight stream of urine, it shot in every direction.

Zoey ducked. "Holy shit he's got lousy aim."

Oliver's urine went up and down and all around.

Zoey's pants took a direct hit, and she hopped off the stool. "Ew!"

Jinx ran screaming from the room.

Dani made a grab for Oliver's collar, but he ran off.

Zoey dabbed at her pant leg with a napkin. "He peed in a circle. How is that possible? Is his peter broken?"

"I don't know. I'm not a vet!"

"You should put a diaper on him."

"He'd just eat it. He's like a goat."

"Maybe you could teach him to write his name when he pees. Then you'll remember it."

"Very funny." Dani finished cleaning and settled in with her pastrami and rye. "This dog pees more in the house than in the yard. Can't we teach him to use a litter box?"

"Fuck if I know."

Oliver wandered back into the room ten minutes later.

Zoey cocked a brow. "Here comes piss boy."

He sniffed around the stools again.

"Uh-oh, watch it, watch it."

* * *

An hour later, Dani sat on the couch with Zoey. Both sported safety goggles and clear, plastic rain ponchos.

Jen walked in and glanced from one to the other, and back again. "You cleaning up a crime scene?"

They just stared back. No one uttered a word for a few moments.

Finally, Jen broke the silence. "What happened?"

Dani spoke first. "It started in the kitchen."

"I can't wait to hear this," Jen mumbled as she took a seat.

Zoey cleared her throat. "At first it looked like your usual doggie accident. He lifted his leg to pee on the stool."

Dani gave her a nod of encouragement and patted her thigh.

"The pee sprayed everywhere. We chalked it up to an excited dog. But the second time, the second time it hit the ceiling. Straight in the air. Then it took a hard-right turn. I've never seen anything like it. I was lucky, my sandwich was safe. But the pastrami…" She glanced at Dani, who, with a quivering bottom lip, slowly shook her head from side to side. "The pastrami was hit. And it didn't make it."

"Where's the dog now?" Jen asked.

They shrugged.

"What's his name?"

"Piss boy," Zoey said.

Dani shot her a look. "Oliver."

"Oliver! Come here, boy," Jen called. The dog wagged his way into the living room and sat down in front of her. "Are those Will's briefs?"

Zoey nodded.

"You put men's tighty-whities on the dog?"

"A maxi pad's shoved in there too," Dani said.

Zoey puffed up her chest. "We made do with what we had. Like MacGyver." She pointed at Jen. "You weren't here. Talk about a golden shower. He must have peed eight times in the last two hours. It went everywhere."

"What's wrong with him?" Jen asked.

"Obviously, his peter's broken," Zoey said.

"Dogs' peters don't break. Hold on." Jen took out her phone.

"Who you calling?" Zoey asked.

"Kara."

Dani cringed. "Oh, shit, the dog police?" She made a grab for the phone. "Don't call her. Hang up, Jen. Hang up!"

Jen pushed her hand away and stood. "I'm not hanging up…Hey, Kara, it's Jen, I'm gonna put you on speaker, hold on. Okay." She placed the phone on the coffee table. "I'm here with Dani and Zoey. Dani's dog has an issue."

"An issue?" Kara sighed. "What's the issue?"

Dani gritted her teeth. She heard it. She heard the sigh.

Jen continued, "When he pees, it's shooting everywhere, right, guys?"

"Yes," they replied in unison.

"When's the last time you bathed him?" Kara asked.

"Bathed him? When was I supposed to bathe him?" Dani was new to all this dog stuff, and quite frankly it was becoming overwhelming. Cats were *so* much easier. And smarter. And cleaner.

"Dogs need baths, much like we need baths."

Dani leaned closer to the phone, pushing the safety goggles farther up her nose. "I can feel you judging me."

"Your dog is young. Young dogs don't clean themselves. He probably has matted hair around his penis. That's why it's important to groom your dog. You should also be giving him a sanitary trim, because if the hair's matted, it can cause a UTI. You do know what a UTI is, don't you, Dr. Clark?"

"Of course I know what a UTI is," Dani snapped.

"Are we picking up Oliver Monday? We can groom him for you."

"How much is that gonna cost me?"

"Well, your wallet is already ripped open, so it shouldn't be too painful. Ninety-five dollars."

"Ninety-five dollars? My hair doesn't cost that much!"

"I can tell."

"Oh, so now I have bad hair. I see. Okay, okay. I get it. What are you doing for ninety-five dollars?"

"We give him a bath, we trim his coat and between his paws, we give him a sanitary trim, we clip his nails. And he goes home with a bandana."

"Oh, well. There's a bandana. Now I get the ninety-five dollars."

"And I suggest you get him to the vet to check for an infection. Are we picking Oliver up Monday or not?"

"Yeah, I guess."

"Are we grooming him?"

Dani waved a hand in surrender. "By all means, groom away. I'll have to get a second job to pay for all this."

"Good, then you can buy yourself a new wallet, and maybe find yourself a new hairdresser."

"Very funny. I have to go."

Zoey's mouth drooped at the corners. "No. This is fun."

Jen disconnected the call while Zoey stared at Dani.

"What?" Dani asked.

"What was that about?"

"What'd you mean?"

"All that snark. Or should I say spark." She wiggled her eyebrows.

"Spark?"

"Seems like you got a boner for this chick."

"I don't have a boner, she's, she's…"

"Hot?"

"No! She's, she's…"

"Sexy?"

"She's annoying as shit. She's condescending and annoying. And aggravating, did I say aggravating? Cause she aggravates me. She's lucky I'm desperate to tire out the dog, otherwise I would've told her to buzz off."

"So you're saying you don't like her because of her hubris?" Jen asked.

Zoey did a double take. "Hubris? That's a big word. You didn't get that from little Jon-Jon."

A haughty expression settled over Jen's features. "Since you told me I was forgetting my adult vocabulary, I found this app that gives you a word of the day. And you're supposed to use it in a sentence five times every day. And today's word was hubris."

"Who's Jon-Jon?" Dani asked.

"One of the kids I'm babysitting," Jen said.

"Oh, right, the nanny job. How's that going?" Dani asked.

Before Jen could answer, Zoey interjected. "Last night we were gonna have sex, and as she's taking my shirt off, she puts my arms in the air and goes, 'Sooo big.'"

Dani flinched. "Ouch."

"Ouch? Ya think? Hard to keep a hard-on after hearing that. Not to mention our bedroom is like a romper room now. She brings home toys and dirty diapers and shit."

"I forgot I put the diaper in my pocket."

"Who forgets about dirty diapers?" Zoey asked.

"I had Oliver's poop bag in my briefcase the other day," Dani said.

"Was there poop in it?"

"Yeah."

Both girls' lips curled in disgust.

"What? It's no worse than a dirty diaper."

"Seems worse," Zoey muttered.

* * *

Late Sunday night, Dani and Will relaxed in bed, each doing paperwork.

"Kevin wants us to come to this charity dinner. It's in a few months." His eyes pleaded. "I'm giving you plenty of notice this time."

Dani groaned. Kevin Murphy. He of the inappropriate comments and unwanted touches. She couldn't stand him and had made up a litany of excuses to miss the last dinner invite. Unfortunately, he was Will's boss at the clinic where he worked. "Do I have to?"

"Why? Kevin always asks about you. And you missed the last dinner."

"He creeps me out. He's always staring and gets all touchy-feely around me."

"I didn't know he did that, why didn't you tell me?"

"Because he's your boss."

"Well, I'll say something to him then."

"No. I don't wanna put you in a bad spot." Dani hadn't been attentive to Will's needs recently, in the bedroom and the proverbial boardroom. In her heart, she knew she should make the effort. "It's fine. I'll go."

"You sure?"

"Yeah."

"Okay. I'll keep my eye on him. Oh, I talked to my parents this morning. Sounds like our moms are planning the wedding."

"And they'll have a blast doing it."

Will chuckled. "I swear, my parents haven't stopped smiling since we got engaged."

"Well, it's their dream come true. They all had us married when we were barely out of diapers."

He laughed. "The prestigious Clark and Kincaid families forging a fantastic union. Sometimes I think they're more excited than we are."

Dani's hand froze over the page. Was Will having doubts too? "Aren't you excited?"

He was quick to reply. "Of course. I didn't mean it to sound like I wasn't." He gave her an apologetic look before turning his attention back to his paperwork. After a beat, he asked, "You're excited, right?"

"Of course. Why wouldn't I be?" Dani nibbled at her bottom lip, not willing to give a voice to her misgivings.

"Did you settle on a date?"

"I don't care, pick one." Dani jotted some notes in the margin of a patient's report.

He shrugged. "How about September nineteenth?"

"Done."

"That was easy."

"What can I say? I'm easy."

Will chuckled. "My dad is insisting I go with him to the hospital board meeting Tuesday afternoon. And then to dinner afterward. Ugh. I hate going to that stuff."

"Tell him you're not going."

"I can't do that."

"Why not?"

He looked at her with lowered brows. "For the same reason you never say no to your mom."

He had her there. "True. We're quite a pair, aren't we?"

"We sure are. Our parents say jump and we say how high." He rubbed the back of his neck and moved his head from side to side to remove a kink. A crack signaled his success. "It's how we bonded. Remember that time I found you in the school library sitting on the floor between the shelves, depressed because your parents told you that you couldn't be an artist?"

"Oh, I remember. I had a big blowout with them the night before, and I was defiantly reading the current issue of *Art Forum*. My way of protesting the fact that they wouldn't let me try for an art scholarship."

"What did your mom say?" Will raised his voice to imitate Dani's mom. "'There'll be no starving artists in our family, Danielle.'"

Dani chuckled and continued the impersonation. "'You'll go to medical school and become a doctor, Danielle.'" The chuckling stopped and she sighed. After fighting with them that night, she'd trudged up to her room and threw herself on the bed, fantasizing about running away with her easels and oils and never coming back.

"And at the library, I had told you I wanted to be a carpenter and make custom tables and chairs…"

"…and your parents told you your hands were made for surgery, not saws."

"Exactly."

They laughed at the shared memory and Dani felt at ease with her life choices. *See? We're good together. Stop doubting yourself.*

Will put his papers on the nightstand, turned off his light, and gave her a chaste kiss on the lips. "Love you."

He fell asleep instantly, his dark hair draped across his forehead. For years he'd worn it closely cropped, but recently he'd been letting it grow, going for the hipster look. A barely-there goatee completed the transformation. He was still handsome despite the changes.

With a groan, he rolled closer, resting a hand on her thigh.

Dani thought about Kara's hands. Long and slender and sexy. Tomorrow would be an early day, so she wouldn't even see Kara. Was that a pang of disappointment?

She shut off the light, and the last image in her head was those sexy hands.

CHAPTER SIX

Monday morning, Kara sat at the kitchen table eating an egg sandwich. Her two dogs stared, hoping for an errant scrap to fall on the floor. "You guys already ate, now stop begging."

The two pit bulls lay down on the ground and cocked their heads, hoping to look pathetic enough for some charity from Mom.

"Nope, won't work. Sorry, boys."

Val popped in to join her for breakfast. She took a bowl from the cabinet and poured herself some cereal.

"I was texting Zoey the other day," Kara said. "She wants to help us put together a website."

"Oh, cool. Maybe we can bring in more revenue."

"Yeah. Hey, listen, I'm going to the school this afternoon, then I have dinner with Travis and the fam tonight, so if you can close up, that would be great."

"Sure, no problem. Does Syd still teach at the school?"

"Yeah."

"She was nice."

Kara shrugged. "I know. We just didn't hit it off, romantically."

Kara still considered Sydney a friend, and still enjoyed going to the Northwest School for the Deaf. It had been Syd's idea to bring the dogs. She'd thought the kids would get a kick out of them, and she'd been right. It was all smiles and laughter when Ziggy and Milo showed up. Some of the kids would throw a tennis ball and chase after Ziggy, because fetch was not his strong suit. Others enjoyed simply petting them. The dogs took everything in stride and enjoyed all the extra attention.

There had been one other bonus to Kara and Syd's short-lived relationship: Kara had met twelve-year-old Travis Walker. They'd bonded over sports, especially football, since they were both big Seahawks fans. They got along so well through Syd interpreting that it motivated Kara to learn ASL, since that was his main form of communication, although occasionally he would speak simple things like thanks, or hi, or touchdown, or drop a curse word when his parents were out of earshot. They had a very big sister-little brother dynamic to their relationship, even though they were separated by over twenty years. His parents, Aaron and Jolie, were thrilled with the friendship, and the Walkers had become a de facto second family.

In between bites, Val said, "You look tired. Didn't you sleep?"

"I had a funky dream."

"What kind of funky dream?"

"My mom was alive, and she told me to take her to the hospital to see a doctor. I take her, and the doctor ends up being none other than our new customer."

"The redhead?"

"Yep."

"Wow, why was she on your mind?"

"Who knows?" She poured another cup of coffee. "Anyway, I woke up and couldn't fall back asleep."

What Kara conveniently left out was the dream turned super sexy. She and the good doctor engaged in some heavy lip-locking. Then kissing led to other things.

"Are you picking up her dog today?" Val asked.

"No, Ellie is." Kara absently stirred her coffee, the spoon spinning round and round, just like the good doctor's tongue did in her dream.

Val's brows rose. "You sure that's all that happened in the dream?"

Kara straightened. "What?"

"Dude, I've known you for years. I know your looks."

"What look?"

"Your sex look."

"I don't have a sex look."

Val slapped the table and guffawed. "You sure do. Did you have sex with the good doctor in your dream last night?" She put her elbow on the table and chin in her hand. "C'mon, give it up."

"Fuck off." Kara tried to hide a grin as a hot flush rushed into her cheeks.

"And now you're blushing. Wow, that must've been some dream. So much for hating doctors."

"I don't hate doctors. I just don't trust them, for obvious reasons."

"Except this doctor, who you're dreaming about."

Kara was already uncomfortable over the dream. She didn't need to be teased about it. "Enough."

"You need to get laid. You broke up with Cathy seven months ago."

"You know, she still texts me."

"Who, Cath?"

Kara nodded. "Yeah, got one a couple days ago." Cathy had taken their breakup hard. The text from the other day was much like the others, with its sad emoji face, asking what was new in Kara's life, which was code for, *are you seeing anybody because I'm still crazy about you.*

"I liked Cath," Val said. "I still don't know why you ended it with her."

"She just wasn't the one. I tried to make her into the one. But...I don't know. Maybe there's no 'one' for me. Maybe I'm that singular person in the universe who doesn't have a soulmate."

"Jesus. You're only thirty-five. You just haven't found her yet."

"I'm already exhausted from looking."

"Maybe you're too picky."

"Picky? I just want a woman who makes my heart race when I see her. Who puts a smile on my face every time I think about her. Someone I can laugh with and take long walks with. Someone I can have totally hot sex with. Who makes me feel like I'm gonna die if I can't be with her. Is that too much to ask?"

"Yes."

Kara balled up her napkin and threw it at Val. "You have that with Jes."

Jesmyn Davani Azar, Val's girlfriend of six years was one of those stunning beings that stood out in a crowd, a second-generation Iranian American with long, black-as-night curly hair. Kara had known her since high school. When Kara was a freshman on the basketball team, Jes was a senior for a crosstown rival. She would flirt with Kara on the court to throw her off her game, and it worked, because Kara had a huge crush on the tall, beautiful girl. A crush that, to a small extent, still existed today.

"Speaking of Jes," Val said. "She has someone she wants you to meet."

"I'm taking a break from women right now. Remember? I don't wanna be in a relationship."

"That's the beauty of it. Neither does this woman. She travels a lot for work, so she's not into commitments right now. She's cute. Her name's Rachel. Come over for dinner and meet her. Then maybe you won't be having X-rated dreams about our customers."

Kara mulled over Val's suggestion. Maybe it wouldn't be a bad thing to have something casual right now, just to take the edge off. She certainly didn't need a repeat of last night's dream. She relented. "Okay. I'll meet her."

* * *

When Kara stepped onto the porch at the Walkers', she smiled. Jolie must've visited her favorite secondhand store. Two distressed rocking chairs sat nearby, price tags waving in the breeze. Both seats needed to be re-caned, but when finished they'd be the perfect complement to the 1920s Cape Cod-style home. Before she could press the doorbell, the door flew open.

Jolie grabbed her hand and yanked her inside. "You're here!"

Kara stumbled through the doorway. "You sound surprised. Tonight's our monthly dinner, right?"

Jolie waved a hand and made a comical face. "Yes. Of course it's our monthly dinner."

"I made cupcakes."

"Thanks. They look delicious," she declared without so much as a glance into the dish.

Kara took in Jolie's slightly disheveled appearance. Her apron had a few yellow stains on it, and her normally tame chestnut bob was sticking out a bit around her ears. "You okay?"

"Yes. I'm great. Give me your jacket."

Kara slipped her jacket off and handed it to Jolie. "Where's my favorite twelve-year-old?"

"Who?"

Kara narrowed her eyes. "Ah, Travis, your son?"

"Oh." Jolie laughed and patted down her wayward hair. "I'm sorry, I've been rushing around trying to get everything ready. I want it to be perfect! He's in the living room."

"Perfect?" Kara mumbled as Jolie snatched the cupcakes and ran down the hallway, leaving Kara to stare after her retreating back. She shrugged off Jolie's hyperactive energy and walked into the living room.

This was her favorite space. Again, Jolie's eclectic style was front and center. A bright yellow couch was the focal point, and a light orange shag carpet covered most of the wood flooring. Kara would never dream of putting orange and yellow together, but in here, it just worked.

She flicked the lights and Travis gave a hearty, "Whoop," before jumping up and hugging her.

Kara squeezed his wiry frame and then ran a hand through his mop of hair. *What's up?* she signed.

Nothing. I'm hungry. He rubbed his belly.

Me too. Found this for you. She handed him a new game for his Xbox.

His eyes lit up and a wide smile split his face. *Thanks! Wanna play?*

Yeah, sure, if your mom lets us. Get it set up. I'm gonna grab a drink.

Aaron Walker poked his head in from the kitchen. "Steaks on the barbie tonight," he said in a playful Australian accent.

"Sweet! Need any help?" Kara asked.

"Nah, I'm good, thanks."

When he went back outside, the aroma of beef wafted into the house, making her mouth water. She joined Jolie in the kitchen. "What can I do?"

"Nothing. I've got it under control." Jolie tossed the salad. "I saw Val the other day."

"Oh, yeah?"

"She said she set you up with someone?"

"Uh-huh." Kara popped a carrot into her mouth. "Her name's Rachel. We've gone out a couple times, but it's nothing serious. We're keeping it casual."

"Oh, good, so you're not off the market?"

"No." Kara rooted around in the fridge for a beer. "What are you getting at?" On a hunch, she wandered into the dining room and counted the place settings. Five. Of course. That's why Jolie was acting odd. "What did you do?"

Jolie giggled.

"Tell me you're not setting me up." When she received no reply, Kara reentered the kitchen. "Jolie?"

"What? I may have invited someone over. A single someone who happens to be a lesbian."

"Oh, Christ," Kara groaned. "You're killing me." There had been a couple of times in the past when Jolie tried to find her the perfect woman. Usually, it turned out to be an unmitigated disaster. Two of the most memorable were Amber the lumberjack, who wanted to toss Kara over her shoulder, and Betsy the wannabe dominatrix, who showed up in leather and chains and kept meowing across the table at her. Kara had no idea where Jolie found these women. She pictured her canvassing for potential lesbians at REI.

Aaron carried a large plate of potatoes into the kitchen. "Potatoes are done, steaks are next."

"Your wife is killing me."

"Relax, Britton, you know she thinks of herself as some sort of modern-day Cupid. It's her romantic nature."

The doorbell rang and the lights flashed.

"I'll get it," Jolie yelled.

Kara raised her eyebrows at Aaron, who clearly enjoyed her discomfort. "Where'd she find this one?"

"Don't know. I think through someone at work." He gave her a wicked grin and hightailed it back to his beloved barbie.

Kara headed back to the living room and steeled herself to meet the fix-up. She inhaled deeply and hoped for the best.

Jolie came bouncing into the room, random lesbian in tow. Kara's first impression was of an imp. Or a sprite. The woman's dark hair was bushy and overly large for her tiny frame. Underneath the hair was a heart-shaped face and blue eyes. But not sky blue, like a certain doctor's.

The woman handed Jolie a large glass baking dish. "I made this for everyone."

They peeked at the contents. It was hard. Or it was soft. It was difficult to ascertain without poking a finger into it. But one thing was certain. It was green.

"Wow," Jolie said. "That's a lot of guacamole dip."

"Oh, it's not guacamole. It's brownies. Although I think I used too much avocado."

Kara had never seen anything that color green before. Or maybe she had. Pond scum came to mind. "You made brownies with avocado?"

"Yes."

"Interesting choice."

"Much healthier for you. I'm Marcie, by the way."

Jolie raised a hand to her chest. "I'm sorry. Marcie, this is Kara."

Marcie's handshake was firm, her eyes wide and unblinking. Which Kara found freaky. She continued to shake, and Kara thought her arm would fall off. Tiny thing was stronger than she looked.

"Kara. Is that short for Karema?"

The shaking stopped. "No, it's—"

But the sprite had turned her attention to the drapes hanging on the dining room window. "These are lovely, how much did you pay for them?"

Before Jolie could answer, Marcie spotted Travis. "Hello, young man!"

Jolie put an arm around Travis and squeezed, then signed and said, "Yes, this is our son, Travis. He's deaf."

Marcie grabbed Travis's hand and the shaking began all over again. "Lovely to meet you, Travis." Every syllable was overenunciated and loud.

"He doesn't read lips very well," Jolie said. "But don't worry, I'll sign everything we're saying."

"Okay." Marcie turned to Jolie. "Tell him he's so handsome."

"You can say it to him. And I'll sign."

"Right." A confused Marcie looked back and forth between Jolie and Travis. "Well. Hello, Travis. You're handsome."

"Hi. Thanks," he said.

Travis finally got his arm back when his dad wandered into the dining room carrying a stack of ribeyes. "I'm Jolie's husband, Aaron."

Jolie waved at the dining room table. "Dinner's ready. Marcie, what can I get you to drink?"

"Do you have any sparkling, distilled water?"

"Um, I don't think so. But we have bottled water."

Marcie's eyes blew wide. "No, God. You read all those stories about how bottled water is not even treated. You should check the caps. I heard some companies refill old bottles, then sell them like new. I think that happened in Wisconsin."

Jolie bent into the fridge. "How about a beer, or wine?"

"No, I'm gluten-free and non-alcoholic."

"Juice?"

"Is it sugar free? Sugar will kill us all someday, right?"

She looked at Kara, who had mentally nodded off after the bottled water explanation. "Ah, sorry?"

Jolie still had her head buried in the fridge. "Soda?"

"I had a friend of mine give up soda and she lost thirty pounds," Marcie declared.

Kara was dumbstruck. "How much soda did she drink?"

"Oh, I don't know."

"Tap water?" Jolie asked.

"That's fine."

Kara hid a smirk. Tap water was the least filtered option in the house.

"So, Kara, what do you do?" Marcie asked.

"I just walk dogs." She hoped that was enough of a turn-off for Marcie the enunciator.

However, the plan was upended because Jolie quickly chimed in. "Kara owns a dog kennel and a store. She doesn't just walk dogs."

"I'm a cat person," Marcie said.

Kara forced a smile. "That's nice. I assume you own a cat?"

"I have eight of them."

"Eight of them? You must have a big house," Aaron said.

"Oh, no, I live in a one-bedroom apartment."

Kara stared, half expecting one of the cats to pop out of her hair. "Wow, sounds crowded."

Marcie giggled. "It does get a bit crowded, yes. Do you like cats?"

"I'm a dog person, to be honest."

"Oh." Disappointment registered on Marcie's face. "You've never owned a cat?"

"Nope."

"Let's eat before it gets cold." Aaron began placing a steak on everybody's plate.

Marcie held a hand over hers. "I'm vegan."

Kara winced. Poor Aaron. He loved sharing his barbecued meats. The devastation was clear in his eyes as he placed the plate back on the table.

Jolie picked up the bowl of potatoes. "Try some potatoes. They're delicious."

"I'll pass. Starchy carbs turn right into sugar."

Kara had never met a potato she didn't like. She glanced across the table at Travis.

Pass the butter, Karema.

She bit back a grin.

Aaron lifted a basket filled with slices of warm focaccia bread. "Bread?" he asked with trepidation.

Marcie fell victim to another case of the giggles. "You're funny, no. I'll just have salad."

Jolie passed the salad and they all watched in wide-eyed wonder as Marcie poked through the bowl, flicking this and that aside. Croutons were pushed to the bottom, cucumbers piled up to the right, carrots to the left. When the poking and picking and prodding were done, two leaves of romaine lettuce lay on the plate.

"Dressing?" Jolie asked.

"No, this is fine. It looks delicious." Marcie cut the lettuce into tiny pieces and happily munched away like a rabbit.

A couple of hours later, Kara said goodbye to Marcie at the front door and ambled back into the living room, plopping down on the couch next to Travis.

Jolie was the first to speak. "What did you think?"

Aaron and Travis snickered.

Kara took a deep breath, absently twirling a finger in her hair. "Well, she was...very nice. But I don't see it going any further."

"Is it the vegan thing?" Aaron asked.

Kara cocked her head to one side. "No, I don't think it was that."

Big hair, Travis signed.

"It *was* big, but no."

"She had blue eyes. Your favorite." Jolie was reaching.

"She did."

Too many cats. Stinky. Travis held his nose.

"She does have a lot of cats, buddy, you're right. But for the right person, I could put up with that."

Green brownies. He pretended to retch.

Kara's head dipped slightly. "They were an unusual shade of green. But no."

They sat again in silence, mulling over all these revelations.

"You see," Kara started. "All of those things, by themselves, don't seem like much. However, once we put them all together, in one person…" She made a blending motion with her hands and nodded at her audience. "It becomes too much."

They acted serious for a moment, then burst out laughing.

Aaron could barely catch his breath. "You need to screen these women better, honey."

"I'm so sorry. Rita said this woman was funny and attractive and would be perfect."

Kara smiled. "It's okay. I appreciate the effort, I really do."

Jolie raised her glass of wine. "I promise, the next woman you have dinner with here, will be the one. I promise."

Kara laughed. "Okay." She raised her glass of water. "Here's to next time, when I'm sure to have dinner with the woman of my dreams, right here in the Walker house."

CHAPTER SEVEN

She pulled back from the kiss and stared into green eyes. Lips and a hot tongue found their way to her neck, nibbling and sucking...

Dani woke with a start, eyes snapping open, breathing labored. *Holy shit.* She lay still for a moment, trying to clear her head. She was groggy but swore she could still feel a tongue.

"Oliver," she whispered, jerking her toes away from him. He gazed adoringly back, his tail thump, thump, thumping on the bed. Will slept soundly and Jinx purred contentedly on her pillow.

Dani covered her face with a hand, groaning softly. *Why does she have to be so attractive?* This was the third dream in the last week. Was she so sexually starved she had to dream about a woman she barely knew? Who annoyed the crap out of her? She slipped a hand down between her legs and touched herself. Her breath caught and she pulled her hand away. She was soaked. A restless, unsatisfied energy coursed through her. An orgasm would be nice right now, just to take the edge off. *Should I wake Will?*

He lay on his back, chest rising and falling softly. He looked peaceful. Probably best to take care of things alone. She slipped a hand back between her legs.

Jinx was having none of it and hopped off the bed, leaving the voyeurism to the dog.

Dani tried to think of Will, hoping to expedite the process, but you-know-who kept popping into her brain. Finally, she surrendered, letting her mind wander, picturing beautiful hands touching her, a beautiful mouth kissing her. Oliver wiggled toward her, cocking his head at the soft noises she made. When finished, she closed her eyes.

She had just masturbated in front of the dog. Surely this was a new low.

* * *

Dani was thankful her besties dragged her out to The Rose. All the stress from the last few months had caught up with her, so a night on the town was just what the doctor ordered. Zoey being the doctor in this case.

They sat around a table nursing their beers while the dance music drummed in the background.

"How's the wedding planning going? I'm your maid of honor, I'm supposed to be helping you," Zoey said.

"I'm not planning it. Our moms are."

"Don't you wanna be involved?" Jen asked. "Sounds duplicitous to *not* be involved. That's one, people!"

Zoey's eyes widened. "Nice. Word of the day?"

Jen nodded.

Zoey high-fived her. "That's my girl!"

An already tipsy Dani was equally impressed. "That's a big word. And to answer your question, I'm crazy busy working, so I don't have a lot of time to do it."

"What about dresses? Would be goddamn duplicitous if we didn't do some goddamn dress shopping." Grinning, Zoey held up two fingers to Jen. "Two, hon."

"Only counts if I use it, babe."

Zoey blew out a frustrated puff of breath.

"Or we can all go down the aisle in scrubs." Dani downed a third beer and started a fourth. "Goddamn duplicitous…less…ly." Dani had no clue what the word meant. "That's three!" She held up four fingers. Maybe "tipsy" was being kind.

"How's Will?" Jen asked.

"He's good."

Zoey cocked a brow. "How's Kara?"

An image from last night's dream popped into her head, and Dani hoped the heat in her cheeks wasn't visible. "I don't know. And I don't care."

"Why don't you like her? She's cool."

Dani shrugged. "I just don't." She didn't know why Kara rubbed her the wrong way. Or why she starred in her dreams. Or why she made Dani want things she shouldn't want.

Jen glanced over Dani's shoulder. "Uh-oh. Here comes trouble. I gotta go wee-wee—I mean pee. I'll be right back."

Someone tapped her shoulder and Dani turned around. She quietly groaned. "Oh, hey, Elena."

"Hi, Dani, long time no see. Where've you been?" Elena's black hair was buzzed close to her head, and she had multiple piercings in her ears and on her face.

"I've been busy. How are you?"

"I'm good. You look great. Can I buy you a drink?"

"I'm still nursing this one, but thanks."

"Okay. But let me know if you need another. Or need anything. Ever." She winked and squeezed Dani's shoulder.

"I will, thanks."

"Like, sexually."

"Okay, I got it, thanks."

Elena walked away, and Dani blew out a breath. "Not very subtle, is she."

"She's in love with you," Zoey said.

Dani looked down at her sloppy self. Not feeling like dressing up, she'd thrown an old hoodie on. "I have no idea what she sees in me. But I guess it's flattering."

"Maybe she needs glasses."

Jen came back from the bathroom with Kara in tow. "Hey, look who I ran into."

Dani groaned again. Nemesis number two. Haunter of dreams and soon to be ruiner of a perfectly good evening.

Kara smiled. "Zoey…and Dani?"

Dani gave a slight nod. "Karen."

"Who's Karen?" Zoey asked.

Dani used the wrong name on purpose, just to annoy, and wasn't prepared for the joyous laughter that burst forth from Kara's lips. Her heart fluttered with…*attraction*? No, it couldn't be. She was developing arrhythmia. Yes, that's what it was. Arrhythmia. And the arrhythmia was now causing a warmth that crept from her belly, slinked through her chest, and settled in her face. Another image from the dream floated into her brain. Lust-filled eyes and long sexy fingers dancing across her hips. She beat the attraction back with a stout, mental stick.

Kara ordered a beer from the waitress and turned back to Dani. "Surprised to see you. Slumming it with the LGBTQ folk?"

"I'll have you know I come here a lot. Not that it's any of your business." Goddamn this woman set her off. And goddamn, why did she have to be so good-looking?

"Yeah, we drag her here all the time to show her what she's missing." Jen looped an arm around Dani's neck and kissed her cheek. "What's up with you, Kara?"

"Nothing exciting."

Kara's eyes lingered on Dani, peering into her soul. Those long fingers tapped the tabletop. It was suddenly hard to breathe. Dani pulled at the neck of her hoodie.

"So, Kara, are you still seeing the chick you met a few weeks ago?" Zoey asked.

"Rachel? We're casually dating, nothing exclusive."

"You mean casually having sex?" Zoey made a comical face.

"Pphhtt." All heads turned toward Dani. "Is that your thing? Casual sex?" Dani tipped back her beer.

Kara's eyes widened. "My thing? No, I wouldn't say it's my *thing*."

"Pphhtt." She tipped the bottle back again but came up empty. That went down quick.

Kara smirked. "How've you been, Dani? We don't get to see each other now that Ellie is picking up the dog. I'm sure you've missed me."

"Oh, terribly." Four beers in and she was ready to spar. "As I'm sure you've missed me. I mean, who do you have to yell at? I'm sure all your other customers know their dog's name."

Kara gave a look that a patient mother would give a toddler who demanded more cake. "I don't think I ever yelled at you."

"Oh, you yelled. At least that's how I heard it. In my head." She tapped her temple for emphasis.

"How's Oliver? Has day care been helping?"

"He's okay. Like slightly better. Just slightly." The dog was much better, but did she have to know that? "Oh, I finally bought a new wallet, no thanks to you." She reached into a pocket, pulled out a shiny black wallet, and waved it at Kara.

"Good. Your hair looks nice. Did you finally comb it?"

Dani ran her fingers through it. "I went to the salon."

"Oh, the Hair Cuttery?"

Zoey waved down a waitress. "We need more beers. And popcorn, do you have any popcorn?"

Dani narrowed her eyes. "Very funny. I see you haven't lost your sense of humor these past weeks."

"No, I'm still funny. How's the fiancé? What's his name? Phil?"

"Will. His name is Will."

"Right, Will."

"He's good. We're getting married in September. And you're not invited."

"Oh, damn, I had your gift all picked out."

The waitress returned with the beers and passed them around. "We didn't have popcorn, but we had nuts."

A rare slow song came on and Jen grabbed Zoey's hand. "C'mon, let's go."

Her mouth turned down at the edges. "But this is getting good."

"No, you guys, don't leave me please," Dani pleaded, to no avail. She stole a glance at Kara, who wore that damn half-smile smirk on her face.

"Afraid to be left alone with me?"

"Oh, please, don't flatter yourself. It's not you." Dani spotted Elena on her way over. "Oh boy."

Elena placed a hand on Dani's arm. "Hey, Dani, come dance with me."

Dani had made the drunken mistake of dancing with her one time two years ago. And ever since, she needed to fend her off whenever the music slowed down. Usually, she had a litany of excuses prepared, but Kara had her all befuddled. Dani could perform the most delicate of surgeries, but she could only handle one annoying woman at a time.

Kara grabbed Dani's hand. "I'm sorry, she promised this dance to me." She gave a small yank and led Dani onto the dance floor. Kara pulled her close. "You're welcome," she whispered into her ear.

"I certainly didn't need you to rescue me," Dani hissed. Kara's arms felt strong. And it wasn't an unpleasant feeling. Dani tried to maintain an acceptable distance from the slightly taller brunette. There was no need for any extra touching.

Kara laughed softly and leaned even closer, her lips brushing her earlobe. "Who was your friend back there?"

A shiver ran down Dani's spine when Kara's breath grazed her ear. *Damn air conditioner.* "Nobody."

"She acted like you guys danced before."

Dani tried to be vague, hoping this line of questioning would end soon. "Maybe we did, maybe we didn't." Kara's hips pressed into hers, and the warmth she experienced earlier moved south. Like, south of the border. The border being her belt. How was this even possible? Wanting to slap someone and rip their clothes off at the same time? All she wanted to do was press her hips into Kara and grind away at the ache that began to throb between her legs. She cursed her traitorous body. And what the hell perfume was she wearing? It was intoxicating but not overpowering, sweet and delicate with a hint of lavender. Dani wanted to bury her nose in Kara's neck.

"You make a habit out of dancing with women?"

Don't say anything, don't say anything. "Sometimes." Dani bit her lip as soon as the words flew out of her mouth. Jesus Christ, the ache was getting stronger.

"Hmm. Have you ever dated a woman?"

"Maybe." *Oh. My. God. Did I just say that?* The arrhythmia came back with a vengeance, only instead of fluttering, her heart pounded like a bass drum. Great. She was having a heart attack. Who would resuscitate her? Would she need mouth-to-mouth? Did Kara know CPR? Maybe a heart attack wasn't such a bad thing after all.

"So, you *did* date a woman."

"I didn't say that." The heat spread to other parts of her body now. Was this a hot flash? When was her last period? Was this early onset menopause? Was the air on in here? *For fuck's sake, turn on the AC!*

"You didn't have to."

"Oh, so you're a dog walker and a psychic?"

Kara laughed again. "What was her name?"

"Suzanne." It seemed she was powerless to stop the flow of information from her lips. She hated her half-drunk self.

"Wow. I'm totally surprised."

Dani became sexually sober in an instant. "Why? You don't think a woman would go out with me?"

"I didn't say that."

"But that's what you meant."

"It's just that...I don't know. You seem a bit uptight for that."

"Uptight? I'm not uptight."

"You're a little uptight."

"I'm stressed, not uptight."

"How long ago were you with her?"

"It was years ago..." Dani caught herself. "Wait, I'm not talking about this with you."

"Aw, c'mon."

"No." The song ended, saving her from further humiliation. She broke away and raced back to the table where Zoey and Jen were already seated.

Kara strolled over. "Ladies, I just wanted to say goodbye. And Dani, thanks for the dance. It was enjoyable."

"Pphhtt. I don't know about that."

"Well, I enjoyed it."

"Well, I didn't."

With a tilt of her head, Kara said, "Maybe you'll enjoy the next one."

Dani gulped. *Next one? I barely survived this one. Quick! Say something clever!* She wracked her brain for a stinging rebuke, but it was too late. Kara was gone. "Damn it," she muttered under her breath, annoyed with the fact that Kara had gotten in the last word.

After she left, Zoey studied Dani. "So how did you end up slow dancing with Kara?"

Dani squeezed her eyes shut. The dance had thrown her off-kilter, and she fought to regain her equilibrium. "It was either her or Ellie, I took the lesser of two evils."

"Who's Ellie?"

"You mean Elena," Jen said.

Dani nodded. "Yeah Elena, what did I say?"

"What didn't you say?" Zoey asked. "I can't keep track of all your women. So, how was it?"

"How was what?"

"The slow dance. Jesus Christ."

"It was a goddamn slow dance. We didn't have sex."

Zoey winked and pointed. "Maybe you should."

"Excuse me?"

"Take her out for more than a slow dance. Sow your wild oats before the wedding."

"Please stop talking. Where's my beer? I need another beer." She couldn't shake the image of Kara doing unspeakable things to her body. She chalked it up to not having sex for a while. Fulfilling sex. Which wasn't a big deal. Was it? Sex wasn't the most important part of a relationship anyway. Right? Communication, common goals, those were the building blocks. *Right?*

Why was she getting married? Because it was expected, that's why. And Dani always did what was expected. The Clarks were not allowed to become starving artists. Check. The Clarks became doctors. Check. The Clarks married within their social circle. Engaged, so almost a check. The Clarks had babies and lived happily ever after.

Yet to be determined.

She sighed. One of these days she'd grow a pair of lady balls, as Zoey liked to say, and do what *she* wanted to do. Someday. When she had the energy. And the lady balls.

CHAPTER EIGHT

"I heard you're doing rounds with your mom today," Kyle said.

"Yeah, can't wait." They had set up a Nerf basketball net last week in the lounge, and Dani found she was embarrassingly bad at it. But no mind, she still enjoyed tossing the tiny ball around. She chucked it and hit the cabinet.

"Maybe she won't be so awful," Kyle said. "She is one of the best surgeons in the city."

"I know. Truth be told, she hasn't been bad lately since the wedding date is set. She's been sort of pleasant. This is probably her way of bonding with me." Dani tossed the basketball at the net, missing again. "Yeah, nothing but air."

"I had a rotation with her. She was…" He rubbed the short stubble on his chin.

"A hard-ass?"

He gave her a sheepish grin. "Yeah. I didn't wanna say that out loud. What was she like when you were growing up?"

"A hard-ass."

They both laughed.

"Her dad was a hard-ass too," Dani said. "And a brilliant surgeon."

"So it runs in the family."

"The brilliant surgeon part yes," Dani joked. "But I'd like to think I'm not a hard-ass."

"No worries. You're not."

"I guess I should cut my mom some slack. She didn't have a great childhood. My grandfather wanted a boy, and my grandmother died before they could try again, so he was stuck with a girl. And my mom was stuck with a father who thought she was something less than. She spent her whole life trying to prove him wrong, trying to be perfect so he'd notice her."

"Which is probably why she rides you so hard."

"True. I guess it's difficult to break the cycle of hard-assery." She laughed at her made-up word. "I remember when I was young, like five or six, and good old Grandpop would visit. Only I couldn't call him Grandpop, or Pop Pop, it was always Grandfather. I would hide behind the furniture because he was so scary. And cold. Not a shred of warmth about him." Dani shook her cheeks. "Brrrr."

"Damn. What about your dad?"

"I love my dad. But. He's a yes-man. Meaning, he worships my mom and basically agrees with everything she says or does."

"Ugh." Kyle raised his bottle of water. "Here's to you breaking away from the cycle of hard-assery!"

"I'll drink to that."

* * *

She spent the morning with her mom, making rounds and discussing upcoming procedures. Dani was to assist on a seven-year-old's tonsillectomy, and today was the meet and greet with the young girl and her parents. While her mom explained the procedure to the parents, Dani sat down on the bed with the young girl, Madison, who had an unruly crop of curly brown hair and big brown eyes.

Dani put an arm around the girl. "Everything will be easy-peasy. Trust me. Dr. Rebecca is my mom, and she's the best doctor in the whole hospital."

The young girl's eyes were wide with worry. "Is it gonna hurt, Dr. Dani?"

Dani squeezed her. "Nah, you're gonna be sound asleep and dreaming the whole time. You're seven years old, right, Maddie?"

"Yeah."

A distant memory drifted back to her. "When I was around your age, I met a girl in the hospital who was having her tonsils out also. And she was as brave as you."

"Really?"

"Yep. She was in the hospital for a few days, and we became best friends. She loved puppies and I loved kittens."

Madison clapped. "I love kittens!"

Dani took her index finger and gently bopped Madison on the tip of her nose. "Who doesn't? And we decided when we grew up, we'd live on a farm together, and we'd get as many puppies and kittens as we wanted."

"That sounds fun."

"I know. I fancied myself an artist back then and I made her a picture book, showing what our farm would look like."

"You made a book?"

Dani smiled. "Uh-huh."

"Are you still friends?"

"No." Dani hesitated as the memory became clearer. The memory of her mom telling her she wouldn't be able to see her new friend again, and Dani crying and asking why. She had been told her new friend lived across town, and doctors worked long hours, and don't worry, she would meet plenty of other friends. "She didn't live near us, so I couldn't see her anymore. You know, I was too short to drive to her house." Dani gave her young patient a nudge with her shoulder. "I wish I had one of those cool battery cars kids have today, then I would've driven to her house."

"I have one of those. I'll let you use it so you can drive and see your friend."

"Aw, thank you, but I don't know where she lives now."

"That's sad."

"Yeah. I was sad for a while."

"What are you two talking about?" Dr. Rebecca asked.

Maddie smiled. "Dr. Dani was telling me about when she was little, and her friend got her tonsils out."

Rebecca's brows creased. "When was that?"

Dani turned away. "It was a long time ago." She brushed a curl from Maddie's forehead. "A long, long time ago."

CHAPTER NINE

Kara sat at the red light, staring into the distance. Last night she'd had another dream. Starring Dani Clark. Jesus Christ, she felt like an adolescent boy. Why on earth was she dreaming about the doctor? Maybe it was because of the surprise meeting at the bar the other night, and the fact that Kara was *happy* to see her. How the hell that was possible, she had no clue. She didn't even like her. She owned a cat. And was annoying as hell. And argumentative. *And utterly unavailable, let's not forget that.*

The car behind tooted their horn, and the dogs in the van grumbled. Her eyes refocused and she hit the gas. A few blocks up Kara sat at another light, and her mind wandered again. She recalled the way Dani's eyes sparkled with a feistiness at the bar, casting a spell on her. And then the slow dance. It'd been invigorating, and the feeling of Dani in her arms felt "right" somehow. Then came the ultimate revelation. Dani had previously been with a woman. She didn't see that one coming.

Barking dogs pulled her back to reality. With a sigh, she tried to banish Dani from her thoughts. Which was hard because she was on her way there now. Kara prayed nobody was home. She wasn't ready to lay eyes on Dani today, not so soon after the slow dance. Not so soon after the dream.

Alas, her prayer went unanswered.

Dani opened the door. "Hey, where's Ellie?"

"She called in sick, so you're stuck with me." Kara's mind concentrated on the task at hand: getting Oliver and getting the hell out of Dodge.

"So, the dog, ah…I don't know where he is."

Kara followed Dani through the living room and came face-to-face with the midget mountain lion, who sat upon his favorite perch. She cowered when he greeted her with his signature hello hiss and swat.

What could only be described as an evil chuckle fell from Dani's lips. "Did you ever meet Jinx?" She scratched Jinx's fluffy ears and cooed, "My good boy. How's my baby?"

"Not formally, no. We usually try to avoid each other."

"Why do you avoid him? He's such a sweetie."

"We have a love-hate relationship. He loves to hate me."

"Really? Good boy." Dani cackled at her joke. "I love cats."

"Of course you do."

"Oliver!" Dani called, and listened. She cocked her head toward the steps. "I'll look upstairs." She took the steps two at a time, calling the dog's name.

Kara stared, admiring her, ahem, agility. In an effort to distract herself from Dani's unavailable ass, she perused the pictures in the dining room. Dani had a warm, beautiful smile in all the pictures, something Kara had yet to see directed at her. Not that she cared. No need to see that megawatt smile. She heard thumping, and a split second later Oliver scooted through the dining room and into the kitchen. "He's down here!"

She followed Oliver into the kitchen and peeked under the table. Something hung from his mouth. That something was a lacy, light-blue bra.

Kara waved a treat at Oliver, distracting him long enough to grab the bra from his mouth. As she straightened, she held it up by the straps and admired the cup size. A tiny pool of moisture settled between her legs at the thought of Dani's breasts filling these cups. What the shit kind of dream would she have tonight?

"Hey!" Dani appeared out of thin air. "That's *my* bra!"

Kara smirked. "Well, I didn't think it was Will's."

"Very funny." Dani's face pinkened.

"Don't be embarrassed."

"Give it." She snatched it away from Kara's grasp. "I'm not embarrassed. It's just a bra."

"Well, I dunno about that." Kara's eyes traveled down to Dani's chest.

"What are you looking at?"

Her eyes snapped back to Dani's. She was caught staring. Not only staring but enjoying the view. She swallowed thickly. "Uh, nothing."

"That was rude."

Kara laughed. "Okay, maybe it was. You should be flattered."

"Flattered? That you were ogling me?" With a scowl, Dani crossed her arms.

"I wasn't ogling." Kara was a breast woman, so of course she ogled. "Okay, maybe I ogled a little bit. It is a nice bra."

Dani's fierce eyes bore into Kara, who found the situation comical. "Evidently, I'm not the only one who likes it." With a playful expression she motioned her head down to Oliver, who sat like a champ waiting for his leash.

Dani continued to glower and added some toe tapping for good measure.

Kara snickered.

"It's not funny. You're not funny."

"So you tell me. All the time." Kara clipped the leash onto Oliver's collar and walked out the door. "We'll catch you and the girls later."

"Who are the girls?" Dani demanded, following her.

Kara laughed again and waved as she walked toward the van.

"Not funny! Karen!"

Kara laughed harder. The Karen thing cracked her up.

CHAPTER TEN

Kara and the dogs sat in her office at the store. She entered the last bill into the accounting program, closed the laptop, and rubbed her tired eyes.

"Knock, knock." Zoey poked her head through the doorway. "Hey, boss. Now a good time to go over some website ideas?"

"It's actually perfect timing. Let me text Val."

"Cool. Jen came too."

Jen waved. "Hi."

Before Zoey and Jen could sit down, Kara's dogs approached to give the new arrivals a sniff.

Zoey held up her hands. "Whoa, big dogs."

Kara smiled. "They're harmless, don't worry. The gray one is Ziggy, and the black-and-white one is Milo. Sit, boys."

"Are they pit bulls?" Zoey asked.

"Yeah. I rescued them about six years ago."

"Are they bilious? That's one, people!" Jen proudly wagged an index finger in the air.

Zoey raised a hand for a no-look high-five. After exchanging hand slaps with Jen, she turned to Kara with a hand up. "Give it up."

A confused Kara obliged. "What are we doing?"

"The word of the day high-five is a thing now," Jen said. "All must participate."

"What's word of the day?" Kara asked.

"Jen, who nannies a few tiny humans, is trying to dumb down the baby talk by using big, smart words," Zoey said. "The kind none of us ever heard of or know the definition of. Which makes them high-five worthy." With a hesitant hand, she patted Ziggy on the head. "Good dog, don't eat me."

Val appeared with Jolie in tow. "Look who stopped by."

After the introductions were made, everyone grabbed a chair and Kara passed around water bottles.

"So, Jolie. I heard you found Kara quite the woman the other week," Val said.

Jolie blushed. "Well, it didn't turn out quite the way I'd hoped. I'm a failure when it comes to matchmaking."

"Ah, matchmaking is my middle name," Zoey said. "Let me know if you need any pointers."

"I may take you up on that. I definitely need pointers."

"Oh, I dunno," Val said. "I think the dominatrix would've worked out if Kara had given her a chance."

Kara blanched. "What?"

The spent the next few minutes teasing Jolie about her matchmaking fiascos and expressing fake outrage at Kara's refusal to date any of them.

When they ran out of horrible blind-dating stories, Jolie rose to say her goodbyes. "You guys have work to do, so I'll head out. It was nice meeting you both."

Val walked Jolie out, leaving Zoey and Jen behind with Kara.

"So." Zoey directed her gaze at Kara. "Last week at the bar."

"Yeah?"

"How did you manage to get Dani to slow dance with you?"

Kara shrugged. "Some woman was hitting on her, so I helped her out. Why?"

Zoey leaned back and linked her hands behind her head. "What do you think of her?"

"Who, Dani? She's okay. I mean, it's no secret we don't get along."

"Don't you think she's cute?"

Kara curled her lip. "Sure, yeah."

"She has nice eyes, right?"

"Um, yeah." What was Zoey getting at? If Kara didn't know better, she'd swear Zoey was flexing her matchmaking muscles. But that would be crazy. Dani was engaged. And a pain in the ass.

"She has a good heart. I know you haven't seen it…yet."

"Yet?" Kara laughed. "I doubt I'll ever see that side of her." She tossed her empty water bottle into the recycle bin. "She told me she used to date a woman."

Zoey's eyebrows popped up. "She was drunker than I thought."

"I was shocked."

"Yeah. Didn't end well. But that's a story for another day. Hey, Saturday Jen and I are going to breakfast at Barjot, on Bellevue. You should join us."

"Sure."

Val returned and they spent the next hour working on the website. Dani wasn't mentioned again, which was fine by Kara. She needed Dani out of her head. Rachel had stopped over last night, and while they were having sex, Kara kept thinking about Dani's blue bra.

She was no sexual rocket scientist, but she was pretty sure that wasn't how things should work.

Although it was a nice bra.

CHAPTER ELEVEN

Dani sat at a table with Jen and Zoey at Barjot's on Saturday morning. The popular eatery was buzzing, and most of the tables were full. The smell of eggs and bacon filled the air and her tummy rumbled.

"You look tired, Dans," Jen said.

"Ugh. I've been having weird dreams."

"What are you dreaming about?" Jen asked.

"The wedding. And other things."

Zoey put her elbows on the table. "What other things?"

Oh, you know, Kara taking my clothes off and having sex with me, just the usual stuff. How a woman she barely knew could play such a prominent role in her subconscious was beyond her. She could barely explain it to herself, let alone explain it to her two best girlfriends. And, it would only be more ammunition for Zoey to tell her to sow her wild oats. "Nothing, forget it, just the wedding. I'm stressing over stuff, as usual."

The roar of a motorcycle distracted them, and they glanced out the window. The rider parked in front of the café, and long, brunette tresses fell from the helmet when it was removed.

"Holy shit," Jen gasped. "It's Kara." She waved enthusiastically when Kara walked in. "Hey, Kara!"

Dani was aghast. *How is it possible to run into her here?* Jesus. She couldn't get away from the woman.

Kara waved and bought a cup of coffee at the counter. After adding some creamer and sugar, she sauntered over. "Ladies."

"What are you doing here?" Zoey asked.

Kara cocked her head to one side. "Ah, you invit—"

"Sit!" Zoey used her foot to shove the empty chair at their table in Kara's direction.

Jen threw an arm around her. "Well, isn't this serendipitous." She turned to Zoey. "That's one!"

"Give it up." Zoey raised a hand for a high-five. Then proceeded to spread it around the table, each girl absently slapping hands.

"You still doing that?" Dani asked.

"Absolutely," Jen said. "It's working. Right, babe?"

"Sure, hon, except for calling my nipples 'nip-nips' last night."

Jen shrugged. "It's a slow process."

"And a buzzkill. Hey, you want anything to eat?" Zoey asked Kara.

"No, I can't stay too long."

"Nice bike," Jen said.

"Thank you. How are you ladies?" Kara's eyes lingered on Dani.

"We're doing good. We were about to analyze Dani's dreams," Zoey said.

Dani gulped. Oh no, no, no, no. She gave a not-so-subtle kick to Zoey's shin.

"Oh, fun. What are you dreaming about?" Kara pursed her lips and blew on the coffee before taking a sip.

Dani caught herself staring at those lips a little longer than necessary. She straightened in her chair. "Nothing. I'm not dreaming about anybody."

Zoey widened her eyes. "Anybody? I thought you were dreaming about the wedding?"

"That's what I said."

"No, you didn't."

Dani sent another kick in Zoey's direction. This time Zoey twitched. "Can we change the subject? Because my dreams are not that interesting."

"Kara, what's going on with you? How's Rachel?" Jen asked.

"She's good."

"Are you officially dating?"

"I wouldn't say that. We hang out. We're not exclusive or anything," Kara explained.

"At least you're getting laid," Zoey said. "How 'bout you, Dans? How's your sex life? Still in a perpetual state of celibacy?"

Dani glared. This time Zoey jumped.

"You okay, babe?" Jen asked.

Zoey scowled and rubbed her shin. "I'm fine."

"I'm not celibate," Dani said. "Our schedules are jam-packed, so sometimes we need to coordinate a little."

"Do you make appointments or something?" Kara asked. "Does a reminder pop up on your phone?"

"Doctors' hours are long, and sometimes they don't match up. He's home, I'm not. I'm home, he's not. We don't work normal business hours like *some* people."

"Ah, you see, us lowly dog walkers have a lot of time on our hands for extracurricular activity."

"I didn't say that. You did."

"Here we go," Zoey mumbled.

"Pretty sure it was implied." Kara smirked. She picked a piece of lint off her jeans. "How long ago did you date a woman?"

Dani hung her mouth open. How did she know that? "Who told you that?"

"You did. At the bar."

Did I tell her that? Dani was toasted that night, so her memory was hazy. The waitress came back with everyone's breakfast.

All these unwanted forays into her personal life made Dani squirm. "How's everybody's dogs?" She grabbed the hot sauce and sprinkled it around her plate, completing her go-to meal here at Barjot's—a bacon and feta omelet with a side of crispy hash browns. Her mouth watered.

"Well," Zoey said, "Rocky ate rabbit poop the other day, and when I tried to pull him away, he rolled in it. Pass the salt, please."

"Roscoe got into the bathroom trash and ate a panty liner. Is there extra butter?" Jen asked.

Dani made a face. "He ate a used panty liner?"

"Yup." Jen slathered the butter on her toast.

"First, he picked it from the trash," Zoey said between bites. "Then he ran downstairs, with Jen in hot pursuit, went out the front door and over to our eighty-year-old neighbor's house. She's sitting on her front porch, and Roscoe decides to sit with her and eat the panty liner. I guess he thought he was dining out or something."

Dani put her knife down. "Oh shit, speaking of eating, that reminds me, I ran out of dog food last night. This morning I had to give him a box of cereal."

Kara's brows shot up. "An entire box of cereal?"

"Yeah. He likes to eat. He's eating us out of house and home. Like he's literally eating my house. Yesterday he chewed the molding off the wall. And then he ate it." She spread raspberry jam on the toast.

Kara tilted her head and narrowed her eyes. "You fed him an entire box of cereal?"

"Geez, calm down. It was granola, not Lucky Charms."

Kara shook her head. "No wonder he's gaining weight."

"How often do you feed him?" Jen asked.

"I just leave food out for him."

"You don't monitor how much he eats?" Jen asked.

"This is what I monitor—his bowl is empty, I fill his bowl." Dani took a big bite of toast.

Kara chuckled while shaking her head. "Is Will the dog lover in the family?"

"Yeah."

"I guess you're more of a…cat person?"

"You say that like it's some horrible thing."

"I find cat people have certain, um…personality traits."

I Dare You to Love Me   69

"Oh, did you do a study or something? Perhaps some scientific research on the difference between cat and dog people?"

"Here we go...*again*." Zoey pulled out a small bag of popcorn.

"I know this," Dani said. "Cats are smart. So, cat people are smart."

Kara's lips set in a straight line. "Dogs are smart."

"Have you seen my dog? He literally likes to lie on his back and pee in the air, then he tries to catch it. In his mouth. I mean, I like him and all, but...dogs are dumb."

"You're dumb." Kara stuck her fingers into her glass of water and flicked some at Dani.

Zoey and Jen were whispering and giggling.

"Is that popcorn?" Dani asked.

Zoey cleared her throat. "Yeah."

"We're eating breakfast."

"So, I like popcorn with my Kardi."

"With your what?" Dani asked.

"Kardi."

"What's that?"

"The greatest show on earth. Carry on, what were you guys saying?"

Dani had no clue what her bestie was talking about. "Uh, I forget. I'm sure it wasn't important."

"Well, here's something important. My birthday's coming up, and we're having a shindig at the house." Zoey dumped the last of the popcorn into her mouth. "You all are invited, by the way. There'll be lots of popcorn."

* * *

Kara sat on a bench a couple of stores down from the restaurant finishing up a call when Zoey and Jen left the café. Dani followed a few minutes later, sliding into the front seat of a faded green Honda Accord while talking on the phone. Kara was surprised at the car, expecting Dani to be driving the latest and greatest, a BMW or Mercedes, not some fifteen-year-old clunker. And from the sound of it, the clunker was dying a slow, painful death.

Dani pulled herself from the car and popped the hood. Kara couldn't wait to see what would happen next. She'd bet a million bucks Dani didn't know a radiator from an air filter. Sure enough, with hands on her hips, Dani blankly stared at the engine and made a show of poking around.

Kara sauntered over. "Problem?"

Dani jumped. "I thought you left."

"Nope. Still here. What's wrong?"

"It won't start."

"Well, there's a surprise. How old is this thing? Is it from the 1930s?"

"Funny. You're so funny. I'll have you know this is the first new car I ever bought."

"Did you buy it when you were ten?"

Dani crossed her arms. "I've had it a long time, and I'm quite attached."

"Like your wallet. You seem to form curious attachments."

"I know you're enjoying this, but I have to get to work." She glanced back at the engine and groaned. "I'm late."

"Why don't you let me give you a ride? I'll get you there in eight minutes."

"A ride? On that thing?" Dani pointed to the motorcycle.

"Yeah, what's wrong with that *thing*?"

"They're dangerous. I'd like to arrive in one piece."

"I'll get you there in one piece. C'mon, the more you talk, the later you'll be. Grab your sunglasses."

Dani nibbled on her lip before nodding. "Okay. Promise you'll go slow."

"Scout's honor." Kara led them to the bike and removed her helmet and jacket from the saddle bags. "Here, you wear my jacket and the helmet."

Dani slipped into the black leather jacket while Kara placed the helmet on her head and tightened the chin strap. She gently patted the lid, then stuck Dani's sunglasses onto her face. "You look hot." She winked.

"Did you just flirt with me?"

"Sorry, momentary lapse of judgment."

"Oh."

Kara swore she saw a flicker of disappointment cross Dani's face.

"What about you? Don't you have another helmet?"

"No, I'll be fine." Kara slung a leg over the bike and lifted the kickstand. "Get on."

Dani half lifted a leg, then put it back on the ground. Lifted the other leg, shook her head, and put that one back on the ground.

"My God. Haven't you ever been on a motorcycle before?"

"No. I told you they're killing machines."

"Okay, *that's* a bit much. Put your hands on my shoulders, lift your leg over, and sit down."

Dani rested both hands on Kara's shoulders and did as she was told. "Jesus Christ this thing's wide. Now what?"

"Put your arms around my waist and hold on. Lean into me when we go around curves, keep your feet up at all times even when we're stopped. Got it?"

Dani nodded and the helmet came down over her sunglasses.

Kara glanced at the rearview mirror and had to bite her lip to stop from laughing at the sight of the helmet covering half of Dani's face. Maybe it wouldn't be a bad thing. She might not want to watch. Nah. It would be more fun to scare the shit out of her. With a quick hitch of her thumb, she flicked the helmet up. "Hello!"

Dani's face pinched with worry. "Thank you."

Kara started the bike and turned. "Hold tighter." Dani's grip increased, but it was still too loose, so she pulled at Dani's arms, patting them when they were in the correct position. Dani was now snuggled close, chin resting on Kara's shoulder.

"Ready?" Kara downshifted into first gear.

"Go slow."

Kara smirked. She released the clutch and the bike surged forward. Dani faded back at first, then she quickly gripped at Kara's stomach to steady herself.

After fifty yards, Dani stiffened behind her. "Slower!"

Kara stole a peek at the speedometer. Twenty miles per hour. At this rate they would make it to the hospital next week. Kara loved to ride with women on her bike. There was nothing like a beautiful woman clinging to her while the wind whipped at their faces. Only this was Dani. And wind doesn't exactly whip at your face when you're going twenty miles per hour.

"Slower, please."

"If I go any slower, I'll be walking the bike."

They made snail-paced progress. Occasionally, when stopped at a traffic light, Kara would purposely jerk them forward as red turned to green. Dani would squeal and grab onto her. The good doc was annoying as hell, but it was still thrilling to have those doctorly arms wrapped tight around her waist, hanging on for dear life. The thrum of the engine between her legs and the press of Dani's breasts against her back was quite the turn-on.

When they finally arrived at the hospital, Kara stopped the bike, pushed the kickstand down, and hopped off. She gave a hand to Dani to help her dismount. "Your destination, madam." Kara bowed and waved her hand. "Sorry, it was ten minutes instead of eight. Next time we'll ride bicycles, might be quicker."

"Thank you." Dani shucked off the leather jacket and fiddled with the helmet strap.

Kara came to the rescue. She gently opened the buckle, her fingers brushing Dani's chin. They locked eyes and a tiny jolt of electricity rippled along Kara's nerve endings. Jesus. Obviously, she needed to blow off some sexual steam. Maybe a call to Rachel was in order.

Dani ran a hand through her hair. "Whew. Thanks again. It was actually pretty nice of you to give me a ride."

"You sound surprised I might be nice."

"Oh, it's surprising," Dani stated as she walked away.

"What about your car?"

She turned. "Oh, crap. I don't know."

"I have a friend who has a repair shop. I can have him tow it there and fix it."

Dani walked back. "Careful, I'm gonna think you like me, what with all this generosity."

"I didn't say I was paying for it. Here, give me your keys."

Dani fished in her jeans pocket for the keys and a couple of poop bags fell on the ground. She snagged them before they blew away and shoved the fistful of bags back.

"Wow, that's a lot of poop bags."

Dani reached around to the other pocket and withdrew another handful of bags.

Kara chuckled. "Whoops, more bags."

"The dog shits a lot." She continued rooting through pockets.

"Probably from all the granola," Kara teased.

"Very funny."

Kara swore she saw a hint of a smile.

"Ah, here they are." Dani handed the keys to Kara. "I'm gonna seriously owe you after all this. I mean, the ride, the tow."

"Don't worry, I'll think of how you can repay me."

"I don't know if I like the sound of that." Dani began walking away.

Kara grinned and admired the sway of feminine hips. Yep. Her body was amped right now. Might as well enjoy the view.

Dani turned before disappearing through the glass doors of the hospital. "It wasn't so bad."

"Me or the ride?"

"The ride." With a huge smile, she turned and headed inside.

CHAPTER TWELVE

Dani crawled into the back seat of Zoey's car. "Thanks for picking me up."

Jen smiled broadly. "Anytime, Dans. How was work?"

"Work is work."

"Why is your car still in the shop?" Zoey asked.

"It needs a new transmission. They're waiting on parts."

"Jesus, maybe it's time for a new car," Jen said.

"No! I love my car. And now it'll be good for another hundred thousand miles." They were going in the opposite direction of their respective houses. "Where are we going?"

"I gotta drop something off," Zoey said.

They turned into a long driveway.

Dani gazed in wonder at the stately stone farmhouse in front of her. It must have been over a hundred years old but had been lovingly restored. Red shutters surrounded all the windows along the front, contrasting nicely with the dark stone. An expansive front porch with rocking chairs reached from end to end. The property had to be over twenty acres. Dani loved the country. As a young child, she dreamed of living on a farm surrounded by cows, chickens, and goats. "Wow, this is beautiful, where are we?"

"This, Miss Clark, is where your dog comes every day."

"Oh, shit. Kara's place?"

"Yep." Zoey parked in front of the store. "Everybody out."

"I can wait here." The motorcycle ride was still fresh in Dani's mind. Well, the sensations from the ride were still fresh in her mind—the way it felt to be pressed against Kara, the way her hair smelled. Dani had made an executive decision a couple of days ago that this had to stop. This, whatever it was, infatuation, this weird physical attraction, needed to be nipped in the bud. Pronto. De-Infatuation!

"Don't be such a stick-in-the-mud. Get your ass out of the car," Zoey scolded.

Dani groaned and the three gals headed into the store where one of Kara's employees greeted them and directed them to the cottage out back.

Kara threw open the front door. "Well, this is a surprise!" They all hugged hello.

Except for Dani, who kept a respectable distance from the hugging. Best not to touch her dream lover when awake. Definitely step one or two of the new De-Infatuation program.

"C'mon in," Kara said.

Dani peeked around the inside of the modest home and found it charming. *Damn it.* She was hoping for a pigsty. Nothing like discovering someone's a complete slob to turn you off, but of course, the place was spotless.

The cottage was cozy with an open floor plan. The living room had a beautiful brick fireplace with a dark oak mantel. The couch was a distressed leather, the kind that enveloped you in softness and warmth. The kind that beckoned you to come and relax and read a book. A large bay window next to the front door let in copious amounts of natural light. Dani wanted to hate everything about the space, but of course her brain had other ideas. An image of herself wrapped in a fleece blanket, lying on the couch, staring at the fire popped into her head. *Damn it.*

Kara encouraged everyone to get comfortable at the kitchen table, but Dani wasn't paying attention, too busy appreciating the decor, walking not watching, and she banged into something big. A squeak of fear gurgled in her throat. Two large pit bulls blocked her way. When she was young, their neighbor had a pit bull, and all the dog ever did was growl ferociously at Dani through the fence, even nipping her once when she stuck her hand through to pet him. From then on, both her parents railed about the dangerous pit bull next door.

Kara sensed Dani's trepidation. "They're harmless. Don't worry."

Not about to be reassured by her nemesis, Dani's hands stayed above her waist. No sense dangling anything in front of those jowls. She quickly slid into a chair.

"The gray one's Ziggy, and the black-and-white one is Milo." Kara smirked at Dani's continued discomfort. "They won't bother you."

As if on cue, Ziggy plopped down in front of Dani and put his meaty paw on her thigh.

"Ziggy, stop. Just push his paw down."

Dani carefully pushed his paw off.

With a growl, he placed his paw back on her leg.

"Maybe he wants to shake. Shake his paw," Zoey said.

"I'm not shaking his paw."

Soon, Milo joined his brother and sat in front of Dani, panting all over her, and then he slipped down and put his head on Dani's foot.

Kara's eyes widened. "Jesus, boys, enough. Sorry. They usually don't bother with new people. I don't know what's got into them."

Dani swallowed the lump of fear that was still wedged in her throat and sat still. Ziggy's paw inched farther up her thigh. "Good doggie."

Jen said, "They must like you."

"Or they're gonna kill you," Zoey added.

"Seriously, they won't hurt you," Kara said.

Dani considered bolting for the door but got distracted by her bestie. "Are you eating popcorn?"

"No," Zoey said.

"Yes, you are."

"No, I'm not."

"There's a kernel stuck to your lip."

Zoey flicked it off.

They all flinched when Ziggy's strong jaws snatched it out of midair.

Dani froze. Sweat trickled down her back. What was it about pitties? Once their jaws locked onto something, they didn't let go? She prayed this get-together would wrap up quickly.

Zoey turned on her laptop and soon both she and Kara were immersed in the new website.

After a few minutes passed, Dani asked, "Where's your bathroom?"

Kara pointed down the hallway. "First door on your right."

Dani cautiously pushed Ziggy's paw down and moved her foot out from under Milo's head. When she stood, both dogs popped up, eyes glued to Dani. She tiptoed around them and scurried down the hallway, the dogs in hot pursuit.

Slipping into the bathroom, she slammed the door shut. She leaned against the closed door, hoping it was strong enough to hold off the dogs. Taking stock of the bathroom, she found it to be as lovely as the rest of the house. An old-fashioned claw-foot tub dominated the room. The walls were a light gray, and rose-colored hand towels hung from the rack. It was incredibly tasteful. *Goddamn it.* Why couldn't her bathroom be disgusting? Why couldn't there be hair in the sink, dirty clothes on the floor, mold in the tub? It was fucking pristine, and she didn't want to leave. She wanted to soak in that tub, wrapped in strong arms, and *oh God*, what was she gonna dream about tonight?

When she opened the door, she had forgotten about her watchful guardians, and tripped over them, landing flat on her face. Now prone on the floor, she was subjected to inquisitive nuzzling about the face. She whimpered, waiting for the imminent bite that never came, instead getting solidly licked, her mouth agape and soon filled with a large doggie tongue.

All three women stood at the door, watching Dani get it on with Kara's dogs.

"Yo, Dani, quit Frenching the dogs, we gotta go," Zoey said.

Dani hustled back into the bathroom to wash the doggie kisses from her face. When she emerged from the loo, her now faithful pooches followed her out the front door, and when she scooted into the back seat, they sat down next to the car, pining for their new love.

Kara had to call them back. "Ziggy. Milo. Jesus. That's enough."

"Damn. Those dogs dig you, Dani," Jen said.

"Great."

* * *

"Dani."

Dani struggled through the fog of her dream. She was in a tub overflowing with bubbles and Kara's lips were roaming freely over her chest, but somehow she knew Kara wasn't the one gently shaking her.

She opened her eyes and found someone leaning over her. "Aaahhh!" She sat straight up. It was Will. "Shit." Dani was instantly frustrated. She was *this close* to having an orgasm. Had she ever had an orgasm while dreaming? No. And it would've been a nice first.

Three pairs of eyes stared: feline, canine, and human.

"Are you okay?" Will asked.

"Yeah," she said, exasperated. "Why?"

"You were thrashing around, then you said Karen. I thought maybe you were reliving some awful surgery you had today. Or had some terrifying interaction with a patient named Karen." He smiled at his own joke.

When Dani's bearings returned, her head hit the pillow. "I'm fine."

"You sure?"

"Yes, I'm sure. Go back to sleep. I'm sorry I woke you up."

"It's okay. I'll hold you until you fall back asleep." He spooned her and fell asleep instantly.

Dani lay awake with Will snoring lightly into her back. She carefully slipped from his arms and rolled away. Now why did she feel the need to do that? Was it because she belonged to someone else in the middle of the night? *No! Don't be silly.* He gave off a ton of body heat and it was hot.

Her thoughts drifted back to the dream and she cursed her stupid luck. Damn it. She almost came in her dream. Was that even possible? She'd have to ask Google tomorrow. And my God how quickly she'd gotten aroused. She was never that quick. What did this woman do to her? What kind of sexual hold did Kara have over her? So much for nipping it in the bud.

And, truth be told, it wasn't the bud she wanted to nip.

CHAPTER THIRTEEN

Dani answered her phone the following morning, still tingling from her dream the night before. "May I help you?"

"What are you doing?" Zoey asked.

"Research."

"What are you researching?"

Dani hesitated. Should she? Why not. "Will and I wondered if it was possible for women to have orgasms in their sleep." There, a harmless white lie.

"Oh, totally possible."

"Really?"

"Used to happen to me all the time, when I was with what's-her-name."

What's-her-name was Zoey's girlfriend before Jen. Zoey broke it off because, "She didn't like when I used the word fuck." And, "She was boring as fuck."

"We would start getting busy, and she was so fucking dullsville in bed I fell asleep. But I still managed to have an orgasm, cause I'm that good."

"You are totally full of shit."

"No, I'm not. Let's go walk the dogs and you can tell me all about your sleep-induced orgasms with Will. Maybe we should set him up with what's-her-name. They can sleep and have orgasms at the same time, like multitasking."

"All right, I'll see you in an hour. But I have to be at the hospital by noon."

"What is it about sunny days?" Zoey asked, inhaling the fresh air as they walked along the paved trail.

"You feel special. Like the gods are smiling on you," Dani said.

"You have enough poop bags?" They both took a moment to double-check their pockets.

Dani revealed her now standard cache of bags. "I have plenty. My poop bags have poop bags."

"Alrighty then, let's go."

Oliver pattered next to Dani, for once not ripping her arm out of its socket. He was better on walks, and she had no idea how that was happening, since she spent zero time training him. But she wasn't going to look a gift horse in the mouth—or a gift dog, as was the case.

"How's the wedding planning going?"

"I have no idea."

"Still? Who's in charge? Rebecca?"

"Isn't she always?"

"Are you sure you wanna go through with this? Just because your parents want you to marry Will doesn't mean you have to. I mean, you are thirty-three. You can live your own life."

Dani sighed. *Here we go again.* "It's fine. Will and I are great together. We're like *When Harry Met Sally.* We practically finish each other's sentences. We're used to each other."

"That sounds horrible. The mad adventures of Harry and Sally, boring each other 'til death do they part."

Were they boring? Dani thought back to the other night when they were both home at a decent hour. They'd spent the evening watching baseball, because they never had time to get wrapped up in TV shows. No. They weren't boring. They fit. They were comfortable. "We're not boring. We're busy."

"Whatever. I've seen you in love. With Suzanne."

The mention of Suzanne brought on the standard tinge of regret and sadness. "I'm in love with Will."

"How many times have you had sex this week?"

"This week?"

"Yeah, do I have to expand the timeline? This month?"

"Lots, we've had lots of sex…this year."

"Aha!"

"I'm kidding. We have sex. How many times do you and Jen have sex?"

"Today? Twice."

Dani had no comeback. "Well, good for you," was all she could manage.

As they walked on, they came upon the baseball fields filled with youth teams.

"Hey, isn't that Kara?" Zoey pointed to one of the fields.

"Where?"

"Over there, walking with a kid. Does she have a kid?"

"I don't know."

"Let's go over and say hi."

Dani panicked. The dream was too fresh. Kara created confusion, and she didn't feel like dealing with it right now. "No, absolutely not." She shook her head emphatically. "Jesus, it's like she's everywhere, I can't get away from her."

"Calm the fuck down. What do you mean she's everywhere?"

Dani, caught up in her own thoughts, ignored Zoey. She was in the middle of being transported back into the dream from last night, and her internal monologue turned external, and she babbled the thing that should never be babbled aloud, especially to Zoey. "She's in my goddamn dreams all the time, we're always running into her everywhere we go—"

Zoey stopped dead in her tracks. "You never said you dreamed about her. When did this start?"

Dani groaned and didn't answer, hoping Zoey would forget everything that just fell from her mouth. But who was she kidding? Certainly not Zoey.

"What happens in these dreams?"

"Can you forget I said anything?"

"Nope."

A defeated Dani dragged Oliver to a bench and collapsed. "Sex. Sex is what's happening in the dreams." She took a deep breath. It felt good to get it off her chest. Maybe now they would stop. Did she want them to stop? *Yes. Jesus.*

Zoey was speechless. For about half a second. "No wonder you don't wanna have sex with Will. I mean, there's no contest. None...nil...naught...zero...zilch—"

"Enough!" Dani ran shaky fingers through her hair.

"What are you going to do?"

"I'm sure it'll play itself out eventually. It's an infatuation. Purely physical. It'll go away. I'll make it go away."

"How you gonna do that?"

"I don't know! Ugh." Dani rubbed her face. "Promise me you won't say anything to anybody. I mean it. Please. Promise, Zoey."

"Yeah, yeah. Wow. How many dreams have you had?"

"I'm done talking about it, okay?" Silence descended again. The dogs had taken a seat and waited patiently for the walk to continue.

"I'm gonna need more popcorn," Zoey mumbled.

CHAPTER FOURTEEN

When Dani made it to the hospital for her shift, she found an emergency appendectomy awaiting her. It was a twelve-year-old boy admitted an hour ago with abdominal pains.

Sue, the head nurse, an older woman with a kind, round face, appeared beside her. "Are you reading your next chart?"

"Yeah. Anything I need to know?"

"Yup, the boy's deaf."

"Is the interpreter in there?"

"Yes. So are his parents. He signs."

"Okay. Thanks, Sue."

Dani walked into the hospital room and nodded at the interpreter. The quiet was almost unnerving as the family signed back and forth. The mother sat on one side, and the father stood on the other. The boy grimaced in pain.

"Hi, everyone, I'm Dr. Danielle Clark, and I'll be doing"—she took a quick peek down at the chart—"Travis's surgery."

The interpreter made quick work of Dani's introduction.

The father extended his hand. "Dr. Clark, I'm Aaron Walker, and this is my wife, Jolie."

"I'm not one for formalities. You can call me Dani." She turned her attention back to the boy in the bed. "Travis, your chart didn't say how handsome you are." She winked and grinned.

Travis managed a small smile at Dani's compliment, and signed, *hello*.

She squeezed his hand. "Let's see what we've got here." She glanced down at his chart. "Brain surgery?" Dani widened her eyes. "Are we removing your brain today, Travis?"

Travis's mouth dropped open. *No. Not my brain.*

"No?" Dani made a play of checking the chart again. "I could've sworn this thing said to take it out. Hmm." She scratched her head. "I could take it out if you wanted me to."

No. I like my brain.

"Okay, we'll leave it." Dani made a note in the chart. "Patient likes his brain, DO NOT TOUCH! I wrote the last part in caps, so I remember." She showed it to him.

For a moment, Travis forgot his pain and giggled at Dani's silliness. *You're taking out my appendix.*

Dani smacked her forehead. "Oh. Right. My bad. Okay, buddy, let me take a quick feel here, see what Mr. Appendix is doing." Dani palpated Travis's side and he winced sharply. "Yep, he wants out." She tapped his baseball mitt that sat on the tray. "Do you play baseball?"

Yeah.

Aaron's brown eyes were full of concern. "He was playing baseball this morning, and after the game he said his side hurt."

"When he said it was his right side, we were worried it might be his appendix," Jolie said.

"Good thing you brought him in. I've taken out a lot of appendixes, so have no fear. I'll take good care of you." She squeezed his arm and gave him another warm smile.

* * *

Kara had arrived at Travis's room right after Dani. She backed into the hallway, holding the cardboard tray of coffees while eavesdropping on the conversation. She smiled as she listened. She'd never witnessed this side of Dani. Playful, silly, and charming. She had to admit, it was heartwarming. This Dani was more in line with the Dani from her dreams. Dream Dani was warm and wonderful and sexy.

Maybe there was more to her than just a verbal sparring partner? Kara was so distracted by her thoughts she was practically run over by Dani exiting the room. They bumped shoulders and Kara steadied the coffee tray.

"Oh, I'm so sorry," Dani said, then recognized who she bumped. "What are you doing here?"

Kara paused, further distracted by how attractive Dani looked. Her hair was tied back at her neck in a messy bun with all sorts of wavy tendrils surrounding her face. "I, um, that's a friend of mine in there."

"You know them?"

"Yeah, little guy's a good buddy of mine."

Realization dawned on Dani's face. "Oh. I wondered how you knew how to sign."

"Well, now you know. How are you, world-renowned surgeon Danielle Clark?"

"I'm good."

Kara had trouble maintaining eye contact because she was flustered by the revelation of this new, sweet Dani. "So. I'm gonna head in there and give everyone their coffee."

Dani misread Kara's awkwardness. "I'll take good care of him. Promise." Her hand brushed Kara's forearm. "I know you think I'm a horrible, dog-hating, cat-loving person, but I am a good surgeon. No worries, I got this." She turned to leave.

"Dani?"

"Yeah."

"Thanks for being nice to him."

"Ah, now *you're* surprised *I* can be nice."

Down the corridor she went, affording Kara a nice long view of her ass again. "Jesus, Kara, cool it. She's engaged," she mumbled as she wandered into Travis's room. "I brought coffee. How you doing, buddy?" Kara asked Travis.

Hurts.

"I know. They'll remove it and you'll feel better."

Hospitals. He made a face and shook his head.

"I don't like hospitals either." She looked around his room. "I was actually in this hospital for surgery when I was six. I survived and you will too. And I know Dr. Clark. You're in good hands."

"You know Dr. Dani?" Jolie asked.

"Her dog comes to day care."

"Wow. Small world," Aaron said.

* * *

Hours later, Travis was recovering nicely from surgery. He was awake, but still groggy.

Glad you're feeling better, little dude, Kara signed.

"Dr. Dani did a good job," Aaron said.

She's pretty. Travis raised his eyebrows and gave the sign for lesbian.

Kara chuckled, knowing his intent. "Well, I know she's bi."

Ask her out.

"Yeah, Britton, you should be moving on that," Aaron said.

Jolie slapped her husband's shoulder. "That's not a nice way to speak about women, husband of mine. She has a name. Now, Kara, why aren't you moving on Dr. Dani?"

"Simmer down, people. She happens to be engaged—"

"I didn't see a ring," Aaron said.

"—and a cat person. And we don't get along."

Jolie pursed her lips. "Well, it sounds perfect, except for the engaged part."

"Perfect? How does that all sound perfect?"

"It sounds like a romance novel, two people meet, they don't get along, then they fall in love."

Kara shook her head. "You need to stop reading those books."

"I love romance novels," she said wistfully. "I'll have to talk to Zoey."

Kara became instantly suspicious. "Why do you need to talk to Zoey?"

"Nothing, never mind."

Before Kara could cross-examine Jolie, Dani popped into the room. "How's my patient?"

Travis gave a small shrug. *Okay.*

Dani checked his pulse. "Your heart is still beating. That's always a good thing." She smiled and he beamed back.

When can I play ball? Travis asked.

Dani dipped her head. "Well, not for at least three weeks."

His mouth turned down at the corners. *When can I ride on Kara's motorcycle?*

Kara stroked his arm. "Soon, buddy. After you heal from this, I'll take you for a ride."

Dani glanced at the Walkers. "Isn't that dangerous? He's kinda young to be on a motorcycle."

Jolie shrugged. "They just go around the block."

Kara chuckled. "Hey, Trav, I gave Dr. Dani a lift on my bike last week."

You rode? he asked Dani, eyes sparkling.

Kara spoke before Dani had a chance to answer. "I wouldn't say we went for a ride, we kinda crawled. She wouldn't let me go above ten miles per hour. And she was scared to death. Clung to me so tight I could barely breathe."

Dani put her hands on her hips. "Oh, please, I wasn't clinging. Exaggerate much?"

"Oh, there was clinging. And squealing. You squealed."

"I didn't squeal. What ride are you talking about? Maybe that was your other girlfriend." As soon as those words fell from her mouth, a red hue rushed into Dani's cheeks.

Kara didn't miss a beat. "Oh, yeah, must have been my other girlfriend. Now, *when* did we become girlfriends? Because I missed that part."

Dani changed the subject quickly. "Well, never mind, motorcycles are dangerous, right, Travis?"

They're cool. You should go again.

Kara chuckled. "Yeah, c'mon. I'll take good care of you... girlfriend. But you might have to lose the cat first, since I don't date cat people. Dani's a cat person," Kara explained to the Walkers.

Dani scoffed. "Cats rule."

"Cats are aloof, and vengeful. Dogs rule. They're loyal, affectionate—"

"My cat's loyal, and he's affectionate. Just because he doesn't like you…that shouldn't be held against him. It actually makes him extremely smart." She made some final notes in the chart and turned to the Walkers. "My Jinx swats at her every time she comes into the house to get the dog."

"Got it." They nodded and snuck glances at each other.

"Swats? More like assaults," Kara mumbled.

"My goodness, the dog whisperer is afraid of a kitten. Ha!" Dani smirked.

A nurse came back into the room, stethoscope dangling from her neck.

"Okay, I have to see some other patients," Dani said. "Sue's going to check some vitals. I'll be back in an hour. Travis, you did great today." Before Dani turned to leave, she took one last glance around the room, her eyes lingering on Kara. With a grin, she headed out.

Kara stared after her, trying to decipher the look on Dani's face. She could've sworn she saw something there, a flicker of something. When she turned around, all the Walkers were giving her the hairy eyeball. "What?"

"Nothing," they said in unison.

Kara did not like the calculating expression on their faces. "Obviously, we don't like each other."

"I don't know if I'd say obviously," Aaron said.

"She's attractive," Jolie added.

"She's outta my league," Kara said. "I mean, if I were even interested, which I'm not."

"Why would you say she's out of your league?" Jolie asked.

Aaron agreed with his wife. "Yeah, nobody's out of your league, Britton."

Kara raised her eyebrows. "Hello? She's engaged."

"So? People break off engagements all the time," Aaron said.

Kara sighed. "There's nothing between the doctor and me. We don't get along."

"Well, I saw the way she looked at you before she left," Jolie said.

So Kara wasn't imagining. Jolie saw it too. "She doesn't like me. Maybe it was her look of hate."

"It wasn't a look of hate."

"Enough! She's engaged, let's drop it." Kara wanted to forget charming Dani because charming Dani was dangerous. Give her rude Dani any day. Please.

Sue cleared her throat to remind them of her presence. "Everything looks good. Press the call button if you need me."

* * *

Dani checked her watch as she stopped at the nurse's station. After a quick check on Travis, she could wrap everything up and be home at a reasonable hour for once. Sue looked to be leaving for the day.

"You out of here?" Dani asked.

"Yep."

"Lucky you. Anything I need to know?"

"No. Oh, your fan club's still here. The Walkers." Sue grinned. "Surprised your ears didn't burn and fall off. You were quite the topic of conversation."

"Oooh. Do tell."

Sue glanced around and leaned closer. "Well, they wanted to set you up with the woman who was in there with them."

"You mean Kara? Ha! She thinks I'm an idiot, and she hates me, so I doubt she took that well."

"I didn't get that impression."

"Why? What did she say?"

"She said you were out of her league."

"Me? Outta *her* league? Oh, that's rich. She thinks I'm a tightwad. And a moron when it comes to dogs. You probably heard it wrong."

"Maybe I did. Maybe I didn't. Have a good night."

Dani made her way to Travis's room. The first person she saw was Kara, and her heart rate increased. Sue's words echoed in her brain. Kara thought Dani was out of her league? No. Sue's hearing was clearly suspect.

A certain dream sequence replayed in her mind, a bathtub with bubbles, and a sudden rush of heat rolled through Dani's body, taking her breath away. Good lord this woman did things to her. When Kara's eyes met hers, a flash of something passed between them, a spark that Dani couldn't explain. Kara turned away, and Dani swallowed thickly.

Jolie and Aaron jumped to their feet when Dani arrived.

"How's my favorite patient?"

Travis's eyes drooped from exhaustion. *Tired. Hurts.*

"That's to be expected. By tomorrow you should be in less pain."

Jolie gave Dani a big hug. "Thank you for taking care of him."

Aaron hugged her also. "You need to come over for dinner as a thank-you. Jolie is a wonderful cook."

"Yes. Please say you'll come to dinner," Jolie said.

"I'd love to. My schedule is crazy, but I'll make the time. Here." She pulled out a business card. "Take my card. My shift is over, but if you have any questions regarding Travis, call me. Any time. And text me a few dates for dinner."

She backed out of the room, throwing one more glance at Kara. As she strode down the hallway, she cursed herself for feeling a twinge of disappointment.

Everyone hugged her.

Everyone except Kara.

CHAPTER FIFTEEN

Kara was working in the office when Val came in carrying a small box. Ziggy and Milo dutifully followed their aunt. Kara pulled off her new glasses, courtesy of her eye appointment the other day.

"We have a problem."

Kara glanced at the dogs, expecting the worst. "Shit, what did they do?"

Val sat across the desk from Kara with the box on her lap.

"I found this behind the barn." Val set two orange-and-white kittens on the desk.

Kara inhaled sharply. "What are they doing here?"

"Don't know." Val gently slid them across the desk toward Kara, like she was all-in at a poker game. "Take them."

"What? Oh no. No, thank you." She slid the kitten chips back to Val.

"Take them, just 'til we can find them a home." And back across the desk they went.

Kara immediately pushed them back from whence they came. "You take them."

"We can't have cats. We foster too many dogs. I called Jes. She'll be here any minute—"

"Jes is coming?"

"Yeah, she's bringing some stuff for you."

"Well, I don't want them. Take them to the shelter."

"It's just for a few days." The kittens made their way back to Kara.

"No." The kitty trail across the desk heated up.

"Yes."

"I can't." Kara searched for an excuse. She pointed at the dogs. "They'll eat them."

"They're the ones who found them."

"What?"

"I saw them sniffing around, and when I got there, these two orange fur balls were climbing all over *your* dogs."

"I don't believe you."

Val took the teeny fluff balls and placed them on the ground near the dogs. Kara peeked over her desk, ready to watch the carnage. Milo gave a sloppy doggie kiss to each of them. One felt a wee bit adventurous and climbed on Ziggy's back. The dog sighed and put his head on the ground.

Kara was aghast at her pups. "First Dani, now this? Did she put some sort of cat spell on you?"

Jesmyn burst in carrying all sorts of kitten supplies, her wavy black tresses cascading down her back and her long, lithe legs wrapped in skinny jeans. "Who's Dani? I hear you're a cat person now." Affectionate with everyone, she planted a kiss on Kara's lips.

"No, I'm not."

"Shut up, you're taking them just until we figure things out. Here's a litter box, litter, kitten chow, food bowl, water bowl, scratching post, and some toys. Who's Dani?" Jesmyn picked up the kittens and smooched them one at a time.

Val smiled wickedly. "She's one of our clients, and Kara has sex dreams about her."

"Sex dreams? Do tell, honey."

"There's nothing to tell." Kara gave Val the stink eye. "Jesus. I told you that in confidence."

"I don't keep things from my girl. Dani's engaged, by the way," Val offered up, piling on now.

"Stop!"

"And she has a nice ass."

Kara was mortified.

"Why am I the last to know all this?" Jesmyn had both kittens under her chin for a nuzzle.

"There's nothing to know. Now please, take your cats and go find something to do. I have to finish the payroll." Kara put her glasses back on and started working on the computer.

Val stood and clapped Kara on the shoulder. "Sorry, buddy, kittens are staying. We're heading to dinner. Oh, they're both boys. And take them to the vet. They're about six weeks old."

"No, wait, you can't leave me with them," Kara pleaded.

Jesmyn poked her head back in the doorway. "Look how tiny they are. You make it sound like they're gonna attack you. Now, pour the litter in the pan, then put them in the pan so they know to use it, simple. Jesus Christ, didn't you ever have a cat? And, fuck you look good in glasses."

"No, I'm a dog person!" Kara yelled, but they were gone. She stared at the orange-and-white things on her desk. They stared back. Kara put her chin on the desktop to take a better look. She was never around kittens. This was going to be a new experience. Poking a finger at the closest one, she smiled when he swatted it. He certainly didn't have the torque of Dani's Jinxie.

The non-swatter came over, sniffed her nose, lifted a hesitant paw, and softly touched Kara's cheek. He mewled softly. The swatter found his courage and came closer. In a blink of an eye, they were in her lap. "What's happening?" And climbing up her shirt. "Oh." And sitting on her shoulders, one on either side. She didn't move. "Okay, but just for a few days." One started to lick her ear, and when she turned, he whacked her on the nose. He had quite the attitude. "Maybe I should call you Dani."

Later in the evening, she crawled into bed and turned off the lamp. The litter box was in the guest bedroom and last she spotted the fur balls they were exploring the living room. Kara fluffed her pillow and shut her eyes. A small quiver rippled along the mattress. She groaned. The living room exploration must have ended. They crept toward the pillows. One sat on her head and kneaded her hair. The other nestled under her chin and purred. Jesus. How could something so itsy-bitsy make such a racket? She was afraid to move for fear of crushing them. Eventually the purring soothed, like white noise, and she drifted off.

* * *

Kara hustled after the dogs, worried they might catch some unsuspecting squirrel or other creature. When she finally found them, she heaved a sigh of relief.

"Dani! What are you doing here?"

Dani had both pooches in her grasp. "I thought you'd be here." She jumped against Kara and crushed their lips together.

Kara reluctantly broke off the kiss. "I thought your shift wasn't over 'til six?"

"I left early. I wanted to surprise you." Dani grabbed her hand and tugged. "C'mon, I'm taking you for some chocolate ice cream."

"I love chocolate ice cream."

"I know, silly."

Kara gradually woke from the dream. Her chest was tight from emotion. Her heart was full. Full of warmth. How was that even possible? Slowly, the feelings she awoke with faded to the background. She felt normal again, but she still had a heaviness in her chest. What the hell? She peered down and two sets of golden eyes stared back. At first, she thought raccoon babies had snuck in, but then she remembered the kittens. She had kittens. Temporarily, at least. One yawned and stretched out his paws, lightly touching her lips.

This dream shook her. It was easier to explain away sex dreams. She found Dani attractive, and she had a fantastic body. That's why they had sex after midnight. But this, this was affection, feelings, happiness. All dangerous emotions. Closing her eyes, she prayed this was a one-time occurrence.

Let's get back to sex, please.

CHAPTER SIXTEEN

Dani stared at the text from Zoey.

I need you to go to the farm and pick up a few tables for the party tonight.

Dani called her right back. "No, no. I'll help you with anything else, but I'm not going there."

"Chill. They're in Kara's office, and she's not even gonna be there."

"Are you sure?"

"Yeah, I'm sure."

She sighed. "Okay."

When Dani arrived at the store, she headed back to the office and peeked inside. Her mouth fell open in shock at the sight in front of her. She leaned against the doorjamb. "Ahem."

Kara—caught mid-nuzzle with a tiny orange-and-white kitten—jumped, and her eyes blew wide.

The dogs rushed over, and Dani patted their heads, all fear of pit bulls gone right out the window when faced with this stunning kitten reveal. "What is that?"

Kara maintained eye contact with Dani and placed the kitten in the drawer, casually closing it. "What's what?"

Dani lost her train of thought because it was the first time she'd seen Kara in glasses, and holy shit. The glasses were superhot. Fuck. *De-Infatuation! De-Infatuation!* She steadied herself and pointed. "What did you put in your drawer?"

"Nothing?"

"You put a kitten in that drawer. The cat hater has a kitten. Oh, this is priceless."

"I'm not a cat *hater*."

"Pa-lease…you might wanna take him out before he suffocates."

Kara's body went rigid. The drawer creaked open and the kitten was placed on the desk.

Dani threw her shoulders back in triumph.

Soon another kitten appeared, and pink dusted Kara's cheeks.

Dani hooted. "Two kittens? My God." She whipped out her phone and snapped a picture. "Unbelievable. I'm gonna post this on Facebook and tag you."

"We're not friends on Facebook."

"I'm sending you a friend request."

"I'm not gonna accept it."

"Why not?"

Kara crossed her arms. "For obvious reasons."

"Such as?"

"One, we're not friends."

"So? I barely know any of my Facebook friends. Accept it."

"No."

"Yes."

"No."

Dani narrowed her eyes. "You are no fun."

"Since when do we have fun?"

Dani leaned over, putting both hands on the front of Kara's desk. "What are their names?"

Kara's eyes strayed downward and stopped.

Dani was perversely pleased with her wardrobe choice today. She had chosen a skimpy black workout tank, and her cleavage was on full display. Kara's slack-jawed expression almost made her laugh.

"What are their names?" Dani repeated slowly.

"Ah…" Kara cleared her throat. She rearranged the stapler and tape dispenser. "Um…kittens."

Dani cocked a brow. "Excuse me?"

"Kittens."

"You didn't name them?"

Her cheeks flushed a deeper shade of red. "No."

Dani cackled and slapped the desktop. "This is priceless. All the berating I took for not knowing my dog's name. How long have you had them?"

"Only a week. And they're not staying."

"You sure about that? You were pretty drooly over that one."

"He's snuggly." Kara adjusted her glasses. "Anyway, I'm just keeping them until we can find them a home."

"Uh-huh." Dani nodded. "Where'd you find them?"

"Out behind the barn. The dogs found them."

"I thought your dogs hated cats."

"I guess they changed their minds. You put the maloiks on them, some sort of cat curse."

"Oh, right, that's what I did. I cat-cursed your dogs. Who love me, by the way." Dani picked up a kitten and smooched him on the head.

"Are you here for the tables?"

"Yeah, Zoey asked me to pick them up. She said you wouldn't be here."

"Is that why you came? Cause you thought I wouldn't be here?"

Dani shrugged. "Maybe."

With a huff, Kara stood. "I'll help you get them into your car."

Kara loaded the tables into Dani's back seat. She then had to unload her dogs, who evidently thought they were leaving with the love of their lives.

"You really need to control your dogs." Dani smirked as she hopped into the front seat and put the window down. "Cat lover." Guffawing, she started the car and pulled out.

"Dog lover," Kara shouted back to her.

Dani waved a dismissive hand out the window and shook her boobs. "Good job, girls."

* * *

When Dani and Will arrived at Zoey's house, the party was in full swing. The alcohol flowed freely, and guests were gyrating to the music pumping from the stereo. Dani puzzled over the bowls of popcorn that were placed strategically around the room. *When did Zoey become such a popcorn lover?*

The guest of honor weaved her way over to them. "'Bout time you two, I'm practically thirty four."

Dani gave Zoey a kiss and handed her a birthday card. "Sorry. Work was crazy."

"It's okay, I forgive you. What do you guys want to drink?"

"Dani probably wants a beer." Will glanced at Dani for confirmation, and she nodded. "And I'll have a Stoli on the rocks, if you have it."

After Zoey left, they found themselves wedged into a sea of bodies in the living room. Will nodded across the room. "There's Kara."

Dani glanced at her dream lover and gulped. Her most recent dream came flooding back to her. Dani at the wheel of her car, Kara in her ear—or she should say, Kara's tongue in her ear.

Tonight, Kara looked incredible, because of course she did. Step one of De-Infatuation just flew out the fucking window. Tight-fitting jeans hugged her hips perfectly. A sheer white button-down long-sleeved top with a black camisole underneath completed the sexy ensemble. An attractive woman with short hair whispered into Kara's ear.

Someone tapped Dani's shoulder, and she turned to find Jolie and Aaron.

Dani hugged them both. "Do you know Zoey?"

Jolie smiled. "I met her a few weeks ago at Kara's."

"Well, that's nice. How's Travis?"

"He's almost recovered. It's been an adventure trying to keep a twelve-year-old inactive. You're coming to dinner soon, right?"

"Yes, text me or call me. I can't wait."

Will cleared his throat and Dani cringed with embarrassment. She'd forgotten all about him. "I'm sorry. Jolie and Aaron, this is Will, my fiancé."

"We love Dr. Dani, you're a lucky guy," Aaron said.

"I am a lucky guy. We were best friends in high school." He looked to Dani for confirmation again, and she nodded while he continued, "Then five years ago, one thing led to another, and we started dating."

That one thing was an after-party drunken kiss that led to sex. Would their lives have turned out differently if they hadn't kissed that night? Will squeezed her hand, bringing Dani back into the present.

"And now we're getting married," he said.

He gazed at her with affection, making her forgetfulness even more painful. In an effort to make amends, she gave his hand a squeeze and kissed him on the cheek. Yes, Harry and Sally. Best friends.

"We're heading over to the food table. Do you guys want anything?" Aaron asked.

"Not right now, thanks." Will turned to Dani. "I'm gonna go say hi to Ethan."

Dani stayed rooted in place, hoping Zoey would be back shortly with her beer. She needed a diversion from a certain brunette in sheer white.

Finally, Zoey thrust a beer into her hand. "Not a bad turnout, huh? Kara's here. Did you say hi?"

"No, I didn't, and I don't need to. I saw her already today, no thanks to you."

"Well, you can't avoid her all the time. It's not healthy."

"It's healthy for me."

"She brought Rachel."

"Oh?" Dani felt a stab of jealousy. It was like a hot pinprick in her temporal lobe. Why in God's name should she be jealous? Fabulous, another emotion she'd have to control.

"You wanna meet her?"

"No."

But Zoey waved Kara over anyway and pulled her close when she was within reach. "Dani wanted to say hi and to meet Rachel."

Kara made the introductions, and with a subtle glance, Dani checked Rachel out. She was pretty. In a delicate sort of way. Her skin was flawless, like porcelain. Brown eyes and dark brows contrasted nicely with her blond hair. Bottle blond, probably. Dani disliked her instantly, which was ridiculous. She was probably a lovely person.

"So how do you know each other?" Rachel asked Dani.

"My dog goes to day care every day."

Kara's arm rested comfortably around Rachel's tiny waist. "Took Dani a while to warm up to the whole doggie day care thing, but it's been working out well for Oliver, right?"

Never willing to give an inch when it came to Kara, Dani raised her brows. "If you say so."

"Oh, c'mon. He's a hundred percent better now."

"Maybe fifty percent."

"Fifty? Please. He's at least ninety percent better."

"I'll give you sixty," Dani countered.

Zoey grabbed a handful of popcorn.

"Eighty-five percent."

"Sixty-five is my final offer."

"I'm not going less than eighty."

Rachel cleared her throat. "Why don't you both compromise and say seventy-five percent?"

Both Kara and Dani paused, then nodded in agreement.

"Dani didn't know her dog's name for, like, a month," Kara said.

"It wasn't a month. You do like to exaggerate. And how are those precious kittens of yours? I'm sorry, what are their names again?"

"I'm not naming them if I'm not keeping them."

Dani ignored her. "Kittens? I think that's what she named them. So creative. There's kitten, and there's…kitten." The last *kitten* had an inflection at the end.

Zoey chuckled and reached for the entire bowl.

"Why would I name kittens I'm not keeping?"

"Oh, I have a funny feeling they're staying. Call it a hunch."

Kara scoffed. "Don't be so sure about that, I'm a dog person."

"I hate to break it to you, but your dogs are cat people. Might wanna join the ranks. Come over to the dark side of cat loving."

"Never."

Two women appeared, and one wrapped an arm around Kara's shoulders. "Who's your friend? I don't think we've met. I'm Jes, and this is Val."

Dani stared at the lovely woman with the long, dark hair. She looked strong and confident and was all sorts of invading Kara's personal space. Was this an ex? Christ, she was gorgeous. And intimidating. The sexual pheromones oozed from her pores.

Kara cleared her throat. "Ah, this is Dani."

With a smile, Jesmyn's eyes traveled up and down her body.

Why did Dani suddenly feel naked? And…flattered? She took a sip of beer, hoping nobody noticed the heat rushing into her cheeks.

Jen popped into the group to create the perfect distraction. "Ladies, are we ready for the golf outing tomorrow?"

"Oh God, another humiliating day is on the horizon. I can feel it," Dani said.

"Relax, Dans," Zoey said. "We're gonna kick ass."

"You mean golf will kick our ass, is usually what happens," Jen clarified.

"Yeah, but there's free beer and food," Zoey said.

Ethan and Will were nearby and joined the conversation. Will looped an arm around Dani. "Did somebody say golf?"

Zoey, Jen, and Dani collectively groaned.

"Hey, I heard they have a prize for last place this year, ladies," Ethan said.

Will chuckled. "Yeah, gives you guys something to shoot for."

"Fuck off," Zoey said. "We're gonna beat your asses tomorrow."

"Yeah, like that's gonna happen. Drink up, girl." Ethan grabbed Will and the two laughed and went off in search of cigars.

Later, Dani stood in a crowd of women while Zoey held court.

"Zoe, what did Jen get you for your birthday?" someone asked.

Zoey, who was two and a half sheets to the wind, snuck a glance at Jen. "Should I tell them?"

"No."

"Oh, c'mon!" Zoey grinned wickedly and wrapped her arms around Jen's waist. "Well, last weekend, this one comes home with a strap-on."

"Zoey, stop!"

Someone brought one of the bowls of popcorn into the discussion, and it was passed around.

"Jen puts this thing on, and she's thrusting and she's biting her lip while she's moving it all around." Zoey's imitation of Jen's technique sent a spasm of laughter through the crowd. With each thrust of her hips, the group's collective heads bobbed backward.

Jen took it in stride and laughed along. "I wasn't that bad. And it was my first time using it. I'll get better."

Jesmyn cleared her throat. "A strap-on is something that takes a lot of practice. Next time, you might wanna try this position. If I may." She turned to Dani. "Would you help me demonstrate?"

Before Dani could answer, Jesmyn bent her over so that her boobs bobbed perpendicular to the ground.

"The best technique is to gently roll your hips like so." Jesmyn rolled and pressed her hips into Dani. "So, you can thrust, but gently, then give a roll." The thrusting and rolling continued for a few seconds while the crowd oohed and aahed.

Back in her parallel universe, Dani wondered how it was she was getting fake fucked by Kara's possible ex. And not feeling too bad about it. She really needed to be more adventurous in the bedroom. When Jesmyn was finished thrusting, Dani stood, put a hand to her throat, and with pursed lips blew out a breath.

Jesmyn gently patted her back. "Nice job."

The popcorn bowl was empty, and the group looked dazed. Some discreetly adjusted their underwear.

"Anybody need a drink?"

"I need a cigarette."

CHAPTER SEVENTEEN

Later in the evening, Kara found herself in the kitchen getting a glass of wine for Rachel. The evening so far had been an awkward mess. Having to deal with two women she was having sex with, even if one was dream sex, could put a damper on anyone's night. Kara had finished a few beers and was quite tipsy at this point. However, the alcohol was not helping her deal with the vision that was Danielle Clark in her low-cut top. That cleavage would be the death of her.

Kara's eyes followed Dani around the crowded room all night. It was like an invisible connection existed between them, a tenuous thread of attraction stretching across the room. Many times she was caught stealing a glance, and it was jarring. At first, she looked away immediately. But the more she drank, the more she held the stare, forcing Dani to turn away.

She re-corked the wine bottle and turned to leave the room at the same time someone was coming in, and the saloon-style door swung open, breaking the wineglass Kara held in her hand. Blood seeped from a cut on her thumb.

"Oh, shit." Zoey grabbed a paper towel. "I'm so sorry. I didn't know you were right there. Here, press on it." She stuck her head into the living room. "Anybody see Dani? Tell her we need her in the kitchen, stat!" She turned her attention back to Kara. "You okay?"

"It's not a big deal." The paper towel turned red.

Jen came into the kitchen with Dani in tow. "Found her."

Dani looked at the red towel wrapped around Kara's thumb. "What happened?"

Kara held the paper towel in place. "Wineglass broke."

"Here, let me see." Dani carefully peeled the towel back. "Well, I think you'll live. You're gonna need a stitch or two, though. You should go the hospital."

"Can't you just put a Band-Aid on it?" Kara asked.

"I could, yes. I could put a Band-Aid on it and leave a hideous scar on your thumb."

"Just stitch it up, Dans," Zoey said.

"With what? I don't have anything with me."

"I don't need stitches," Kara insisted.

"Ethan always has EMT stuff in his car," Jen said. "I'll go get him."

Dani continued to inspect the cut. "You may have glass in there. We'll have to check before I stitch you up."

"Is this wise? Have you been drinking?" Kara didn't need a drunk surgeon sticking her full of holes, even one with incredible cleavage.

Dani waved her off. "No, I had one beer, I'm fine."

Ethan rushed into the kitchen with a large first aid bag. "What's going on?"

"Kara got cut, and Dani's gonna sew her up!" Zoey said with more glee than the situation called for.

Ethan peered at the bloody appendage. "You want me to do it? I love stitching people up."

Zoey was quick to interject. "No! Dani can handle it. Right, Dani?"

Dani nodded. "I live for this. It's my jam. Okay, where should we do this?"

Jen pointed to the steps. "Go upstairs to our bathroom. Nobody will bother you and the lighting's good."

"The upstairs bath it is. Let's go." Dani rewrapped the thumb and grabbed Ethan's bag.

Dani ushered Kara into the bathroom and took charge. "Sit on the toilet and put your hand over the sink." She poked through Ethan's bag and pulled out a syringe. *Perfect.* Next came a stitching needle and thread, a small bottle with some liquid in it, a pair of tweezers, and a large pair of glasses.

"What's the needle for?"

"Lidocaine."

"I don't need lidocaine."

"Oh, really? I'm gonna be putting three or four stitches in your cut, and you don't think you'll need it?"

"Nah, just stitch it up, Doc. I can handle it."

Dani pulled Kara's hand under the spigot and turned on the water.

Kara's face paled and she almost fell off the toilet. "Oowww, shit!"

"Still don't want the lidocaine?" Dani blinked with feigned innocence.

"That wasn't very doctorly." Kara stared at the needle. "I may need to be drunker for this. You got any beer in your bag?"

Dani took the syringe and positioned it near the cut. "Ready?"

"Are you sure you need to stick a needle in there?"

Dani sensed her patient's trepidation. It was slightly endearing. "Are you afraid of needles?"

"Maybe?"

"Well, well. The cat lover is afraid of a needle. I can't believe you're a closet cat lover. All those times you made fun of me for loving cats. What did you say about them? They're aloof? Vengeful? Are your new kittens vengeful and aloof?" Dani asked.

"Not my kittens. They're angels. Not like your mini mountain lion."

"Done."

Kara's mouth fell open. "You stuck me already?"

"Yup."

"I didn't feel a thing."

"What can I say? I'm good." Dani put on the headband with large magnifying glasses attached to it and turned on the LED light.

Kara giggled. "Wow, those are attractive. You wear those out? Bet you get a lot of action."

"Very funny." She turned the water on again and let it rinse over Kara's hand.

"Ouch."

"And, I don't need action. I'm engaged, remember?" Dani held up her hand, realizing too late she forgot to put the engagement ring on.

"Oops, no ring."

Dani glanced at her naked ring finger. "Shit."

"You know what they say…No ring, no engagement."

Dani turned the water on again.

"Ouch."

"We'll give it a minute." With chin in hand, Dani rested her elbow on the vanity, waiting for the local anesthetic to take effect. Her eyes kept straying to the camisole under Kara's shirt. *Talk about not being doctorly.* Dani flicked her finger at Kara's cut.

"Hey, that could've hurt."

"Sit still. I need to look for glass."

Kara settled in. "Do you have your blue bra on?"

Dani took a quick peek down at her chest, wondering if her bra was even visible. "None of your business."

"Aw, c'mon, Dani." Kara's mouth hovered close to Dani's ear. "What color is it?"

A tingle of excitement awoke deep in her gut as Kara's breath brushed over her ear. She fought the sudden urge to lean into her. "Hold still." She fished a shard out and prepared the needle and thread. With steady hands, she began stitching.

"You were in my dream, Dr. Clark."

Dani stopped for a brief, almost imperceptible second, then continued stitching. "Oh yeah? Were you yelling at me?"

"No."

She locked eyes with Kara, who had a shit-eating grin on her face. The heat crept into Dani's cheeks. "Sit still." She tried to concentrate on the task at hand, but curiosity got the better of her. "What was your dream about?"

"Let's just say you were wearing the bra. And only the bra. While sitting on my motorcycle."

Dani bit her lip and steadied her hand. "Oh, I was sitting on your killing machine?" Could this be possible? They were both having sex dreams about the other?

"Don't you wanna know what we did?"

An image from Dani's last sex dream popped into her head and a trickle of sweat rolled down her back. Did someone turn the thermostat up? "Not really."

Drunken Kara was not to be deterred. "You kissed me. Then you started taking your bra off—"

"All done." Dani finished and put a bandage over the area. She needed to stick her head in a bucket of ice. Hell, her whole body needed to be submerged. "You've obviously had too much to drink. It's delusional, thinking I would ever want to kiss you. That is not gonna happen. Ever."

Dani stood and repacked Ethan's bag. She needed to get out of this space as soon as possible and find a large walk-in freezer.

"I think the lady doth protest too much."

Dani froze. "Boy, you are full of yourself. How does your head even fit through a doorway?"

Kara laughed. "Are you afraid?"

Dani zipped the bag closed. "Afraid of what?" Her eyes strayed to those luscious lips.

"Of what would happen if you kissed me?"

"Afraid? Of kissing *you*? Unbelievable, you're a, a—"

"Just a dog walker? A little beneath you?"

"No…you're—"

"Not in the right tax bracket?"

"No, I wasn't going to say any of that."

Kara approached Dani. "What were you going to say?"

Dani's heart thumped inside her chest, and a tight knot of desire coiled in the lower part of her belly. Kara was close, too close. So close she could smell her perfume. This scent was different from the one she wore at the bar. It had a hint of vanilla, and something else. Something sexy. This fire needed to be extinguished before it engulfed her. "Argh! You are so arrogant. And pompous. And annoying!"

"I'm arrogant? I'm pompous? Ha! That's a good one." Kara moved closer, her face inches from Dani's. "At least I'm not a spoiled brat, raised with a silver spoon in my mouth."

Dani's dander rose. The nerve of this woman! She might be hot as shit, she might have the most beautiful eyes ever, but no one called Dani a spoiled brat. She didn't move away; in fact, she shifted closer. "Did you just call me a spoiled brat?" Their lips were millimeters away.

"I did."

"That's what you think? I'm some spoiled, rich kid?"

"You're a doctor. Your parents are doctors. You live in a big house. How could you not be rich and spoiled?"

"You don't know me at all."

"I know enough."

And Dani did the only thing she could think of to shut her up, engagement be damned. She kissed her. She slammed her lips into Kara's so hard Kara crashed backward into the door. In a hot second Kara's tongue jammed into her mouth, and she grabbed Dani by the back of the neck to pull her closer. It was violent. It was angry. And it was sexy. Their mouths slanted across each other's. Teeth knocked together. They couldn't get enough. Kara's free hand grabbed Dani's ass and she moved them across the room, banging into a shaker cabinet and sending its contents all over the floor. Kara's lips and tongue found their way to Dani's neck, and they left a hot, wet trail down to her pulse point. Dani threw her head back and moaned.

Then, as quickly as it started, it stopped. Dani pulled away, horrified. "Shit." It took all her might to disengage her sex-crazed body.

Kara grabbed the sink to steady herself. "Holy hell, you kissed me."

"I did not. You kissed me!"

"You kissed *me*!"

Dani covered her face. "Jesus Christ. We were drunk. That's why this happened."

"You said you weren't drunk."

"Look, this didn't happen, got it?" Dani paced around the small room. She needed to banish this whole episode from her mind. "There was no kiss."

Kara slumped against the wall. "Oh, there was a kiss. A pretty fucking good kiss."

Dani waved her hands back and forth, thinking they could cool the heat that rolled through her. "I'm engaged! There was no kiss."

"If you say so."

They both fell silent for a few seconds.

"Maybe we should kiss, to make sure it wasn't a kiss," Kara said.

Dani stopped pacing. "What kind of half baked logic is that?"

"It makes perfect sense."

Panic rose in Dani's chest, because right now, that's exactly what she wanted to do. "It would be stupid to kiss again." *God, so stupid.*

"Stupid is a red-flag word."

Dani battled her inner demons, battled this sudden hunger that had flared up, that was all consuming. Willpower slowly ebbed away. Maybe Kara was right. Maybe they needed to kiss again to establish the first time was not a kiss. Maybe it *was* sound logic. *Fuck it.*

She moved in and captured Kara's lips. Once again, they stumbled into the shaker cabinet, and the last remaining bottles and lotions fell to the floor. Dani pressed her body's full length into Kara's, who moaned into her mouth. Suddenly Kara's lips left hers and found their way to her exposed chest. Those long, elegant fingers grasped her breasts through the soft cotton of her shirt, and a skilled thumb teased an already hardening nipple. An inhuman sound gurgled in Dani's throat. How incredible it would be to feel Kara's lips against her bare skin. She'd never wanted something so bad.

"You guys still in there?" Ethan asked through the closed door. "Is everything okay?"

The sudden interruption startled them, and they broke apart. Dani stepped away and put a hand to her heart. "We're finishing up. We'll be out in a minute." She hoped her voice sounded normal, that it didn't quake like the rest of her body was doing right now.

"Okay, see you downstairs." Ethan moved away from the door.

Dani closed her eyes and willed herself to beat back the minor panic attack that wanted to take hold. "Jesus Christ. What am I doing? I'm engaged, for God's sake. This cannot happen. This did not happen. Listen to me. You can't tell anyone about this. There was no kiss."

"What kiss?"

"Exactly. We finally agree on something. Now, I gotta go find Phil."

"You mean Will?"

"Shit." Dani rubbed her temples, completely flustered by the situation at hand. Down was up. Right was wrong. Black was white. Will was Phil. She reached for the door and opened it. Only it was the door to the linen closet.

"Wrong door."

"I see that," she hissed.

Dani hurried out the correct door and flew down the steps, running away from the best kiss of her life. She headed toward the back door. Once she hit the crisp evening air, she took several deep breaths, trying to calm the storm raging inside her. With a groan, she collapsed onto one of the chaise lounges on the deck.

She had to kiss her, right? Kara practically dared her to do it. And Dani Clark never backed down from a dare. Never. Also, she had a beer. It was an alcohol-fueled kiss. One beer could do that to people. Couldn't it? And all those sex dreams. Let's not forget about the sex dreams. Her subconscious made her do it.

Dani felt better. Number one, Kara made her do it, number two, the Corona Light made her do it, and number three, her subconscious made her do it. Who else could she blame? She could blame this chaise lounge. One, Kara, two, beer, three, subconscious, and four, this chaise lounge. With so many things conspiring against her, there was no way she could avoid kissing her. Why, she should be congratulated. Four unstoppable things made this happen, the chaise lounge being the straw that broke the camel's back. *Whew.* She was fine.

* * *

After Will and Dani returned home, she relaxed on the couch in the living room, absently stroking Oliver's head. Will had gone upstairs, but she was still too charged from the earlier events. Kara's lips were as good as advertised in her dreams. Had she ever been kissed like that? No. But she needed to forget about it. It was a one-time thing and couldn't happen again. It won't happen again. The guilt from the dreams was heavy enough, she didn't need the added weight.

"Hey, babe, Where's my red golf shirt?" Will called down. "I wanna wear it tomorrow."

"Check the laundry basket." Well, that was sobering. Her fiancé was upstairs, in their bedroom, and she was down here, fantasizing about a woman. *Pull yourself together. You'll be married in a few months. To Will. It's your destiny. It's what you're supposed to do. De-Infatuation plan goes on as scheduled.* Although she better add a step, right after number one—or maybe it should be number one. No kissing the object of your infatuation.

Yes, that should be number one all right.

CHAPTER EIGHTEEN

Dani sat in her lap. The light-blue bra was the only thing between Kara's lips and nirvana. She slipped the straps off Dani's shoulders and almost lost her mind at the sight before her. Here she could stay forever, worshipping at the altar that was Dani Clark. She needed no other sustenance…

As the dream faded, Kara struggled to hold on to it. Something sandpapery and wet was in her ear. Was it Dani's tongue? She heard purring. Was Dani satisfied? She opened her eyes and was immediately swatted across the nose. A loud, frustrated groan echoed around the bedroom. Kara rolled onto her stomach and put the pillow over her head. Mother of God. That was hot.

She swallowed to erase the fetid taste of stale alcohol that was still in her mouth. She was hungover, and her head pounded. The events of the previous evening remained fuzzy. How did she get home? Rachel had driven her own car because she had to catch a red-eye to the East Coast last night for work. Kara vaguely remembered saying goodbye at one point in the evening, and remembered Rachel wasn't too pleased with her.

What happened? Tiny paws walked along the pillow on her head. Voices drifted in. Was she still dreaming? A knock on the bedroom door confirmed she had company.

"You getting up anytime soon?" Val called through door.

"Why are you so loud?"

"Somebody had too much to drink last night. Get her up."

The bedroom door opened, and Jesmyn strolled in. The kittens scattered.

"Hey, sexy. Get up. I'm gonna make breakfast."

"Please leave me alone."

"Here, take these." She lifted the pillow and handed Kara a glass of water and some Advil.

"Ah, I'm naked under here." Kara struggled to sit up and not flash her friend.

"Yeah, I know. I put you to bed last night."

Kara spit some water onto the bed. "What? You, you…did what?" How Jesmyn still had the power to reduce Kara to a babbling idiot was beyond her. And goddamn her thumb was throbbing. Suddenly the memory of the kiss in the bathroom came rushing back. Dani had kissed her.

"It smells like sex in here. Did you have another sex dream?"

Warmth crept into her cheeks. "Please go away."

"Starring Dani?"

Kara lay back down and put the pillow over her face. "Where are my dogs?"

"Outside. So, you had another sex dream about Dani?"

"Who else?" Kara lamented into the pillow, resigned to the fact that Jesmyn would only drag it out of her anyway. She wasn't the top detective at the Southwest district police department because she was pretty.

"What were you two doing upstairs for so long last night?"

"She was stitching my thumb." She produced the bandaged appendage as evidence.

"Doesn't take that long to put a couple stitches in a thumb. What else happened?"

Kara was caught off-guard by this new line of questioning. "What do you mean?"

"Well, first Dani came flying down the steps like she was running away from something. Then you came stumbling down looking like somebody stole your cookie…or your Dani."

"I did not."

"Yes, you did. You looked dazed."

"She had to stitch me up. We didn't do anything else."

"Did you have sex?"

"No! I'd like two eggs scrambled, please." Surely if she placed her breakfast order, Jesmyn would vacate the bedroom and the sexual inquisition would stop. She hugged the pillow tightly to her chest for moral support.

"Did I ever tell you I was sorry for giving you that black eye when you were a freshman in high school?" Jesmyn asked.

Ah yes. Her one and only black eye. It was the first time Kara had been on the basketball court with the imposing senior. They'd both been centers, but Jesmyn had towered over her at the time. Kara had her back to the basket, waiting for a pass, and Jesmyn had bumped her from behind and whispered, "You're fucking hot."

Kara had frozen, stunned and embarrassed. The pass came and Jesmyn had reached around and an elbow had connected with Kara's orbital socket. She stole the ball and started a fast break the other way. Kara had sported a black eye from that elbow for a week afterward.

"No, you never did apologize."

"Well, I'm sorry. So, who kissed who?"

"She kissed me." It slipped out. She didn't mean for it to. It was an involuntary reaction, like when a doctor tested your reflexes by hitting your knee with a rubber hammer. *Damn it.* Jesmyn and her powers of interrogation.

"The kissing part was quite obvious. What are you gonna do about it?"

Damn it. Jesmyn and her powers of observation. "I'm gonna try and stay away from her." Kara paused, then added, "Which should be easy, because we don't even like each other."

Super sleuth Jesmyn kept interrogating. "If you don't like her, why do you have to *try* and stay away from her?"

"Isn't somebody supposed to be making breakfast? Two eggs scrambled? Wheat toast?"

"Kara?" Few could refuse to answer Jesmyn when she turned her steely, amber gaze upon them. "Why do you need to try and stay away from her?"

Kara's head continued to pound. Her not-so-steadfast resolve crumbled right before her eyes. "Because she's sexy as fuck. There, I said it. I wanna do unspeakable things to her body. Happy? I wanna hear her scream my name in ecstasy. And she's engaged. Anything else?"

"Nope. Scrambled eggs coming up."

And with that Kara was left alone with thoughts of sexy Dani running through her brain.

"You owe me twenty bucks," she heard Jesmyn say to Val.

* * *

Kara washed the breakfast dishes, careful not to get the stitches wet. Luckily, the Advil had taken the throbbing away. The kittens sat next to the sink, waiting patiently for a bubble to float up from the dish soap. She feared she'd soon have to come up with names, because quite frankly, they weren't going anywhere. But she wouldn't admit that to anyone else right now.

As she placed the final dish in the rack, her mind circled back to her decision made earlier. Stay away from Dani. If she stayed away, there would be no more danger of kissing. If there was no more kissing, well, she'd be devastated, but maybe the dreams would stop. Maybe she would stop aching to touch her. Touch her breasts, obviously. That was all. She appreciated her breasts. She was a breast woman. There, that was it. No more Dani Clark. Her phone buzzed with a text from Zoey.

Our fourth bailed, Dani and Jen suck, I need you. Tee time is 1230pm. I know you got a band-aid on your thumb but suck it the fuck up.

I'm in. She put the phone down.

So much for that decision.

* * *

Dani made it to the country club early so she could limber up. Will and Ethan were in the restaurant enjoying the free lunch. His group would be in front of Dani's, and she could only imagine the trash-talking that would take place. And to make matters worse, Kevin Murphy would be here.

She took a club and swung it, waking up muscles that had been sleeping soundly an hour ago. She didn't fall asleep until after four a.m. because of a certain brunette. And a certain kiss. And a certain grope of her breasts.

Hopefully, the rest of her foursome would arrive soon. She felt like a loser on the practice range, surrounded by people who clearly had a better grasp on the game than she did. And not just any people, but colleagues, superiors, and staff. Her phone vibrated with a text from Jolie.

How about this Wednesday for dinner?

Dani smiled. What a nice surprise. *Absolutely. Let me know what to bring.*

Soon a tired Jen and Zoey appeared.

"Hey, girls. Ready to play some golf?" Dani asked.

"If you mean are we ready to cheat at golf, you bet your ass." Zoey shucked the golf bag off her shoulder.

"How you feeling?" Dani asked. "You were pretty tipsy last night."

"I'm good, no worries. Gonna have a little bit of the hairy dog."

"You mean the hair of the dog that bit you?"

"What the fuck ever. What about you?"

"I only had one beer, so I'm fine. Where's Hannah?"

"Yeah, she bailed. Couldn't get out of bed."

"Great!" Dani threw her hands up. "Now we don't have a fourth."

"Relax, we have a fill-in." Zoey stretched. "So, ah, Dans. Did you happen to knock into our cabinet in the bathroom last night?"

Dani's stomach muscles clenched, and she bit her lip. Her denial came quick. "No, I wasn't anywhere near the cabinet. Why would you ask that?" She put a ball down and made a show of addressing it.

"Things were on different shelves. Like somebody rearranged it, or accidentally knocked it over and put stuff back."

"It was probably your dogs."

"Dogs don't put things back on shelves."

"Yeah, but I bet cats could." Dani made a half-hearted attempt to hit the ball. And missed. She changed the subject. "I have a great idea. How about we don't finish last this year? Maybe we could stay sober until at least the fifth hole." Every year they finished last, and the year before at the dinner afterward, Will and his group teased them mercilessly.

"Dani, the beer's free," Jen said. "It would be abhorrent to not drink free beer. That's one, ladies. One!" She waggled a finger in the air.

"Word of the day, word of the day!" Zoey gave her a high-five, and they chest-bumped for good measure.

"But, wouldn't it be nice to not finish last for once?" Dani asked.

"I've been practicing. I'm ready to tear it up out there," Zoey said.

Jen began to warm up. "I'm surprised you're not banned from this place."

"Why would they ban *me*?" Zoey asked.

"Oh, I don't know, for yelling 'watch the fuck out' instead of 'fore'?"

"Nobody heard it. Everybody's old and deaf at this place."

"You said it on every shot, because every shot almost killed somebody," Jen said.

Dani agreed, "Everybody heard it."

Zoey looked over Dani's shoulder. "Whatever. Here's our fourth."

Dani turned and her heart stopped, either from lust or anger—she couldn't tell which. "Oh my God, you invited her?" Panic rose in her chest.

"Who? Karen?" Zoey smirked.

"But, but, she has stitches in her thumb," Dani said. "She can't play."

Zoey scoffed. "Fuck that, she's an athlete. She's gonna gut it out."

"She could rip open the stitches." Dani grasped at any straw to save herself.

"Then you'll stitch her back up."

Kara made her way over to them and set her bag down. "Ladies."

Dani was instantly mesmerized by The Lips. Last night they were incredible. Plump and soft and God help her she wanted to feel them in other places. Her chest heaved at the thought.

"Dani!" Zoey yelled.

"Huh, what?" She looked up from The Lips and met a pair of bemused green eyes.

"Kara's a real golfer and is gonna give us some pointers. Pay attention. You wanna be *not* last, right?" Zoey addressed the ball and Kara readjusted her grip and posture, touching her hands and lower back.

Was there always so much groping with golf lessons? Dani swallowed her dread and turned away. Maybe if she ignored everybody, she'd be safe.

"Dani, if I may?"

She groaned inside as Kara slipped behind her and rearrange her hips. Tiny electrodes began firing off between her legs.

"Stick your butt out more." Hands grasped her ass. "Bend over a little."

Last night's dildo demo came rushing back, and Dani's body temperature ticked upward.

"Don't be so stiff. Go ahead, swing." Kara's hands still rested on Dani's hips.

She promptly shanked the ball. "Shit."

"Here, let me help you." Kara arms wrapped around Dani. "How did you sleep last night," she whispered.

Dani shivered, her legs nearly gave out, and she may have creamed her panties. She had to get ahold of herself quickly. "Like a baby," she fired back.

Kara was back in her ear. "Liar." She softly laughed and stepped away.

"What are you guys talking about?" Zoey called over to them with a mouthful of popcorn.

"Nothing," Dani said. "What is it with you and popcorn lately?"

"What? It's a vegetable."

"Corn has absolutely no nutritional value."

"It's in the vegetable aisle of the grocery store. Whole Foods wouldn't lie."

A horn blared, calling all the golfers back to their respective carts. "I'm riding with Jen this year," Dani said quickly. There was no way she could spend an entire afternoon in the same cart as Kara. Her heart wouldn't survive it. Neither would her underwear.

Zoey would have none of it. "Nope, I need to ride with my girl." Zoey and Jen shared a cackle and sped along to the first hole.

Kara smiled. "Might as well make the best of it. Probably gonna be a long round." When Dani didn't answer, Kara shrugged and hit the gas on the cart.

Dani plotted the next moves in her head. She went over the steps to De-Infatuation. Step one, stop thinking about her. No, wait, step one was no kissing. She sneaked a peek at Kara. She wasn't all that. Her ears were way too small. And she was too thin. And too athletic. Her eyes traveled down to the steering wheel on the golf cart, studying the fingers wrapped around it. Overrated. She glanced at her profile. Her green eyes were too green. Dani started to feel stronger. More hopeful she'd make it through the day without a sexual breakdown of some sort. Like dragging Kara off into the trees to make out with her.

They pulled behind Zoey and Jen, who were in the midst of an animated discussion with Will and his group about how they were gonna kick each other's asses.

Will came over to check on them. "Hey, babe. Zoey's betting dinner at the Metropolitan Grill that you guys are gonna beat us. You in?"

"Sure." Well, that's one expensive dinner lost.

Kevin Murphy with his slicked-back dark hair and amber-colored Ray-Bans sauntered over. "How are you, beautiful?"

Dani's skin crawled. "I'm fine."

"Don't I get a hug?" He spread his arms wide.

She had to behave herself because he was Will's boss, but one of these days she was going to slap his face. As she hugged him, he pulled her much closer than necessary, and his hands wandered down to her ass. She extracted herself as quickly as she could without actually shoving him away.

Kevin glanced at Kara. "And who's this lovely vision? I'm Dr. Kevin Murphy." He reached across the cart to shake Kara's hand.

"Kara Britton."

"You guys gonna tee off, or what?" Zoey said.

Will's group made their way to the tee box.

Ethan turned and chuckled. "Here's a free lesson for you ladies. Pay attention."

"Screw you, Ethan," Zoey yelled back at him.

As Dani sat back down in the cart, Kara asked, "Who was that douchebag?"

"Will's boss."

"He shouldn't have touched you like that. He needs to keep his hands to himself."

A bemused smile settled on Dani's face. Kara sounded concerned, and a warm glow bloomed in her chest. "Careful, you almost sound protective."

Kara shrugged. "He shouldn't touch any woman like that."

When it was their turn to tee off, Zoey jumped from the cart, first beer in hand. "Okay, let's giddy up and get this party started." She put down the beer, teed up the ball, and hit a beautiful slice, right out of their fairway and onto the next. Cupping her hands to her mouth she yelled, "Watch the fuck out!"

"Jesus Christ," Dani said. "Already with the F-bomb?"

Kara was next, and she hit a beautiful drive, straight down the fairway.

"Whoa, nice. Watch out, second to last, here we come." Zoey finished off her first beer.

Dani made her way to the tee box. She bent over to put her tee in the ground and happened to catch Kara watching with what could only be described as a longing look. Dani stood back up, wanting to glare at her, wanting to berate her for daring to look at her that way, but she was secretly thrilled. It was gonna be a long day. *"De-Infatuation!"* she silently screamed in her head.

Addressing the ball, she took a swing and missed entirely. The day just got longer.

"Keep your head down," Jen instructed.

"Do you need me to help you with your setup?" Kara asked.

"No, no." *Please God, no.* "I got it." She took a deep breath, steadied her hands, and swung, sending the ball well over to the left.

"Watch the fuck out!" Zoey yelled.

They piled into their carts to search for balls.

When Dani sat down, she couldn't even make eye contact with Kara. "Don't say anything."

"I wasn't." Kara put the golf cart in motion. "Keep your head down."

Dani huffed. "I thought you weren't going to say anything."

After finding their respective balls, they came back to hit from where Kara's ball had landed. The scramble format of the tournament meant everybody in a foursome hit from the spot of the best ball.

Kara took her stance, swung, and sent a beautiful arcing shot onto the green.

Jen sent a line drive into the bunker. With a curse, she went in search of her shot.

Dani hit her ball ten feet. "Don't anybody say anything."

"You need to relax. Have another beer, Dans!" Zoey placed her ball on a tee.

Kara's eyes widened. "You're teeing it up in the fairway?"

"Chill. Nobody's watching." She grabbed a three wood.

Dani's jaw dropped. "We're only fifty yards out. Isn't that too much club?"

"Nah. I've got this." Zoey took a wild swing and the ball sailed, and kept sailing, and sailing, eventually out of view. "Watch the fuck out!" she hollered. She turned to Kara. "I think I'm on the green," she stated with some certainty.

Kara winced and shook her head before calling out to Jen, "She thinks she's on the green."

"Oh, she's on a green, all right," she shouted back. "Two holes over."

They all ran up to see where her shot landed. It was indeed two holes over.

Zoey waved to the group on the other green who had all turned to stare at her. "Yo!" she yelled at them, waving her hands. "That's my fucking ball." She gestured to try and convey what she meant. "Yeah, no, what? That's my ball. Leave it there. Pretty good shot, right? What? Yeah." She turned to other gals. "I have no fucking clue what they're saying."

Dani cowered behind Jen, realizing who was on that green. Only the CEO of the hospital, getting F-bombarded by her bestie.

"Dr. Clark?" an elderly gentleman with white hair called over.

Dani sheepishly left her cover and waved. "Hi, Dr. Kentman. Sorry about that."

"Kenny, dude, leave my ball there," Zoey yelled.

If the hole on the green were bigger, Dani would've crawled into it. Dr. Kentman waved and his group left Zoey's ball on the green.

After much fanfare, and many duffs and whoops, they managed to put the ball in the hole. If not for Kara, it would have been a comedy of errors. But they wrote a five on the scorecard.

"That's the first single-digit number we've ever recorded," Jen gushed. "Legally."

As they sat in their carts at the next hole, Kara quietly asked, "Should we talk about the elephant in the room?"

"What elephant?"

"The kiss. You seem agitated. Maybe if we talk about it, you might feel better."

"There's nothing to talk about. It was just a kiss. It wasn't even good," Dani lied. And it was a big one.

Kara laughed. "Oh, please. Not good. Really?"

"Really. Do you find that hard to believe? That maybe you're not a good kisser?"

"I've never had any complaints."

"First time for everything."

"What are we talking about?"

Both girls jumped at the interruption. Zoey had magically appeared in front of their cart, popcorn in hand.

"Jesus Christ, you scared me," Dani said.

"Did I hear someone say kissing?"

Kara's eyes snapped open wide. "No, no kissing." She looked to Dani for reassurance.

Dani spoke quickly. "Nobody said kissing. We said hissing. Hissing."

"Dani saw a snake," Kara blurted out. "Back there...at the last hole."

Dani continued with the alibi. "It was a snake, and it was hissing. We didn't say kissing. We said hissing. Maybe you have popcorn in your ear."

Zoey absently stuck a finger in her ear while staring at them. After a beat, she said, "Carry on," and headed back to her own cart.

Dani scowled. "A snake?"

Kara gave as good as she got. "Hissing? What was I supposed to do with that?"

At the next hole, Zoey glanced at the picture on the scorecard. "Shit. Water hole, ladies. We always have trouble on water holes."

"You mean you always have trouble on water holes," Dani said.

Zoey's balls had an unhealthy attraction to the wet stuff. No matter where it was, eventually Zoey's ball would be sitting in it. One time, they found it in a bird bath.

"Where's the water?" Jen shielded the sun from her eyes and searched the fairway.

Kara studied the card. "It's behind our tee box, so you should be good."

"Famous last words," Jen mumbled to Dani.

"Dani, you're up!" Zoey called.

"Why am I first?"

"To scare all the snakes away. Let's go."

Dani grimaced. "Very funny." She knew Zoey wouldn't buy that story, but it was the best she could come up with on such short notice. She put her ball on the tee, stood up, and with snakes on the brain, hit a lovely tee shot that traveled all of twenty feet.

Zoey stepped up next and stared down the fairway. She waggled and wiggled over her ball, bit her bottom lip to concentrate, and swung as hard as she could. The ball headed straight into some rocks, hit them square-on, ricocheted backward, sailed over their ducking heads, and landed in the creek behind the tee box.

Zoey's mouth hung open. "Did that just happen?"

Jen smirked. "That was abhorrent." She held up two fingers, then fist-pumped in solitary celebration.

"You jinxed me, Dani," Zoey said. "You said water."

"I did no such thing." Dani threw down her second beer and reached into Zoey's cart for a third.

By the time they finished the ninth hole, they felt jazzed. Their score was surprisingly good, probably due to two things. Number one, Zoey would walk up to each green and accidentally on purpose roll a spare ball toward the hole, showing the line of the putt. One time she rolled it in, shouting, "That's a birdie, bitches!" and they carded a three. Number two, Dani putted like a champ when she was drinking.

So, at the halfway point, the girls found themselves five under par. Rarefied air indeed, the likes of which this group had never experienced. A heady feeling enveloped them. Suddenly, a free steak dinner at the Metropolitan Grill was not wishful thinking, and Zoey, who was competitive as the day was long, let Will and Ethan know about it as she drove up to them on the next hole.

"Hey, jackwads. What's your score?"

Ethan gloated. "We're three under par."

"What are you guys, like thirty over as usual?" Will laughed, elbowing Ethan at what he thought was a funny joke.

Zoey circled them in the cart, staring, with her middle finger raised. When she completed her circle she shouted, "I like my steak medium rare, bitches!"

Dani, witnessing the whole exchange, merely shook her head. The golf gods would not look kindly on such boastful behavior. It was going to be a long back nine. She glanced at her cart partner. Suddenly her ears were adorable, her body fantastic, her fingers sexy, and her eyes dazzling.

Jesus Christ.

CHAPTER NINETEEN

Kara stood with her foursome as they stared down a long par five. Will's group was already hitting their approach shot to the green.

Zoey wandered back to her bag and brought out the driver. She lovingly removed the Shrek head cover Jen had gotten her for Christmas.

Jen groaned. "Not the driver. Put the driver away."

Balls hit by Zoey's driver were rarely ever seen again. Some of them ended up on milk cartons.

"It's a long hole. I gotta get the ball out there." Zoey lined herself up, gave a butt waggle, took the club back, clearly over-swung, and sent the ball to the right—at an almost unheard of angle, breaking all the laws of physics—straight into a large oak tree. All sorts of things dropped out of the tree. Everything except her ball.

She whipped her head around to her playing partners. "Did you see my ball?"

"No, but I think you killed that squirrel," Jen said.

"He just fell. I'll hit another one."

"No!" they yelled in unison.

"All right. Calm the fuck down. Somebody else go."

Kara stood next to Dani waiting for her turn. Dani's earlier statement stuck in her craw. Of course she was a good kisser. All her previous girlfriends lauded her kissing ability. She refused to let doubt creep into her brain. "Maybe you're the bad kisser."

"No way, I'm a great kisser," Dani whispered.

Kara knew firsthand the truth of that statement, but she was too stubborn to give Dani the satisfaction of agreeing with her. "Maybe I should ask Will."

"Go ahead. I'm sure he'd agree. I'm a first-class kisser."

"So am I."

"Oh? I'll ask Rachel next time I see her."

"You do that."

"You're up, Kara," Zoey said.

Kara glared at Dani as she stepped up to the tee box and smashed the ball.

"Wow, girl, what a beaut!" Zoey yelled. "Dani, go."

Dani placed her ball on the tee and hit it twenty-five feet.

"That's five feet farther than last time. Getting better, girl."

When they pulled up to Kara's anger-fueled, monster drive, the guys were still on the green. Ethan and Kevin turned and gestured at the girls, daring them to hit it to the green.

Zoey turned to Kara. "Are they taunting us?"

"Looks that way," Kara said.

"What?" Jen asked.

"They're taunting us." An agitated Zoey glowered as the guys continued to make fun of them. "I should take out my driver and cream it. Take one of those fuckers out."

"You can't hit them from here. It's over two hundred yards," Dani observed.

Zoey ignored her. "I should try."

Kara, who had been shocked and awed with Zoey's long shots all day, knew one of two things would happen. One, she would clock someone on the green, preferably douchebag Murphy, or two, she would put it on the patio of the clubhouse restaurant, probably in someone's shrimp cocktail. "Tee it up, girl."

A slow, evil grin overtook Zoey's face. A fist pump and a cackle followed as she grabbed the big dog. She placed the ball on a tee in the middle of the fairway, took the club back, and whaled on it.

It was a perfect storm of mechanics. Swing plane, tempo, contact. The ball came off the club face like a rocket, flying straight toward the green, the straightest shot Zoey hit all day.

"Oh, shit. WATCH THE FUCK OUT!" Dani screamed.

The boys must have thought it was careening out of bounds, because they turned their backs to finish the hole. But it didn't go out of bounds. Instead, it hit Murphy square in the back. He collapsed onto the green like he was shot.

Zoey dropped her club, spread her arms wide, and in her best homeboy voice yelled, "Take that, mother fuckers."

All the gals guffawed.

When they reached the green, Dani dropped the putt, and they carded a three.

After their euphoria of the elusive eagle, Dani and Kara headed into the bathroom at the thirteenth hole. It was quite nice for a golf course restroom. There was a table near the door, with a comfy wicker chair next to it. Golf-related pictures hung on the wall, and some toiletries and tampons sat in a basket on the granite sink counter.

"My first girlfriend told me I was the best kisser she ever kissed," Kara said from her stall, still smarting from the earlier discussion. "Said I was a natural."

"Sounds like someone can't take constructive criticism."

"There was nothing constructive about it."

They both left their stalls with their panties in a bunch.

Kara washed up at the sink. "I'd like to hear from your alleged ex-girlfriend. Until I do, I'll have my doubts about your kissing ability."

"Alleged? Alleged? You don't think I had a girlfriend? I had a girlfriend for two years. And she had no complaints. None." Dani looked at Kara in the mirror as she turned on her water. "I don't know why you're being so defensive. Not everybody can be a good kisser."

"I'm not defensive. I'm merely stating a fact. *I am* a great kisser. I make women's knees weak."

"Ha! I'd like to see that."

"I can prove it."

"Oh, how you gonna do that, Karen?" Dani walked over to the paper towel holder.

Kara was fed up and, damn it, she needed to make a point. And goddamn she was tired of being called Karen, and God fucking damn it, Dani was hot, even while being a pain in the ass. She stared at Dani's back and weighed her options.

Fuck it. This was for bragging rights. Nothing else. She walked up, grabbed Dani, spun her around, and smashed her lips into hers. She held Dani's head still while her mouth and tongue and teeth had their way with Dani's mouth.

The momentum of the kiss sent them backward, and they banged into the sink. Dani's hands flailed around, perhaps looking for anchor, or something to hold on to, knocking the toiletries and tampons all over the floor. She settled for the small of Kara's back, and she pulled her closer. A small moan escaped from deep inside as Kara's tongue continued its assault.

They breathed heavily into each other's mouths as they both came up for air. As soon as they caught their breath, they went right back to it.

When Dani sagged against her, Kara pulled back. "Ha! Your knees are weak, and you moaned. I heard you." She stepped away, breathless from the kiss, and tried to reel in her pounding heart. She had to fight the ache to pull Dani back into her arms.

"My knees aren't weak. I slipped." Dani gasped for air. "And it wasn't a moan of pleasure, it was pain. You nearly broke my back when you threw me against the sink."

Kara crossed her arm defiantly. "It was a great kiss."

Dani merely shrugged. "It was, maybe, okay."

Kara huffed in disbelief. "Right. You keep telling yourself that. Meanwhile, over here in the real world, I know it was a great kiss, so why don't you admit it? And while you're at it, you can admit I'm a better kisser than you. Because, I know for a fact, you can't do better than that."

"Was that a dare?"

"What?"

"Did you just dare me?"

"No, I don't think I—"

"You want great? You want *great*?" She hooked her fingers through Kara's belt loops and yanked her forward. "I'll show you great." Her lips latched onto Kara's and her tongue pushed its way into her mouth, battering Kara's tongue, chasing it around her mouth. She pushed her whole body against her, sending them both back a couple steps and into the trash can, which couldn't withstand the onslaught and toppled over to the floor. The wall stopped their progress as Dani pinned Kara against it, her shoulder knocking against a picture, sending it down to the ground. Dani mashed her breasts into Kara's chest, and Kara whimpered softly. Dani broke it off and stepped back to put some distance between them. "Now, tell me that wasn't great."

It took a few moments for Kara to answer. "I've had better." She could lie just as well as Dani.

Dani narrowed her eyes. "What?"

Kara raised her chin, her breath still uneven. "I've had better."

Suddenly the ante was upped in this little kissing contest.

"I can do better." Dani nodded. "I know I can do better."

"Prove it, let's go." Kara waved her on. "Show me what you got."

Dani growled, she actually growled, and she came in again, tangling her hands in Kara's hair, pushing her into the other wall, and knocking into the paper towel dispenser. A cascade of Kleenex one-ply multifolds piled up on the floor. As their mouths melded together, Dani's tongue traced Kara's bottom lip, and then she sucked it into her mouth.

Kara's whole body quivered. She grabbed Dani's ass and pulled it up and in, creating unexpected friction. Moans echoed around the room. Kara's hips twitched into Dani's as a hot jolt of desire shot through her lower belly.

They broke apart, and a triumphant Dani poked a finger into Kara's chest. "Take that." She gave a quick tug to her shorts.

Conceding was not an option for Kara. "You think that was better? Really? I feel sorry for you if you thought that was better." She grabbed Dani's neck again and hit her with an open-mouth kiss that would have dropped any ordinary woman.

Evidently, Dani Clark was no ordinary woman, not when there was a dare involved.

Now the game was on, each exerting their will on the other, each trying to prove their prowess as a top-notch kisser. Their bodies strained together around the small confines of the bathroom like two teenagers groping on a dance floor, swaying to music. If objects weren't bolted to the floor, they were upended or knocked off-kilter. The table by the door ended up rolling under one stall.

Hands began to get minds of their own and wandered over heaving body parts. Hips thrust. Lips locked together. Kara fell onto the chair next to the sink, and she pulled Dani down. Now she had Dani right where she wanted, in her lap, like her dream.

* * *

Dani lost all inhibitions as she invited Kara's hands to wander up her shirt or up her shorts—she lost track of them, they moved around so quickly. And she wanted them everywhere at once. Kara's lips moved down her neck and onto Dani's chest, kissing and nipping through her golf shirt. Dani moaned. A couple of *oh Gods* slipped from her lips as she was transported back to every dream she'd had in the past months. All thoughts of a kissing contest were long forgotten as things had escalated almost to a point of no return. So much for De-Infatuation.

Suddenly, she heard the creak of the door shutting, and they both froze. Somehow, that soft sound had penetrated the sexual haze that enveloped them. Dani peeked back at the door. "What was that?"

"I don't know."

"Did you hear it? Fuck, did someone come in?" Reality seeped back into Dani's consciousness. She felt Kara's fingers pressing against her soaked panties. Kara's other hand was also occupied, ensconced firmly underneath her bra. Panic rose in her throat and her gut clenched. How did this happen? How did they get this carried away? She was engaged, for God's sake.

With guilt washing over her like a monster wave, Dani stood and adjusted her clothing. "Let's go. They're gonna be asking questions."

A dazed Kara struggled to get to her feet.

"Hurry up!" Dani needed to put as much distance as possible between them and the bathroom. Hoping to leave whatever happened in there far behind, she flew out the door and into the golf cart.

Kara sat down heavily. "Well, that escalated quickly."

Dani brushed some imaginary dirt off her shorts. "Perhaps we got a little carried away." She waved a hand. "Let's go."

"I think we can put that argument to bed."

"What argument?"

"Who's the better kisser. I mean, I know I make women weak in the knees and all, but Jesus."

Dani jammed on the brakes in her head, and all thoughts of rushing off came to a screeching halt. "Oh, so you think it was your kiss that caused the escalation?"

"Absolutely."

"My, my, my, that oversized ego of yours strikes again. It was clearly my last kiss that sent us over the edge. And when I sat down in your lap, you were a goner."

Kara slowly shook her head. "Nope, don't think so. I pulled you onto my lap, and *you* were the goner."

A shrill whistle from the next tee box pierced the air. Jen could stop a cab three blocks away with that whistle. Zoey gave an impatient wave.

Dani sighed. "We should get going. They're probably freaking out, wondering why we're taking so long."

Kara refused to budge. "Not until you admit I'm a good kisser."

"You wanna do this now?"

"I can sit here all day."

"In the interest of moving this along, let's call a truce. We both admit the other is a good kisser. I'll go first. I admit it, yes, you're a good kisser."

"So, you're retracting your earlier statement?"

"Yes, it's retracted. And replaced with, you kiss pretty damn good."

The corner of Kara's lip turned up. "Okay, my turn. You are also a good kisser."

"Should we shake on it? The truce?" Dani asked.

Kara took Dani's hand and gave a soft shake. "Truce."

"All right. Let's go. Zoey's already suspicious. That snake tale of yours will haunt me 'til my dying day. We're not telling anybody about any of this, right?"

"No!" Kara said emphatically, then hesitated as she hit the gas on the cart. "Well…"

"Well, what?"

"Jes and Val know. Jes dragged it out of me."

Dani curled her lip up. "Jes dragged it out of you."

"She's good. She's like a super cop."

"A *super* cop." Dani's voice dripped with sarcasm.

"Yes."

"Unbelievable. Just go!"

* * *

After the round was complete, the girls cleaned up in the ladies' locker room and joined Will's group in the ballroom.

Still wracked with guilt, Dani went straight to Will and kissed him on the cheek. *That's who you're supposed to be kissing.*

"Ladies, what did we end up with this year?" Ethan asked.

Zoey tossed the scorecard onto the table. "Read it and weep, losers."

He glanced at the score, and a flush settled on his cheeks. "Nine under? No way."

"You couldn't have been nine under," Will said. "I don't believe it."

Zoey threw her shoulders back. "Oh, believe it."

"How did you guys do?" Jen asked.

"We were six under," Ethan mumbled.

"I'm sorry, what was that?" Zoey asked.

"Six under."

"Ha! Get ready to pony up some dough when we hit the Met Grill. Filet mignon all around. And champagne. I like champagne when I eat steak. And for dessert…what's the most expensive dessert on the menu, babe?"

"The nine-layer chocolate cake at sixteen dollars a slice."

"Ka-ching! Slices all around. I need two pieces, because I like to have a spare for later."

"That's almost a hundred dollars' worth of dessert," Ethan stammered.

"Oh, that's the first course of dessert."

"The first course?"

"Yeah. We get three courses of desserts."

While Ethan and Zoey went back and forth about how one could or could not possibly eat three desserts in one sitting, Will leaned into Dani. "Hey, babe, I'm gonna check out the silent auction items."

"Hold on, Will, I'll go with you," Jen said.

Kara picked up her drink and followed. "I'll go too."

Dani admired Kara's outfit as she walked away. Who knew the masculine look of a vest over a dress shirt could be so devastatingly feminine? Her eyes trailed down and landed on Kara's ass as she sauntered toward the front of the room. She caught herself biting her bottom lip. *Stop it!* This had to be a De-Infatuation step, no ass staring. Probably number three or four. She'd already failed number one in a big way.

Kara chatted with an older woman who was standing in front of the auction items. Her face was animated and the way she smiled at the woman warmed Dani's heart. She had a wonderful smile. Why didn't she notice this before? Because noticing that was a rabbit hole she couldn't go down. Dani was startled out of her thoughts by Murphy, who placed a hand on her shoulder and murmured into her ear, "Can I get you a drink, beautiful?"

"No thanks, I'm fine."

"How's your back, Murph?" Zoey asked.

"It's fine, thanks for asking. Next time try yelling 'fore.'"

"Dani yelled, 'watch the fuck out,' didn't you hear her?"

"No, I didn't."

After Murphy left, Zoey stared after him. "He was totally eyeballing your boobs."

"He always does. He's disgusting."

* * *

Kara and Zoey headed to the bar to get the next round. They sat on stools as they waited for their drinks. From their position, they could overhear Kevin Murphy talking to a few other doctors.

"Did you see what Dani has on tonight? Shit, I'd like to tap that."

"Kincaid is a lucky man."

"Yeah, he gets to touch those tits every night, right?" Murphy said.

Kara's blood boiled and she started to get off the stool.

Zoey placed a hand on her shoulder. "Easy girl."

"He's a pig, and I swear to God, I'm gonna punch his lights out."

Once again Murphy's voice floated over to them. "Her ass is grade A also."

Kara closed her eyes and tried counting to ten.

"If she were mine, I'd fuck her five times a day. That body is made for fucking."

Zoey shot an angry look over at the offenders. "Okay, you're right. That bastard needs to be popped in the mouth."

Kara smiled, stood with her drink, and with her purse tucked under her arm, sauntered over to the group. It was time to shut this guy's mouth.

Murphy spotted her immediately and smiled. "Kara, is it? I was watching you today. You have a beautiful swing."

"Thank you, Dr. Murphy. I'm glad I caught your eye."

Murphy's grin turned lecherous. "Oh, you caught more than my eye." The rest of the group chuckled at his comment. He caressed her thumb. "What happened here? It looks painful."

Kara batted her eyelashes seductively. "It's just a minor cut."

"Do you need me to check it for you? I know someplace quiet where we won't be disturbed."

"Oh, my goodness." Kara grasped his forearm, forcing out a small laugh. "It's so sweet of you to be concerned, but I think it's okay. Maybe another time." She casually dropped her purse on the floor, and the contents scattered around everyone's feet.

"Oh, my." Kara bent over and started picking things up. "I'm so clumsy sometimes."

"Here, let me help you," Murphy said. "You might hurt your thumb." He knelt next to her. The other guys also bent down to help, each grabbing things and stuffing them back into her purse.

Kara grabbed her keys at the same time someone else did, and they got into a tug-of-war. "I've got them." She yanked them back with much more force than needed. The momentum caused Kara's elbow to fly backward, connecting perfectly with Kevin Murphy's nose.

"Ow!" He stumbled backward, his backside landing heavily on the ground. Blood gushed forth.

Kara turned. "Oh, I'm so sorry." She glanced around. "Is there a doctor in the house?"

Zoey witnessed the whole thing and almost fell off her barstool laughing.

Kara pulled a tampon out of her now refilled purse. "Isn't this what athletes use?" She tried to shove it up Murphy's nose, none too gently, which only led to more moaning from Murphy.

"Ouch, ow! No, don't do that," he groaned.

"Aren't you supposed to pinch the bridge of your nose when it's bleeding?" Kara pinched his nose, which caused more blood to spew forth, and more painful moaning from Murphy. "No, wait, maybe it's ice. You're supposed to put ice on it." She reached into one of his friend's glass, grabbed a couple of ice cubes, and smacked them on Murphy's crooked nose.

"Oh my God," he wailed.

Zoey hopped off her stool and joined in the fun. "Aren't you supposed to put your head down between your knees?" She shoved his head down, hard enough to bang it on the ground. "Oh shit, who put the floor there?"

"Oww!" His eyes rolled up and the lids slammed shut.

"Don't pass out. If you have a concussion, you have to stay awake." Kara threw her drink in his face.

Zoey took a pitcher of water from the bar and threw the whole thing on an unsuspecting Murphy. "Wake the fuck up!"

He sputtered and howled.

His friends finally came to his rescue and helped him up as the girls walked away.

"Tragic situation. Could be disfiguring," Kara said.

"Good thing he's in plastic surgery," Zoey replied.

They made it back to the table in time for their salad.

Will craned his neck. "What was going on over there?"

"Kara broke Murphy's nose," Zoey said casually, sipping her beverage.

Dani's eyes popped open. "What?"

Kara winked. "It was an accident."

Dani put a hand over her mouth to hide a smile.

Murphy eventually made it back to the table. A wad of cotton was shoved up his nose, his tie was askew, and there were bloodstains on his shirt.

Ethan clapped him on the back. "You okay, buddy?"

"You need me to take a look at it?" Will asked.

"No, I'm good," he said with a muffled voice. "It's not broken."

Jen glanced over at the mess that was Kevin Murphy. "That's abhorrent."

* * *

A few minutes later, Dani watched as Dr. Kentman approached the podium and spoke into the microphone. "Before I announce the winners, the club asked if anyone saw anything or anybody suspicious around the ladies' restroom by the thirteenth hole. Evidently it was vandalized. Ladies? Did any of you notice anything strange?"

Zoey raised her eyebrows at Dani and Kara. "Maybe your snake made it in there. Messed some shit up."

"Probably. Snakes can be…destructive," Kara said, and Dani sent her a hot glare.

Dr. Kentman continued, "We'll start with fourth place. This year, fourth place goes to the group of Dani Clark, Zoey Callahan, Jen Rowe, and Kara Britton, coming in at nine under par. Congratulations, ladies. Please come up for your prizes."

A boozed-up Zoey whooped and threw her arms into the air. When the foursome made it to the podium, she tried to grab the mic from Dr. Kentman, and a small tussle ensued. Eventually, she managed to wrestle it from his hands.

"I'd just like to thank my teammates. Great job, ladies."

Dr. Kentman tried to take the mic back, but Zoey pushed his hand away. Dani intervened, and with Dr. Kentman's help managed to almost pry it from her hands.

"All right, calm the fuck down." Zoey loosened her grip.

Both Dr. Kentman and Dani assumed they had freed the microphone and they relaxed, long enough for Zoey to grab it back and quickly say, "Drinks on Murphy!" And with that, she raised her hand in the air and literally dropped the mic, which caused a screech of audio feedback to reverberate around the room.

Everyone covered their ears and cringed. Some cried out in pain. Drinks spilled. A set of dentures dropped on a salad plate. Dr. Kentman teetered and tottered and face-planted next to the podium.

With his finger in his ear, Ethan hollered, "What the hell?"

Will's old-fashioned landed in Murphy's lap, and he tried to pat it dry—accidentally touching his family jewels in the process. With a glare, Murphy pulled the napkin from his grasp and tried to sop up the excess liquid.

A mortified Dani helped Dr. Kentman to his feet, then yanked Zoey down the aisle.

"I always wanted to drop the mic," Zoey said with pride, unaware of the auditory destruction she wrought.

Jen and Kara howled with laughter and shared a jubilant fist bump.

The ladies' exhilaration was not shared when they returned to the table. Ethan scowled, his finger still in his ear, checking for damage. Will moped, possibly because his recent fondling of his boss's junk left him scarred for life and probably headed for a demotion. Murphy had scurried off to the men's room to use the hand dryer on his cotton briefs.

"Well, that was fun!" Zoey boasted to the Brothers Grim.

Kara raised her glass for a toast. "Ladies, it was a pleasure golfing with you today. Drinks on Murphy!"

They all cackled.

The boys were not amused.

After all the winning groups received their prizes, it was time for the silent auction.

"Did you bid on anything?" Dani asked Will.

He leaned in and gave her a lingering kiss on the lips. "I did, babe. Something for you."

"Our next item up for bid is six free private dog training lessons, courtesy of Kara Britton, certified dog trainer."

The whole table turned to Kara, who smiled and shrugged.

"And the winner of the bid is…Will Kincaid."

The color drained from Dani's face. Will wrapped his arm around her and squeezed. "I got them for you. You always said you wished Oliver would behave better, and you wanted to learn how to train him. Well, now, maybe Kara can help you." He left the table to pick up his prize.

Jen leaned toward Zoey. "Babe, ain't enough popcorn in the world, know what I mean?"

Zoey smiled. "I love you, baby." They started making out at the table.

Meanwhile, Dani was having a mini mental meltdown. How was she going to survive six private dog lessons with Kara? She barely survived five hours on the golf course. She cast a glance around the table. Kara smirked, Zoey ate popcorn, and Jen had a shit-eating grin on her face. She heaved a sigh.

So busted.

CHAPTER TWENTY

Dani was on her way to dinner at the Walkers', the De-Infatuation Playbook left safely at home. No need for it tonight. She almost missed the turn because she was too busy admiring the quiet, quaint streets filled with modest homes, each with its own unique style and architecture. It was an older neighborhood, with charm and character and stately trees, not like the mini mansions in her area with their ornate columns, grand entrances, and manicured landscapes. Nothing was ever out of place in her neighborhood. But here, bikes were scattered along sidewalks, dogs ran in front yards, and kids played ball in the streets.

She pulled into their driveway and instantly fell in love with the house in front of her. It was a Cape Cod-style home. It looked welcoming. And warm. And lived in. Everything Dani secretly wished for.

She walked along the bluestone pavers to the front door and rang the doorbell. She was instantly greeted by a smiling Jolie.

"Hi! It's so good to see you again."

Dani was pulled into a tight embrace. "I brought my world-famous rice pudding for dessert."

Travis ran to greet her. *Dr. Dani.* He gave her a big hug.

When they pulled apart, Dani signed *hello*, followed by *how are you?*

His toothy grin stretched from ear to ear as he turned to his mother and signed.

"What did he say?" Dani asked.

"He's excited that you signed," Jolie said. She pulled Dani in for another hug. "I know how much it means to him. Thank you so much."

"I only learned a few basics."

Travis grabbed her hand and led her to the living room, where a large blue sectional faced a flat-screen TV that hung over the fireplace.

Aaron came in from his grill to greet her. "Now, Dr. Dani, I have an important question to ask." Aaron's expression became grave. "The question is…" He paused. "Do you eat red meat?"

Dani laughed. "Hell, yeah. I like my steak medium."

He pumped his fist. "What are your thoughts on potatoes?"

Dani mimicked his serious expression. "Potatoes were put on this earth to be slathered in butter and salt and consumed in great quantities."

Aaron whooped. "We'll get along just fine." He headed back outside to worship at his grill.

Dani laughed. "He's kinda easy to please."

"He is." The love Jolie had for her husband was evident in her eyes. "Follow me, I'm going to put the rice pudding in the fridge."

They took the short walk from the living room into the kitchen. "What do you want to drink? We have wine, beer, soda, water?"

"I'll have a glass of wine, whatever you have open." Dani leaned against the counter and looked around with appreciation at the eclectic style of the small galley kitchen. The cabinets had shaker-style doors, the top row painted a colonial blue and the base ones stained a honey brown.

"Cabernet okay?" Jolie asked.

"Perfect."

As they continued their conversation in the kitchen, the doorbell rang and the lights flashed.

* * *

Kara felt the stress of the day melt away on her motorcycle ride to the Walkers'. A nice, normal dinner would be a welcome escape. It had been three days of unwanted fantasies since the kiss. She made a mental note to keep away from bathrooms when Dani was around.

She banished all thoughts from her mind and turned her attention to tonight. Maybe this was another setup by Jolie. Another attempt to find her the woman of her dreams. It would be perfect timing. Just the thing to snap her out of these Dani fantasies. The conversation she had with Rachel last night had a finality to it. Evidently, she didn't like the way Kara was looking at Dani during Zoey's party. So, if Jolie was fixing her up, that would be fine. Kara briefly flashed back to the last blind date at the Walkers', and the promise made at the end of the evening. Jolie's promise. The next time Kara had dinner there, she would meet the one. The *one*. As if such a person existed.

Another car was parked in the driveway, which meant someone else was here. A pulse of excitement coursed through her veins. A feeling of anticipation swelled in her chest. Was she about to witness fate? Was her destiny on the other side of that door?

She pressed the doorbell and walked in as usual.

Travis ran down the hallway to greet her.

She gave him a quick hug. *Hey, dorko, brownies are here.*

He stuck his hand underneath the aluminum foil to steal one.

That's dessert. She tried to look perturbed. She missed badly, and with a mischievous smile, signed, *Where's mine?*

He pulled one out and shoved it in his mouth. After inhaling it, he signed, *Take me for a ride?*

After dinner. Is someone here? Kara shucked off her leather jacket and hung it in the hall closet.

Maybe. He yanked her down the hallway.

They walked into the living room at the exact time Jolie and Dani entered from the kitchen.

Jolie's mouth dropped open in shock. "Kara? Wha...what are you doing here?"

Kara took a second to answer, because her eyes were locked on the blue ones across the room. "Ah, I was invited?"

"How...who?"

She looked to Travis, who was all smiles, enjoying the awkwardness of the adults in the room. *You invited your friend, so I invited mine.*

"Uh, okay, kiddo, but how about we give Mom a heads-up next time." Jolie turned to Dani and Kara. "I'm sorry, I had no idea."

"It's fine," they both said.

Aaron was the last to join the party. "Steaks are looking fabulous. Dinner will be ready soon, did anyone—" He stopped short. "Did I forget who was on the guest list?"

Jolie put an arm around Travis. "No. It seems our son took it upon himself to invite Kara, which is fine. We'll set another place at the table."

"Sweet! I'll slap another steak on the barbie. Travis, come help your old man."

Father and son headed onto the back porch.

"Kara, beer?" Jolie asked.

"Yes, thanks."

"Be right back."

After Jolie had gone off to fetch a beer, Kara and Dani were left to stare uncomfortably at each other. Kara had certainly not expected to see Dani so soon after their adventures on Sunday.

Kara cleared her throat. "Did you get a new car?"

"No. I drove Will's."

"Oh." No wonder she didn't recognize it. She glanced toward the kitchen, hoping for Jolie's reappearance. The silence dragged on, making an awkward situation more so. There was no escaping this woman. Was this some cross to bear? A punishment for some dastardly crime she committed? So much for meeting the woman of her dreams tonight. Instead, she'd be spending the evening with the very taken Dani Clark. "Well, here we are. Again."

Dani rocked back on her heels and blew out a deep breath. "Yep."

"Should we continue our truce? I mean, we don't wanna spoil dinner. Let's agree to be civil, okay?"

Dani raised her eyebrows. "I can be civil."

"I didn't mean you couldn't be—" Kara cut herself off as Jolie came back into the living room, empty-handed.

"How is everyone?" Jolie asked while wringing her hands.

Kara had no idea why Jolie was suddenly acting weird. "Did you get my beer?"

Jolie's mouth formed a silent O. "Be right back."

Kara turned her attention to Dani. "So, deal? Civil?"

"Deal."

Jolie returned to the living room, again no beer in her hand. "Dinner's ready!" She disappeared as quickly as she had appeared.

Kara and Dani were befuddled by Jolie's odd behavior.

"Are we supposed to follow her?" Dani asked.

"I guess so."

"Where's your beer?"

"Maybe she drank it."

"Does she have a drinking problem?"

"She didn't yesterday."

After taking their seats, they passed the food around. Jolie's phone buzzed.

"Who's that, honey?" Aaron asked.

She glanced at the phone and nibbled on her bottom lip before turning it facedown onto the table. "Nobody."

Aaron shrugged and pointed a fork at the disappearing food. "Well, this is a damn sight better than the last dinner we had with you, Britton."

"Why, what happened last time?" Dani took a healthy spoonful of roasted potatoes.

Jolie spoke up. "I tried to set Kara up with some woman, and she didn't eat meat. She didn't eat potatoes. It was a disaster."

"What *did* she eat?" Dani asked.

Lettuce. Travis smirked.

"You don't have to worry about that with me. I love to eat." Dani smiled at the faces around her, landing on Kara's. The warmth of her smile reached her eyes and Kara responded in kind. "Did you go out on a date with her?"

"Ah, no, I didn't. She wasn't my type."

"You have a type?"

"I do."

"Well, please share," Dani said. "Maybe it'll help Jolie in the future."

"She likes red hair and blue eyes," Jolie blurted out. All eyes landed on her. She put her head down, cut a piece of steak, and shoved it in her mouth.

"Oh?" Dani cocked a lone eyebrow at Kara.

Dani has red hair and blue eyes, Travis signed, and Jolie interpreted.

The eyes were now on Kara. She cleared her throat. "Um, yeah, lots of people have red hair and blue eyes, buddy." Kara ruffled Travis's hair. "Just to be clear, I've dated people who've had brown eyes, and dark hair also." Kara still felt everyone's gaze upon her, making her squirm. A quick flash of Dani in a light-blue bra popped into her brain.

Aaron put his beer on the table after taking a swig. "So, Dani, what made you wanna be a doctor?"

"Well, truth be told, I didn't want to be a doctor."

"Really?"

"No. I wanted to be an artist. When I was a teenager, I used to paint and draw all the time."

"How come you didn't become an artist?" he asked.

"In my family, you had one career choice. Medicine. My mom and dad are doctors, and my mom's parents are doctors. There was no way I could be anything else. I tried, believe me. Eventually I just gave in."

"That's a shame," Jolie said. "You couldn't be what you wanted to be."

"It's fine. I certainly have nothing to complain about." A tinge of sadness was visible around her eyes.

"Couldn't you have told your parents to butt out of your life?" Aaron asked.

Dani chuckled. "You don't tell Rebecca Clark to butt out of your life."

"Who's Rebecca?" Jolie asked.

"My mom."

"Didn't she want you to be happy?"

"She wanted me to get straight As. One time, I came home with an eighty-nine on a test, and I was grounded for a month."

"Jesus," Aaron said. "Was your dad hard on you too?"

"Oh, yeah. My one ally was my Gram Evelyn, my dad's mom. She wanted me to go to art school. It led to some lively discussions around the dinner table. Mom and Dad usually won the arguments." Dani waved it off. "But it was fine. They wanted excellence. I gave them excellence. I'm a good doctor because of them." She turned to Kara. "What about your family?"

Kara had an inkling there was more to Dani than she previously thought. Childhood dreams dashed. Demanding parents. Perhaps there was no silver spoon after all. "I never knew my dad. But my mom was wonderful."

"Was?"

"She died eight years ago."

"What happened?" Dani asked.

"She had surgery, and the surgeon clipped an artery. By the time they figured it out, it was too late. The surgeon was… under the influence."

"That's awful." Dani touched Kara's hand.

"It was devastating. She was the only family I had. I sued the surgeon, and the money from the lawsuit helped me buy the farm."

Dani's hand still rested on Kara's. "Not all surgeons are bad."

"I know."

The look they shared spoke volumes. These tiny, new revelations about each other resonated, at least with Kara. Her previous rash judgment of Dani's character started to fade. She hoped Dani felt the same.

"Okay, let's talk about something else." Aaron said. "How was the golf outing?"

Dani smiled. "It was fun."

"I ended up playing." Kara raised her beer in the air, toasting Dani with a big smile. "And we took fourth place!"

Dani clinked her wineglass against Kara's beer bottle. "Which was a huge deal, by the way. We usually finish last, and everyone makes fun of us." She took a quick sip of wine. "Zoey was in rare form the entire day."

"What did she do?" Jolie asked.

Kara chuckled at the memory. "She almost beaned Dani's boss, Dr. Kentman, in the head."

"And then she dropped the F-bomb all over him," Dani continued with a giggle.

"And then she went all WWE on him at the awards dinner." Kara barely contained her laughter as she watched Dani.

"She got into a tug-of-war over the microphone with him. He's, like, eighty." The giggle fest continued.

Kara only had eyes for Dani at that moment, and it looked like Dani was caught up in that bubble as well.

"And then, she literally dropped the mic and burst everyone's eardrums." Kara guffawed.

"Poor Dr. Kentman." Dani grabbed her sides, she laughed so hard. "He got Zoey'd." And with that, she almost fell out of her chair.

Kara wasn't doing any better as she slapped at the table. "Stop it, you're killing me." Tears slid from her eyes.

"Sorry." Dani tried to catch her breath.

Any cool prizes? Travis asked.

Kara's eyes found Dani's. "I donated dog training lessons for the silent auction."

"Who won them?" Aaron asked.

Kara paused as the ramifications of being alone with Dani hit home. "Ah, Dani won them." She nodded at Dani. Smiling Dani. Playful Dani. This newly revealed Dani.

Travis waved a hand at Kara. *How's Ziggy and Milo?*

"The dogs are good, buddy."

Dani raised a hand. "Wait. Didn't she tell you?"

Everyone fell silent, expecting, perhaps, bad news.

"She has two new kittens at home."

"When did that happen?" Jolie asked.

"I got them a couple of weeks ago."

"Ha!" Dani pointed at her. "You said, 'I got.' Means you're keeping them."

"No, it doesn't, and no I'm not."

"Did you name them yet?" Dani's eyes sparkled with every lighthearted dig. "She refuses to name them."

"Cause I'm not keeping them."

"Maybe we should brainstorm some names for her," Dani said. "How about Fluffy and Muffy."

"I'm not naming my kittens Fluffy and Muffy."

"You said, '*my* kittens.' You are so busted," Aaron said.

Jolie nodded. "Yeah, you're keeping them."

Kara *was* busted, but she wasn't going down without a fight. "Nope. No cats."

"Pooh and Tigger," Aaron volunteered.

"I'm not keeping them." Kara tried to look perturbed, but she secretly loved the brainstorming session.

"Speaking of Tigger, here's a story for you," Dani said. "When I was young, I used to like to draw picture books—"

"You drew picture books?" Jolie put a hand over her heart. "That's adorable."

Kara's mind briefly went on hiatus. Someone gave her a picture book once. A long time ago. She was pulled back to the present by Travis whacking her arm. "Huh?"

"Those are great names, aren't they?" Jolie asked.

"What?" Kara had no idea what had been said. "I'm sorry, what are great names?"

"Thumper and Tigger. Dani's favorite animal names when she was young," Jolie said.

Kara was embarrassed she lost track of the conversation. "I zoned out, sorry."

"Pay attention!" Dani playfully scolded. "They were the characters in my story. A tree frog named Thumper and squirrel named Tigger."

"I love those names!" Jolie exclaimed.

"Calm down, people. If I keep the kittens, and that's a big if, I will consider all the names presented tonight."

They had finished dinner by this time, and Dani stood. "Can I use your bathroom?"

Jolie stood also. "Yes, of course. It's upstairs. Kara, show her where it is."

"Why can't she use the powder room down here?"

"It's broken!"

"What happened to it?" Aaron asked.

Jolie shook her head. "It's too abstruse. Kara, take Dani and show her where the upstairs bathroom is."

Kara's heart leapt into her throat. Bathroom and Dani? No! "Why don't you show her?"

"I'm doing the dishes." Jolie gathered the empty plates. "Now go!"

"Okay, geez. Dani, follow me."

Kara and Dani traipsed upstairs.

Kara began mumbling, "I have no idea what's gotten into her tonight."

* * *

When they reached the bathroom, Dani yanked Kara inside and slammed the door. Kara lost her balance and stumbled into her. Their faces were inches apart.

Dani's intention was to question Kara about Jolie and Zoey, but the proximity of those lips rendered her mute. Her mind went on holiday and she did what now seemed to be perfectly normal bathroom behavior—she leaned in and pressed her lips to Kara's. When Kara moaned and pulled her closer, the vacation was over, and her brain screamed, De-Infatuation! The battle was on. Dani's body waged war with her head. Her body wanted to taste the sweetness of those soft lips, while her head flooded with guilt and shame.

This kiss was different from the previous ones. It was soft and exploring as tips of tongues touched and breathy sighs echoed around the room. The effect was staggering. Dani needed to exercise some self-control, stat, or they might end up in the bathtub.

Willing her mind to victory, she put an iron grip on her attraction, an attraction heightened by their shared moments at the dinner table. She silenced it. She strangled it. She had to. She was engaged, for God's sake!

Placing a hand on Kara's chest, she reluctantly pulled away and almost chuckled at the expression on Kara's face. With lips slightly parted, eyes dreamy and unfocused, Kara looked like she was in never-never land. And it was adorable. Dani wanted to drag her off to a bedroom right now. She took a quick peek at the tub. No! De-Infatuation! Fucking right fucking now. She took a couple deep breaths.

Dani stepped back. "We shouldn't..." Shouldn't what? Shouldn't kiss at all, or shouldn't be kissing in here? She had no clue.

Kara jammed her hands into her pockets. "Ah, no, we shouldn't. I doubt they could afford the renovations."

Dani tried to hide a smile, but the corners of her mouth turned up on their own.

Kara leaned against the closed door. "So, if you didn't pull me in here to make out, why did you pull me in here?"

Dani slowly came back down to earth. Her brow furrowed with contemplation. "Uh...I don't remember." Evidently, she needed to add short-term memory loss to the list of things that happened to her when she was around Kara. "Oh! I remember. Do Jolie and Zoey talk?"

"I think so."

"Aha!" Dani pumped a fist. "I knew it."

"What?"

Dani began pacing the small room. "Abstruse? What the heck was that?"

Kara shrugged. "I don't know what it means."

"Exactly!" Dani pointed at her. "Nobody does. It has word of the day written all over it." She twirled her pointing finger in a big circle for emphasis. "She's been talking to Zoey. And that was probably who texted her." She continued pacing and nibbled on her fingernail. "I bet Zoey told her we kissed. Damn it. I *knew* she knew."

"I'm confused."

"The bathroom. Jolie insisting you take me to a *bathroom*."

Kara's eyes widened. "So, you think Zoey told her to get us into a bathroom."

"Yes!"

Kara laughed. "That's kinda funny."

Dani frowned, trying not to enjoy the joke. The last three days were spent dealing with a massive amount of guilt, and just when she thought she wouldn't let it happen again, here she was. In a bathroom. Recovering from another mind-blowing kiss.

She didn't know what to say next. Suddenly the air in the bathroom crackled with electricity. Dani needed to break the spell, or they *would* end up in the tub. "We should probably get back."

* * *

Later, they all relaxed in the living room, listless from the sugar rush of rice pudding and brownies. Kara found herself reliving their recent kiss. It was much more tender than the last one and had shaken her.

Travis startled everyone by jumping off the couch. *Kara, take Dani for a ride.*

"I don't think Dani wants to do that," Kara said.

"What don't I wanna do?"

"He wants me to take you for a ride on my bike."

Dani's mouth dropped open. "Oh, no. I'm not getting on the death machine."

Kara chuckled. "See, buddy? She has a healthy fear of motorcycles." She felt confident Dani would pass. It would be like throwing gasoline on a fire. And surely, the last ride would be fresh on her mind since it was only a few weeks ago. At least it was fresh on Kara's mind. The feeling of Dani's breasts pressed against her back, her arms around her waist, her chin on her shoulder. Add to that the fact she knew Dani could kiss her into oblivion, and an involuntary shudder of desire shot through her. *Please say no, Dani,* she silently pleaded.

Travis was not to be deterred. He pointed to his mom. *Mom says face fears.*

Jolie shrugged and gave a sheepish grin. "I do tell him he should face his fears."

"It's too dangerous," Dani insisted.

Travis narrowed his eyes. *Chicken?*

Aaron cleared his throat. "He called you chicken."

"I'm not chicken. I choose not to get on it."

Travis tilted his chin up. *Dare you.*

Dread settled in Kara's gut. The last time Dani felt dared was almost her undoing. *Dani Clark should not be dared,* she wanted to scream.

"He, um, just dared you," Jolie said.

"You're daring me?"

A small groan gurgled up from Kara's throat.

Double dog dare. Travis folded his arms. The gauntlet had been thrown. The double dog dare.

"Oh." Aaron shifted in his seat.

Dani's eyes darted toward Aaron. "Oh, what?"

"He just…double dog…dared you."

Dani's mouth opened slightly, then shut. A muscle in her jaw twitched. "Just around the block?"

Aaron signed to Travis, and he nodded.

A look of steely determination settled over her features. "Well. I never back down from a dare. We're doing this! Game on!" She raised a fist in the air.

Kara's mouth dropped open. She certainly didn't see this coming. Another ride with Dani's arms around her? After what happened tonight and this past weekend? Surely this was some sort of cruel torture.

Travis hooted and threw his arms in the air.

The gang hustled out the door, leaving Kara alone. She swallowed the lump wedged in her throat. It was unclear whether to be stoked at the thought of Dani so close or petrified. Images from the evening washed over her, Dani smiling, Dani laughing, Dani sad because she wanted to be an artist, Dani teasing her.

"I promise, the next woman you have dinner with here, will be the one. I promise."

She put on her jacket and zipped up.

Yep...she was fucked.

CHAPTER TWENTY-ONE

Kara walked out of the house toward the bike.

Travis bounced around with excitement. *Go fast!*

Kara made sure Dani's helmet was secure, her fingers softly brushing her chin. She caught Dani staring at her with a look of determination. "You okay?"

"I'm more than okay. Let's get this party started." She whacked Kara on the ass.

Kara raised her eyebrows. "Well, somebody's fired up."

"A dare's a dare, and I've been dared, so let's…"

Kara slowly closed the visor while Dani was talking, silencing her, and slung a leg over the bike. "All aboard."

Dani did her motorcycle dance, much to the amusement of the Walkers.

"Do you need help?" Jolie asked.

"Throw your leg over it," Aaron suggested.

"Give her a minute." Kara put the key in the ignition.

Travis got a major case of the giggles as Dani hopped about.

Kara checked the brake lights and blinkers. "Getting dark. Any day now." As Kara waited for Dani to figure it out, she tried to numb her body for the onslaught of sensations soon to come. She tried to recall every awful thing Dani had ever said to her. But the only image in her head was Dani in the blue bra. Which wasn't helpful.

All thoughts ceased immediately as Dani finally got on the bike. She wrapped her arms around her waist and snuggled against her back. Kara's body temperature shot through the roof. Somehow, Dani's hands made their way under her jacket and shirt, which meant Dani's bare hands were on her bare stomach. She waited for her to remove them, because there was no way she was going to be able to function with Dani caressing her abdomen. The hands stayed put and Kara took a deep breath and clicked into first.

"Slow!" Dani yelled.

Kara needed to address the fondling, or they'd end up in a hedge on someone's front lawn. "Are you going to remove your hands from my stomach?"

"No, they're cold. You give off a lot of body heat."

Great. "You ready?"

"Hit it!"

Kara popped it out of first and took off.

They reached thirty miles per hour in a few seconds.

Dani shrieked, "Slow down!"

The caress on Kara's stomach became a clutch and a squeeze, less of a turn-on, so she slowed down.

"Slower, please," Dani pleaded.

The speedometer registered twenty.

"Slower."

"You're kidding."

"I'm not kidding. I don't wanna die tonight."

"This ride's not gonna kill you. I may, but this ride won't."

"Very funny."

They chugged along at a comfortable twelve miles per hour, and Dani's grip relaxed.

Kara heard a shout and glanced to her left.

Travis churned past them on his bicycle, laughing and pointing and waving, making fun of their inept velocity. He snapped a picture with his phone.

"He just passed us. On a bicycle!" Kara said.

"Don't take the bait. This speed is fine. I feel almost safe at this speed."

Dani's fingers lightly stroked her belly. Kara had a brief image of grabbing those hands and putting them to better use somewhere else. "When do you want your dog lessons?"

Dani shifted closer and rested her chin on Kara's shoulder. "Soon, I guess. When I get a free Saturday. Maybe you could teach me sign language too."

"Let's see if we survive the dog lessons, first."

"Why wouldn't we survive the dog lessons?"

"Well, as long as we steer clear of bathrooms, I guess we will." Sleep would be hard to come by tonight. Between the feeling of Dani snuggled against her, those wandering hands, and the soft kiss they shared, she'd be lucky to find any peace at all in the overnight hours. She had a wild idea of gunning it, taking Dani back to her place, and showing her what she wanted those hands to do.

She was saved from further sexual anguish as she coasted to a stop in front of the house.

All three Walkers stood in the driveway waiting, including Travis, who had clearly returned from his bike ride some time ago. He rushed over to them. *Beat you.*

"Did you have fun?" Jolie asked.

Dani dismounted and removed the helmet. "It wasn't so bad."

Kara heaved a sigh filled with relief, guilt, and doom. Relief to put some distance between her and Dani, guilt for harboring an attraction for someone who was engaged, and doom because she was powerless to stop the attraction.

They wandered back into the house and spent the next half hour covering every detail of the ride.

Later in the evening, Dani stood. "I should probably head home. I have an early day tomorrow."

"Thanks for coming," Jolie said. "Maybe we can do it again?"

"I'd love to." After hugging Aaron and Jolie, she embraced Travis. "Thanks, bud. I had a great time."

He gave her a squeeze.

"I'll walk you out," Kara said.

The two women walked down the driveway to Dani's car.

"I'll text you about the dog lessons," Dani said.

"Okay." Kara was unsure if a hug was in order. Or a handshake, which would involve minimal touching. She was at a loss on how to proceed. How could a simple goodbye be so complicated? *Just hug her already. Or shake her damn hand. My God, you've kissed. More than once. Like, multiple times. Surely a small peck on the cheek is in order.* There, simple. A hug and kiss on the cheek goodbye.

She extended her arms and leaned in to place her lips softly on Dani's cheek. What was the saying? The best laid plans? Because Dani didn't expect a kiss, just a hug, and she turned her face in the same direction Kara was heading, leading to not a kiss on the cheek but one right on the mouth. And then Kara's lips moved of their own volition, because that's what they did when encountering Dani's lips. They couldn't be blamed. But then they kept moving, and to top it all off, she may have moaned.

She pulled back immediately. "Shit, sorry, didn't mean to do that." She shifted backward and extended a hand to initiate a goodbye handshake, then realized how idiotic it must have looked and let the hand fall back to her side. The whole thing was a mess. A sloppy, haphazard, inelegant mess. "Well, that was moronic."

Dani laughed as she slid into her car, a rich, lighthearted sound that took Kara's breath away.

Double-dutch fucked for sure.

* * *

Dani clung to Kara as they flew down the road on the motorcycle. When they pulled into the driveway, Kara parked the bike and they both hopped off. Dani started toward the front door, walking backward, beckoning. She slowly unzipped her jacket and shrugged it off as Kara followed.

She opened the door and Kara grabbed her and they shared a passionate kiss. Soon Kara's lips were nibbling along Dani's throat, and she murmured, "I love…"

Dani fell to the ground with a thud and woke up. At first, she was disoriented because the dream was so vivid. Her mind zeroed in on the last words spoken. "Love? Loved…what?" she said out loud. "What do you love?"

Oliver gave her some wet, sloppy kisses, clearly concerned about his mommy. She pulled back from the slobbery onslaught. "Okay, Ollie. I'm good, thank you though. Not the kisses I want, but thank you."

How did she get on the couch?

Slowly her memory came back. After coming home from the Walkers', she relaxed on the couch with Oliver and Jinx to watch TV, still feeling slightly buzzed from the wine. And the ride. Will had come home late, and they chatted. When he headed upstairs, she stayed down to finish watching a movie and must've fallen asleep. And dreamed. Boy, did she dream.

Should she analyze it? Or chalk it up to the fact she and Kara kissed again? This time the dream went further than it ever had. *I love…*what? Riding a motorcycle? Eating nachos? Dani loved nachos. Who doesn't say *I love nachos* while kissing someone? She was sure it was something like that and nothing to do with her. She put it out of her mind. No sense driving herself crazy over some half-spoken sentence—from a dream no less.

With eyes closed, she thought about last night's kiss and the feeling of being pressed against Kara on the motorcycle. A new sexual flush rushed through her. And then a tsunami of guilt struck, drowning her.

It was time she made a conscious effort to rein this in, whatever this was. She had to make a conscious effort to stop it. Yes, Kara was attractive. Yes, Dani's body reacted every time she was near. But she needed to draw a line in the sand. She was going to marry her best friend. He didn't deserve this. It was time to recommit to her future husband. No more kissing.

CHAPTER TWENTY-TWO

Dani came home early Friday morning from the hospital, around four a.m. to be exact. She shuffled through the door and collapsed onto the couch. Oliver bounded up next to her. She absently stroked his head, thankful for his companionship. Dog ownership was certainly growing on her. Even Jinx had been won over. Well, maybe not won over. He would still give a whack to Ollie's nose on occasion to make sure Ollie remembered the pecking order in the household.

Dani had lost a patient tonight. It wasn't the first time, and it wouldn't be the last time. But it still hit her hard. It was a bullet wound, and the patient had already lost a ton of blood by the time he made it to the hospital. He was only ten years old. His life was just beginning, and now it was over.

She rested her head on the back of the couch and recounted every move made in the OR. Did she miss something? Did she do something wrong? Silent tears slipped from her eyes. He was so young.

A couple of hours later, the doorbell chimed and woke her up. With a jolt, she lifted her head and looked at the clock. It was eight a.m. She rubbed the sleep from her eyes and opened the door, surprised to find Kara standing there. "Oh, hey. You're picking up today?"

"Someone called in sick." Kara took in Dani's disheveled appearance. "Long night?"

"I lost a patient."

Kara's eyes softened. "I'm sorry. That must be hard." Kara tucked an errant curl behind Dani's ear.

"I know, my hair's a mess." Dani waved her inside. "Go ahead and tell me how awful it looks."

"I'm not gonna kick you when you're down. I mean, give me a little credit. I'll tell you that next week." She must have sensed Dani was too far gone to banter, and her tone softened. "I'm sure you did all you could."

"It wasn't enough." Dani bit her lip to stop it from quivering. "I don't know where Oliver is. Which I'm sure doesn't surprise you."

A soft smile played around her lips. "That you always lose track of your dog? It's gotten kind of endearing, actually."

The twinkle in Kara's eyes brightened Dani's mood. "I'm sure he's around here somewhere. Wanna help me look?"

"Yes! I live for these adventures with you. Where's Will?"

"He's not here." Dani led the way through the house, toward the back door. "Maybe he went out the doggie door."

"Will?"

Dani grinned. "No, silly. He's at a conference in Portland. He'll be back tomorrow."

They peered through the kitchen window, and there was Oliver, in all his muddy glory, digging away. From the size of the hole, he'd been digging for a while.

"Welp, there's my dog, digging a monster-sized hole."

"Maybe he's burying a bone."

"Like a brontosaurus bone?" Kara laughed, and Dani felt a thrill in her own bones and a familiar, tingling sensation in her groin. "About yea big." She stretched her arms wide but realized dinosaur bones were probably much bigger. "Only I'm too short to give the visual."

Kara's smile lit up her whole face. "I got the visual."

A wonderful warmth permeated through Dani's chest. Not the lustful heat, but a genuine, caring warmth. A warmth that scared her. The lust was easily explained away, but this wasn't. Was it an offshoot of the lust? Did something shift in their relationship? Did the shift happen at dinner the other night? And what should she do about it? Ignore it, probably. Or try to ignore it. It was lust and nothing more. She drew her line in the sand the other morning, and it was best not to cross it.

Dani opened the back door. "Oliver, come." He picked his head up, and with tongue lolling, raced back to the house.

"Oh, might not wanna do that," Kara warned.

"Why?"

Oliver barged through the doorway, bringing half the backyard in with him.

"Oh, shit!"

Muddy paw prints tattooed the kitchen floor and splattered along the hallway. The trail ended on the couch.

Dani watched helplessly. Of course the dog had muddy paws. He was digging a ginormous hole. Christ. Once again, she looked like a dog-owning moron in front of Kara. "Oops?" She giggled at the absurdity of the situation.

"Oops is right. That's a lot of mud." Kara bit back the laughter. "I can stay and help you clean."

"No. I'm the idiot who let the muddy dog into the house. You must think...I don't know what you must think. Of me. I am getting better. I know his name," she said in a small voice.

Kara chuckled. "Yeah. And, he did come when you called him. Don't be so hard on yourself. You're just not dog savvy. Yet. I'll be giving you those lessons, and you'll be an expert in no time."

"I'll never be dog savvy."

"Look, I'm early. There's nobody else in the van right now. I'm gonna help you clean this mess up."

Dani relented, and they got out mops and a bucket with soapy water. When they finished, they put all the cleaning supplies away, and Kara headed to the door with Oliver in tow.

Before opening it, she stopped short, and Dani almost bumped into her. "You sure you're okay?" Kara asked.

"Yeah, I'll be fine." She paused. "He was ten years old."

"I'm so sorry."

"It's part of the job. But it's something I'll never get used to." Moisture pooled in her eyes as she gazed back at Kara. Neither spoke. The silence became deafening.

Dani wasn't sure who reached for who, but somehow, she found herself in wrapped in Kara's arms, and she melted into them. It was exactly what she needed, and it took her a few moments to pull back.

A host of emotions played across Kara's face.

Dani knew what was coming. Could sense it a mile away.

Kara dropped Oliver's leash, cupped Dani's face, and kissed her. A soft, exploring kiss. She pulled back, probably waiting for Dani's hand to come between them again. When it didn't happen, she moved in to continue.

Dani placed a hand on Kara's back to keep her close. When the tip of Kara's tongue caressed Dani's upper lip, a soft sigh escaped. When the kisses became deeper, when passions flared, Dani broke it off and leaned her forehead against Kara's. Her heart flopped all over her chest cavity. Were infatuations supposed to feel like this?

They stayed in this position for another minute while their breathing slowed and their pulses returned to some semblance of normal. Guilt assaulted Dani. She pulled away from Kara's embrace and slid down the wall to sit on the floor.

Kara joined her and they both stared straight ahead, each lost in their own thoughts. Dani's hand was in Kara's. She wasn't sure when it slipped in there, but it was so warm and comforting, she didn't want to remove it.

"Kara…" Dani hesitated, not knowing what to say. She glanced at their clasped hands. This was wrong. This whole thing was wrong. The kissing was wrong. The dreaming was wrong. The hand-holding was wrong. But why did it feel so fucking right? She had to fight the urge to lead Kara upstairs to her bedroom. Her inner voice hissed, *Stop it. It's an infatuation. You're committed to Will.*

She slowly let go of Kara's hand and sighed. What should she say to this woman who had shaken her very core?

Kara pulled her knees tight to her body and rested her arms on them.

Dani fought back the urge to push a wayward strand of hair away from her eyes. She was overwhelmed by a feeling. A feeling she wanted to get to know her better. No, she *needed* to get to know her better. She wanted to spend time with her. The physical attraction had to be curbed, that was all. How hard could it be?

"Maybe we should call another truce," Dani said.

Confusion clouded Kara's features.

"You know how sometimes you meet someone, and you find them attractive, but then, the more you get to know them, and the more you become friends, that initial physical attraction fades, into, just a…friendship." *Was this idiotic? Asking for Kara's hand in friendship?* "Maybe we could be friends. Get to know each other better. Then, maybe this—" Dani struggled with the words to describe this intense lust, without actually saying lust. "Whatever *this* is, will stop."

Kara took a moment to process what Dani proposed. "Uh, okay, I guess. I'd like that."

"Really?" Dani tried to read Kara's expression. Was there a hint of resignation? Disappointment?

"Sure. Friends. No more arguing. Which was kinda fun, by the way."

Dani cocked an eyebrow. "You thought that was fun?"

"Yeah."

"I guess it was kind of fun." Dani took a deep breath. "We'll try the friendship thing then?"

Kara nodded. "Yeah, why not?"

"No more kissing. We have to stop that."

"Don't friends kiss?"

Dani laughed. "Not like that."

"I'm gonna miss the kisses." Kara's voice held a tinge of regret, but her eyes sparkled.

"Stop it." Dani gave her a playful shove.

"No, you're a good kisser."

"Oh, now you admit it," Dani teased. "Took you long enough."

"I was stubborn."

"I told you I was a good kisser. You refused to believe me."

"I should've listened."

Dani shook her head. "You are stubborn. But you're also a good kisser."

"Truth be told, I was crushed when you said I wasn't."

"I was being bitchy. I'm sorry."

"Forgiven. Now, I hate to break up our friendship party, but I do have to get to work." Kara rose and pulled Dani from the floor. She retrieved Oliver from the sofa, where he had settled back down to nap. "All right. I'm leaving. Without my goodbye kiss. Call me when you wanna get together for your doggie lessons."

"I will."

CHAPTER TWENTY-THREE

Dani was putting away the groceries on Sunday morning when her phone rang. "Hello?"

"You home?" Zoey asked.

"I don't go in to work until tonight, why?"

"We have your steam cleaner. We'll drop it off in a few. And we're bringing our dogs so they can trash your house."

"Great."

"And Jen's on the rag, just so you know."

"What does that mean?"

"She's got her monthly, Dani, what do you think it means?"

"I know what it means, I meant…" She sighed. "Never mind. You gonna want lunch?"

"We always want lunch. What a silly question. See you in five."

Dani hung up. Good thing she went shopping. She had plenty of lettuce and vegetables, so she'd make everyone a salad. Five minutes did not give her a lot of time to contemplate whether she should come clean about the Kara situation. She was mentally exhausted from keeping it inside. Might be time to lay it all on the table. Good thing Will was working.

The doorbell rang and all hell broke loose. In charged Roscoe and Rocky, followed by Jen and Zoey.

Zoey lugged the big steam cleaner through the doorway. "This is heavy."

"Be careful!" Jen said.

Roscoe and Rocky bounced all over the furniture. Rocky chased Jinx onto the dining room table. Roscoe grabbed a throw pillow from the couch and ran around the room like he had a prized squirrel in his mouth.

Dani observed the mayhem with hands on hips. "Your dogs could use some discipline."

"They're energetic," Zoey said. "Where's Ollie?"

"Out back."

Jen gathered up the pups and ushered them into the backyard while Dani set the table.

When they finished eating their lunch, Dani walked to the cabinet and pulled out the biggest bowl she owned. She placed it in front of the girls, who looked at her questioningly. Heading back to the cabinet, she returned with a bag of popcorn. After pouring it into the bowl, she sat down heavily in the chair.

Jen and Zoey shifted in their seats with anticipation.

Jen murmured, "Popcorn means Kardi."

Again with the Kardi? Dani let it go and cleared her throat. "As I'm sure you're aware, there has been some, uh, physical interactions between Kara and I."

Zoey's hand snaked into the bowl. Jen put an elbow on the table, chin in hand.

"Please continue," Zoey said.

"We have…kissed."

"And?" Zoey asked.

"That's it. We kissed."

Disappointment registered on both their faces.

With a sullen expression, Jen turned to Zoey and whispered, "I thought we were gonna hear about something other than kissing."

Zoey consoled her. "I know, babe, it's okay." She rubbed her back sympathetically.

Dani widened her eyes. "What? We kissed."

"Everyone knows you kissed." Zoey stroked Jen's hair.

"Everyone? Who's everyone?"

"Does it matter?" Zoey used her eyes to direct Dani's attention to Jen, who held back tears. "The damage is done."

"Oh my God, you're both ridiculous. Are you crying? Is she crying?"

"She's on her period," Zoey chided. "Show some compassion. You know she's extra sensitive this time of the month."

"And I have mood swings," Jen mumbled through sniffles.

"It's okay, baby," Zoey cooed. "She's sorry. Say you're sorry, Dani."

It was unclear as to what Dani was apologizing for. "I'm sorry." She could tell from Zoey's look that the apology was not sufficient. "For...upsetting you. For causing your mood to... swing...down?"

Zoey handed Jen a napkin from the table, so she could blow her nose.

Dani continued to watch them battle their despondency. Desperate to be relevant, she blurted out, "We kissed multiple times!"

Zoey became mildly interested. "Define multiple."

"More than once."

"Like, ten times?"

Dani was quick to answer. "No. Not ten times."

Jen perked up, her mood visibly lifting. "More than three?"

Dani scrunched up her face in concentration, picturing each kiss and counting. "Yes, more than three."

"More than twenty?" Zoey asked.

"No! Not more than twenty."

"Just checking. You guys have been in bathrooms an awful lot lately. So, more than five?"

"No, not more than five."

"Huh. That would be, what..."

"Do you need a calculator?"

"No. Let's see, more than three, but less than five. That makes four." Zoey began ticking off the times she knew about. "Our bathroom, that was obvious. The golf course, although I would consider that more than a kiss." Zoey arched a brow suggestively.

"Ah, so it was *you* who came in?"

"Yes, and I still haven't recovered from your little burlesque show. Might wanna try locking a door once in a while. Then, Jolie's house."

Dani narrowed her eyes. "You two talked, didn't you? Were you texting her that night?"

"We all talk. So that's three, when was four?"

Dani was determined to get to the bottom of who exactly "we" was. "Who all knows?" she demanded.

"That's not important, when was the fourth kiss?"

"This past Friday. Here."

Zoey and Jen exchanged a look.

"Two days ago? You kissed here? In your house?" Jen asked.

Zoey rose and checked the powder room. "All clear," she called out. "Do I need to check the bath upstairs?"

Dani filled her lungs with air and exhaled. "We didn't kiss in the bathroom."

Zoey sat back down. "Where did you kiss?"

"By the front door. But that was the last time. We both made a decision."

Zoey reached for more popcorn. "You're getting married."

"What? No. We're gonna try and get to know each other better."

"So, you're gonna start dating," Zoey said.

"That's not what I meant. We're gonna be friends."

"So, friends who have sex." Zoey pointed a finger at Dani for emphasis while grabbing more popcorn with the other hand.

"That's not what I said. Just regular friends."

"Who have sex." Zoey nodded, making sure everyone was clear.

Dani's frustration spilled over. "Ah! Nobody's having sex. And nobody is kissing anymore! I'm engaged."

"To...Kara."

Dani was at her wit's end.

Jen raised a hand. "So, to *encapsulate*." She wiggled her fingers, looking for recognition, her mood on a violent upswing.

"Word of the day, word of the day!" Zoey shouted, and the conversation halted as they completed their ritual.

Jen continued, "So, to encapsulate. You think if you become friends, you'll stop being attracted to each other?"

Dani spread her arms wide. "Exactly. Thank you." She took a deep breath and let it out. Finally, someone understood.

"That is the dumbest thing I've ever heard," Zoey said.

"Red-flag word, babe," Jen said.

"Well then, it's the stupidest thing I've ever heard."

Jen sipped her water. "Still a red flag."

"Well, it's pretty dumb and it's pretty stupid. I don't know another word for dumb and stupid."

"It's not dumb." Dani tossed a few kernels at Zoey's head. "It's actually smart. We'll be buds in no time, like you and I are buds."

Zoey tapped her index finger against her lips and then pointed. "I'm a little confused with your definition of buds. I don't think I've ever had my hand up your cooch."

Dani opened her mouth, ready to deny with a sharp retort, but Kara did have her hand on Dani's lady bits at the golf course. She closed her mouth and recalculated. "Kara and I will become friends, and we'll look back on all this kissing stuff and we'll laugh." Dani was sure everything would work out. Well, she hoped it would work out. Okay, she prayed it would work out.

Jen's eyes puddled. "Well, good luck with that." Her voice was tinged with sadness and her mood started to plummet. She reached for another napkin.

"What's happening?" Dani asked, befuddled. Wasn't Jen happy a moment ago? Her eyes sought out Zoey for an explanation.

"Welcome to my world. Every month for five days." She turned her attention to her now sniffling girlfriend. "Babe, it's okay. I'm sure Dani will fix all this." She rubbed Jen's head. "And don't you worry, I'm still bringing the popcorn. Like, everywhere I go. Just to encapsulate."

CHAPTER TWENTY-FOUR

Kara lay in bed early Saturday morning, feeling lethargic. Another night spent tossing and turning. Which had been the case ever since she last saw Dani a week ago. Their last kiss played over and over in her mind. It was soft and searching and sexy as hell.

At the time, Kara felt compelled to kiss Dani. She had ached to kiss her. Kiss away her sadness. Provide comfort. Lift her spirits. She longed to see the smiling, teasing Dani from dinner at the Walkers'.

When did this happen? How did she go from disliking her to this?

With a groan, she stretched her arms above her head. Maybe friendship Dani would be enough. Maybe that was the way to end this thirst, this craving. She prayed for Dani to be right. Prayed the attraction would fade the more they got to know each other. A small sliver of doubt existed. Who was she kidding? It was bigger than a sliver. This had the potential to end badly.

Her dream last night had been a doozy. She was walking with Dani, a child between them, a tiny girl with a mass of curly red hair. They each held one of the girl's hands and swung her back and forth, much to the child's delight.

Great, now she was having babies with Dani.

Rubber-duck fucked.

A kitten interrupted her thoughts. The swatter walked along Milo's back, swaying this way and that but never falling off. She snatched her phone and took a quick video of the high-wire act.

Her fingers hovered. She itched to send it to Dani. They hadn't spoken since last Friday. She was hesitant and had no idea why. Maybe this was the icebreaker needed.

The instant reply made Kara laugh.

Cat lover.

I give up. They've melted my cold dog-loving heart.

Aha! I knew it! Now about those names.

Oh, I named them, Kara typed.

What are they?

Guess you'll have to visit sometime to find out. What are you doing?

Just got out of surgery.

Did it go well?

Yes.

So you don't need any "friendly" comfort?

LOL. I'm good.

Kara sent another video, of a kitten fetching a ball of paper.

They fetch better than Oliver, Dani typed.

Don't you worry, lil lady. We'll learn that dog some fetchin'.;)

LOL. Learnin' and fetchin' sounds like a plan.

Great. Talk soon?

Def. Bye K.

Kara exhaled. See? Friends. Everything would be fine. She dragged herself from bed and jumped into the shower. As she ran a soapy loofah over her breasts, her mind went rogue. Suddenly it was Dani's hands on her. A small, quiet moan escaped as her hand dipped lower, between her legs. Only they were Dani's hands, searching and coaxing. The rational side of her brain knew this was not something that happened between friends, but picturing Dani's hands roaming her body completely short-circuited all rational thought.

She continued to stroke herself as the fantasy continued. She leaned her forehead against the wall of the shower. The warm water running over her limbs only added to the dream-like quality of the moment. Her breath quickened in response to her touches, Dani's touches. *Her* fingers pinching and pulling her nipples. *Her* hand sliding through silky folds. The image of Dani, naked and grinding against her, whispering encouraging words into her ear, sent her into overdrive. She was close now, only a few more seconds…

The bathroom door opened. She jumped, knocking the handheld shower attachment off its perch, and it crashed to the tub floor, but not before bouncing off her foot. She cursed. The moment was lost. And her toe hurt. Pulling back the curtain, she poked her head out.

Jesmyn sat on top of the toilet seat. "Hey. You okay in there?"

"Uh, I'm showering."

"Is that all you're doing?" she asked with raised eyebrows.

Jesus Christ. Jesmyn was in super-detective mode. "What do you mean? I'm showering." Kara quickly whipped the curtain closed, making herself invisible to Jesmyn's prying eyes. That's all she needed, to be forced to confess to whacking it in the shower while thinking of her newly minted friend. "Close the door." Crankiness crept into her voice.

"It's hot in here."

"Hello? It's because I'm taking a shower."

Jesmyn half shut the door. "I haven't talked to you in a while. Thought I'd check in."

Kara poked her head out again, making sure to keep the rest of her body covered. Anybody else and she wouldn't care, but this was Jesmyn. "You saw me a couple weeks ago."

"Seems like a long time. Nice shower cap."

"It's not hair-washing day. I didn't wanna get it wet." Kara loved her shower cap, although it might be construed as dorky. It did have tiny ducks on it.

"How's Dani?"

Kara closed the curtain and continued with her shower, not liking the direction of the conversation. "She's fine, why?"

"Val said you golfed with her."

"Yeah, so?"

"Did you kiss again?"

"What?"

"Did you kiss again?"

Kara hesitated. Maybe if she didn't answer, Jes would leave. "You did, didn't you?"

My God, how does she know? "Maybe?"

"Maybe?"

Kara decided to conserve her mental energy. No sense in delaying the inevitable. "Yes, we did."

"I thought she was off-limits."

"She is." Kara started to shave her legs.

"So why did you kiss her?"

"Which time?" The razor hovered over her kneecap. *Crap.*

"Jesus. How many times have you kissed?"

"Four times. But it won't happen again. We've talked about it. Dani just wants to be friends."

"Friends with benefits?"

"No, just friends."

"You're crazy about her. How's that gonna work?"

"I'm not crazy about her." This was said with more emphasis than needed. Shit, who was she trying to convince here?

"You couldn't take your eyes off her at the party. Hey, kittens. Hey, babies."

Kara peeked out from behind the curtain. The kitties milled around the bathroom.

Jesmyn picked one up. "Did you name them yet?" She went eyeball to eyeball with him and received a whack on the nose for her trouble. "Well, aren't you feisty."

"That's Thumper."

"Thumper?"

"Yeah, because he likes to whack you."

"How about this one?" Jesmyn put Thumper down and went to grab the other one, but he high-stepped away from her. "That's Tigger."

"Why Tigger?"

Kara couldn't bring herself to say both names were Dani's favorites. That would leave her open to ridicule for sure. She winged it and said the first thing that came into her head. "Cause he's bouncy, bouncy...bouncy." Kara closed the curtain and turned her attention back to shaving.

"Knock, knock," Val said. "Do we want breakfast? I can make it."

"Babe, Kara and Dani are gonna try and be friends."

"What? Like fuck buddies?"

For what seemed like the hundredth time, Kara peeked around the curtain. "No! Jesus, don't you two have someplace to be?"

"Nice shower cap," Val said.

Milo and Ziggy were the next visitors to jam themselves into the bathroom. The space was not quite big enough for three adults, two kittens, and two dogs.

Kara was on the hot seat and needed to escape. A change of subject would do the trick. "Paintball should be fun tomorrow. Everyone will be there."

"How you gonna be friends with Dani?" Val asked. "You dig her too much."

She gnashed her teeth together. So much for vacating said hot seat. "I don't dig her, it's a physical attraction, that's it."

"Isn't that digging?" Val asked Jesmyn.

"Definitely digging. I said she was crazy about her."

Kara cleared her throat. "Let's be clear here. I am not crazy about her." Lie number one. "I am not digging her." Lie number two. "And we'll be fine as just friends." A complete trifecta.

"Sounds like a clusterfuck to me," Val said.

Kara turned off the shower. "I don't wanna talk about it anymore."

"Okay." Val stood. "We're leaving." She ushered the pups out the door as Jesmyn followed, a kitten on each shoulder.

Their voices floated back. "Zoey's gonna have a field day with this," Val said.

Jesmyn agreed. "She's gonna be Jiffy Popping her ass off."

Kara whipped open the curtain and glared at the now-empty space. Jiffy Pop? Were they all talking? Were the interactions between her and Dani common knowledge? Goddamn it.

Royally rubber-duck fucked.

CHAPTER TWENTY-FIVE

Dani and Will were the first to arrive Sunday morning at the paintball fundraiser. Jolie had invited everyone to the yearly event hosted by Travis's school. The money raised enabled them to buy laptops and other supplies for the students, and Dani was only too happy to contribute.

This would be the first time Dani would see Kara since their friendship talk a week ago, and she was apprehensive. She still had doubts about how this new relationship would work, especially when random images of Kara popped into her head, which was frequently. Kara at the Walkers', laughing not at her but with her. The smell of Kara's hair when they rode on the motorcycle. The feel of Kara's abs under her fingers.

This truce would probably be the death of her.

Soon the rest of the gang arrived. Jen and Zoey brought their friend Hannah. Ethan brought Kevin Murphy and his EMT partner, Brian.

Kara waved and Dani cursed the increased pressure inside her chest. How could she miss her so much?

They embraced, and Kara stepped back. "I feel like I haven't seen you in forever."

"It's only been a week." Dani tried to act cavalier.

"Seems longer somehow."

They all checked in at the office and received their guns, helmets, gloves, and kneepads. Protective vests were available, and the girls made sure to get one, but the boys decided to tough it out.

Next, they gathered around for an explanation of the rules. They would play on a large outdoor field the size of a soccer pitch. Today's game would be "Capture the Flag." Each team's flag would be at their home base located at opposite ends of the field. The object of the game was to steal the other team's flag and bring it back to their base without being shot.

They geared up, most of the helmets perching precariously on their heads so they could talk.

Zoey waved her gun around. "I look badass."

"Whoa." Ethan raised his hands. "Maybe you shouldn't wave that thing around until we start the game."

Zoey scoffed. "Relax. I'm cool." She lowered the gun and accidentally pulled the trigger. And shot Jen's foot, which in turn set off a ripple effect, like a stone tossed into a lake.

"Ow!" Jen screamed. When her arm flew into the air, her fingers pressed the trigger.

"Shit!" Dani took a direct hit square to the nip, and her hand spasmed, sending a shot toward Will's head, who ducked and accidentally pulled his own trigger, resulting in Kevin Murphy yipping at the splat of blue paint near his belt line.

"Everybody put the safety on," Ethan demanded.

After a few sheepish grins and mumbles, they all did as they were told.

Dani scowled and rubbed her breast. "I thought you weren't supposed to feel anything through this vest."

Kara interrupted the target practice. "How about we do girls against guys again?"

"Losers buy dinner," Zoey said.

"Why don't we do double or nothing on the last bet from golf?" Ethan asked.

Zoey pointed. "You're on! Double or nothing, losers buy two dinners at the Met Grill. That's double the dessert."

"All right. Girls against guys it is," Ethan said. "Me, Will, Murph, Brian, who else?"

Kara spoke up. "Aaron, Travis, and Travis's cousin Joffrey will be here."

Ethan nodded. "Cool. Then it's Zoey, Jen, Dani, Kara, Hannah? Hardly seems fair."

"Aaron's wife, Jolie. Oh, and Jes and Val are coming," Kara said.

"That's eight girls against seven guys," Will said.

"It's okay. They'll need the extra person." Ethan fist-bumped Kevin and Brian.

"Here comes the Walker clan," Kara said.

Kara introduced everyone. "We're doing guys against gals," she told the newcomers.

Aaron took in all the blue paint splattered on everyone. "Did you guys play already?"

Kara smirked. "No, we had some, ah, equipment malfunctions."

Zoey stood next to Travis's cousin. "Joffrey, like *Game of Thrones*?"

He nodded. "Yeah."

"I hate you already, little dude."

Dani nudged her. "He's a kid."

Joff's eyes narrowed. "I'm coming for you," the youngster said brashly.

"Come and get it, Joff. I got a paintball with your name all over it."

Two employees of the paintball center approached the group and introduced themselves.

"Hey, everyone. Glad to have you with us today. I'm Robert, this is Dave, we'll be your referees today." He checked out the amount of blue paint on display. "Do we need another lesson on our guns?"

Quite a few looks were thrown in Zoey's direction.

"Maybe," she mumbled.

When Robert was done reviewing gun safety, they all made their way over to the field where they would spend the next two hours. It was a wooded area filled with "bunkers," a fancy term for things to hide behind. Some were man-made, and some were natural, like fallen tree logs and rock formations. A flimsy orange construction fence surrounded the perimeter. The dead zone was roped off and located midway out-of-bounds. Anyone shot had to immediately leave the playing field and stand in this area. Before giving the flags, Dave reminded them they would play three games, lasting thirty minutes each.

When all questions were answered, the groups took their flags and headed for their home bases.

As the girls walked to their base, Jen said, "First one to shoot Murphy in the nuts gets ten bucks."

Zoey put a fist in the air. "Make it twenty!"

"I'll go fifty." Kara gave Dani a soft smile.

"You guys are awesome." Dani was happy her crew had her back in all things Kevin Murphy. Especially a certain someone.

"Hey, Kara, when's Jes coming?" Zoey asked. "She's a total babe."

"She should be here soon."

Jolie's eyes blazed with excitement. "Oh my God! Jes is coming?" She and Zoey slapped hands and exchanged a few woo-hoos.

Dani leaned into Kara's ear. "Somebody's excited."

"Mm-hmm. I suspect both have fallen prey to what I like to call 'The Jesmyn Effect.'"

"What's that?"

"An unhealthy obsession-slash-fangirling of one Jesmyn Davani Azar."

"Oh."

"I imagine the dildo demo at Zoey's party may have triggered it. You remember the dildo demo, right?" Kara's eyes sparkled.

Dani felt a prickly heat spring to her cheeks and looked off to the right. "I don't recall."

"Mm-hmm." Kara gave a playful nudge to Dani's shoulder before addressing the group.

"Okay, listen up. We need two people to stay back and defend our flag. Jolie and Hannah?"

They nodded their agreement, and Kara continued to strategize. "Zoey and Jen can provide cover, and Dani and I will go after the flag."

"Great," Jen said. "I'm assuming since Zoey and I are providing cover, we must move in a surreptitious manner." She paused to let the word soak in. "That's one, folks. That's one."

"Woo!" Zoey raised her arms in the air, and everyone ducked. "Relax, bitches, the safety's on." The high-five circled around the group.

Dani slapped Kara's hand with a smile and did a grab also. Any contact was welcome, even a brief high-five and clutch. And it felt good touching her. She started plotting how to get in some more feels before the day was out.

Dave blew the whistle once, which meant to get ready.

Kara rallied her troops. "All right, ladies, we're shorthanded for this game, so let's do our best."

The second whistle blew, signaling the start of the game.

The boys fanned out across the field, heading toward them.

"Let's try to get to that pile of rocks." Kara pointed to the middle of the field.

They zigzagged toward their destination while paintballs whizzed past their heads. When they made it safely to the rocks, they fell to their knees.

Joffrey, partially protected by a fallen log, shot at them repeatedly.

"That damn Lannister is shooting at us," Zoey growled.

"That's what he's supposed to do." Dani returned fire, aiming at Ethan and Brian.

Joffrey began moving closer.

"Come and get it, Lannister!" Zoey stood, ready to fill the boy with paint, only to find she'd forgotten to turn off the safety. "You've got to be kidding me!" She was promptly peppered with paint. "Damn it." She waved a hand in surrender. "I'm out," she said, and was plunked one last time in the head from Joff, just for good measure. "Motherfucker." She stomped off the field.

"All right, Jen. Dani and I will try to get over to that shed," Kara said. "Cover us."

They managed to make it to the shed without being shot, and they hunkered down behind it. The enemy flag was still forty yards away.

They both spotted Aaron and Will creeping toward Jen and immediately started shooting. The guys dove behind a man-made bunker and remained out of sight.

Dani ducked back down. "Damn, I'm not hitting anything."

"Paintballs drop in flight, so you have to aim higher."

Dani tried again and failed miserably. "Damn it! Let's hope we're not gonna depend on me to do anything."

"You'll be fine. Let's get to that log pile. Go slow."

"Can't we go out like Butch and Sundance? Guns a-blazin'?" Dani asked.

"Let's just make it to the log pile, then we'll talk about guns blazing. Ready, Sundance?"

"Ready, Butch."

They began moving forward.

Dani put a finger to her lips. "Shh, surreptitiously." They giggled, not paying attention to Brian, who had snuck up on them.

Too late. They were sitting ducks.

"Watch out!" Kara pushed Dani onto the ground and shielded her with her own body. Paint splattered all around them.

Brian was ready to complete the kill, but Dani shot off a few rounds, hitting him squarely in the chest. "I got him! I got him!"

Brian raised his hand. "I'm out."

"Hey, did you see that?" Dani lifted her visor.

Kara rolled away from Dani, her back covered in paint.

"Oh no," Dani wailed. "You're hit."

"Afraid so." Kara took off her helmet.

"You took a paintball for me. You saved me. That's the sweetest thing anyone's ever done for me." It was just a game, but somewhere, in her heart, it mattered.

Kara smiled. "You would have done the same for me, I'm sure."

"Well, I dunno." Dani laughed. "A couple months ago I would've pushed you right into the line of fire." She stood and helped Kara to her feet.

Kara closed Dani's visor. "Stay safe. You may be our only hope." Kara waved to the group and moved to the dead zone.

"Bye, Butch." Dani sighed. She had no clue what to do. Maybe she should rush the flag. Go down in a blaze of glory, continuing the Sundance theme from earlier. Sounded pretty damn romantic. She searched for her other teammates. Jen got lit up by Aaron and Will. Back at home base, Joff and Travis had stolen the flag and pranced across the field. Jolie and Hannah trudged toward the dead zone.

Dani was alone. The last one standing. This was it. Her time to shine. She checked her hopper, which was full. Taking a deep breath, she ran as fast as she could toward the enemy flag, firing at will, hitting mostly trees and shrubs, but hey, that didn't matter, at least she hit something. She ran past a rabbit, frozen in place. Did he have a spot of blue paint on him? Shit, did she shoot a rabbit?

She ran closer and closer. Why, she might just pull this off! Suddenly, the theme music from *Chariots of Fire* ran through her head—or maybe it was the *Six Million Dollar Man* theme, she wasn't sure. She liked to watch the *Six Million Dollar Man* and *Bionic Woman* on Netflix. She just liked it, damn it. Although six million dollars wouldn't get you much today in the way of prosthetics, but back then it was enough to build a man!

Paintballs struck her vest, one after the other, and she threw her arms out wildly, dropping the gun and crumbling to the ground. "I'm hit, I'm hit!" She slumped into the grass.

From the dead zone, Zoey yelled, "What the hell was that, Dani?"

"You ran right into them," Jen said.

Dani stood and dusted herself off. "Shut up. You're ruining my *Chariots of Fire* moment." With a pout on her face, she plodded over to her teammates.

Kara's eyes were filled with mirth. "Nice try, Sundance."

"Thanks, Butch."

Kara threw an arm around her. "You'll get 'em next time."

Dani's heartbeat pitter-pattered in a happy rhythm. The day was full of free feels, and she was enjoying it immensely. She slipped an arm around Kara's waist. "I hope so." When she looked around, her eyes landed on Will, who stared back with a curious look. She dropped her arm, realizing how it must look to him. The guilt that had once been a constant companion but lately had faded since the friendship pact, accosted her again. She shifted away from Kara.

The other guys hooted and hollered in victory, creating a perfect diversion. They slapped hands and asses. They taunted.

The first game was in the books. One-nil, the guys.

Robert and Dave informed them that there would be a five-minute break before the next game, and that they should change their hoppers to a new paint color. They all straggled over to the sidelines to hydrate.

Suddenly, Zoey perked up as she gazed into the distance.

Jesmyn approached, sauntering in knee-high black boots, ripped jeans, and a bulletproof vest with the letters *SPD* in bold white. A helmet dangled from her hand. Two pistols were strapped to her thighs, and two bandoliers were slung across her chest. As she got closer, they turned out to be three rifles of varying sizes. When she made it to the group, she crossed her arms. "Who's on my team?"

CHAPTER TWENTY-SIX

Zoey screamed, "Me!"

Dani laughed at her bestie's exuberance. Maybe she needed to institute a De-Infatuation plan for Zoey.

Jen scowled. "Jesus, babe. What the hell?"

"Babe. It's Jes."

Kara chuckled. "Welcome to The Jesmyn Effect. I think it's pheromones or something."

Jen crossed her arms. "Between The Jesmyn Effect and my period, I'm about to go postal."

Zoey wasn't the only one agog over the new arrival. The guys stared with eyes wide and mouths agape.

Will pointed at the array of armaments. "You know this is paintball, right?"

"Yeah, um, those aren't, uh, real, are they?" Ethan asked.

Jesmyn gave them each a contemptuous glance. "If you had a vest on, it wouldn't matter."

A vestless Ethan and Will visibly gulped.

In an instant, she was all smiles. "I'm fucking with you, boys."

"Whew!" Ethan returned her smile. "Damn, those pistols look real."

"Oh, these are real." She pulled one from the holster, checked the clip and slammed it back in. "Glock nine-millimeter Luger." She pointed it at Will, who yelped and turned his back.

She chuckled. "I'm fucking with you."

"Ah, is that...ah...a grenade launcher?" Brian stammered.

Jesmyn re-holstered the pistol and pulled the heavy rifle off her back. "Yeah, it's a beauty, isn't it?" She lovingly caressed the barrel.

Ethan pointed at the grenades attached to her belt. "Are they legal?"

Her eyes narrowed. "Who are you again?"

He extended a trembling hand. "I'm Ethan, Jen's brother. We met at Zoey's party."

She slung the grenade launcher onto her back and shook his hand.

Val joined the group, looking equally badass in tight, black jeans and a formfitting camo jacket. "What are the teams?"

"Guys against gals," Kara said. "Best of three. We already lost the first game."

Val adjusted her kneepads. "Well, the cavalry has arrived, ladies. Let's do this."

The boys walked to their end of the field, and the ladies walked back to theirs.

"What's the plan this time?" Dani asked Kara.

"Well, Jes has the long-range rifle, so she should take a few people with her, set up in the middle of the field, and provide cover."

Jesmyn nodded, took the sniper rifle off her back. "Who's with me?"

An exuberant Zoey waved her hand. "Pick me, pick me."

"All right, you come with me."

"Yes!" Zoey pushed her boobs out for a chest bump, ramming herself into Jolie, who was caught off-guard and stumbled backward, landing on the seat of her pants. After the chest bump, Zoey stood next to Jes.

Jesmyn's eyes traveled over the group. "Who else should we take?"

"Let's take Kardi," Zoey said.

Kara looked over her shoulder. "Who's Kardi?"

"Cool. Kara and Dani, you come with us."

"Hannah and I will guard the base," Jen said. "Probably safer for everyone with me back here. I'm inclined to lay down some friendly fire in the direction of my Jesmyn Effected girlfriend."

Val tightened her helmet. "I'll take Jolie and we'll drive the boys toward Jes. Easy pickings, babe."

Dave blew the whistle, and the game was on. Jesmyn raced toward the bunker of logs in the middle of the field, rifles in hand, covering the forty yards in record time. Dani, Kara, and Zoey huffed and puffed to keep up. When Jesmyn got close to the logs, she executed a perfect dive, drop, and roll, airborne for a second, tucking in midair and rolling forward, popping up right behind the bunker.

Zoey tried the dive, tuck, and roll maneuver, but all she managed to do was belly flop on the ground and skin her chin. "Damn it!" She crawled the rest of the way on her elbows, military style.

Dani and Kara chose a less dramatic arrival. No diving, dropping, or rolling needed. They slid to the ground once they reached the bunker.

Jesmyn produced a bipod for the sniper rifle and set it on top of the logs. She locked the rifle into place and put her eye to the scope.

Aaron ran down the left side of the field.

She turned the rifle and took the shot, hitting him square in the chest.

A wide-eyed Zoey grinned at Dani. "Booyah," she said in a soft tone that belied her enthusiasm. Dani found it both amusing and a tad unsettling as she watched Zoey grab the grenade launcher.

"Be careful," Dani said.

"Yeah, that has a recoil," Jesmyn said. Zoey nestled the launcher against her shoulder and pointed it in the general direction of...nobody, really. She pulled the trigger and was promptly recoiled back onto her ass. The grenade hurtled toward the big, majestic oak tree standing in the middle of the field. It exploded in the top of the branches, sending a flock of starlings streaming for the heavens. Two squirrels ran down the main trunk, yellow flecks of paint stuck to their fur.

Zoey high-fived Kara. "Nailed it."

Brian ran toward Jolie and Val. Jesmyn calmly took aim, hitting him right in the helmet. She swung the rifle to the opposite side. "Zoey, shoot at Ethan," Jesmyn said. "Maybe he'll poke his head out."

Zoey stood and emptied her hopper in Ethan's direction, then quickly sank back down behind the logs. "I got you, Ethan."

His head popped up. "No, you didn't." A perfect shot of yellow paint spattered on his visor.

Zoey whooped in victory.

Travis bobbed between barriers and Dani took aim. *Aim higher, aim higher.* She pulled the trigger and a splat of paint hit Travis in the arm. "I hit him!"

Kara threw an arm around her. "You did!"

"Boss, bogey at two o'clock," Zoey said.

Kevin Murphy slunk toward their position.

"A nut shot earns you fifty bucks from Kara. If you do it with the grenade launcher, I'll kick in a hundred," Zoey told Jesmyn.

"I could use a cool hundred and fifty." Grabbing the grenade launcher, Jesmyn took aim. "He needs to turn around."

Zoey took off toward Murphy, hootin' and hollerin'.

When Murphy turned, his face lit up with revenge, and he cackled as he raised his rifle. However, his euphoria did not last long, as Jesmyn launched a direct hit, square to the junk.

Mouth open in a silent scream, he dropped his rifle and grabbed his jewels. He remained upright for a brief second, then tipped over, writhing on the ground.

"That's gonna leave a mark." Kara smiled at Dani. "But it's fifty dollars well spent."

Dani grabbed her hand. "Thank you." Her eyes locked with Kara's, and for a moment she forgot where she was. A movement over Kara's shoulder caught her eye. "Zoey, get down!"

Joffrey rose from the grass, a paintball bow and arrow pointed in Zoey's direction.

"You've got to be kidding me!" Zoey pulled her trigger. Nothing happened. The hopper was empty. "Motherfucker!"

Joffrey let loose the arrow and paint smeared across her vest. Up went her hand. "I'm out!" As she walked off, another arrow struck her back.

Joffrey's maniacal laughter rang out as she continued walking to the dead zone. His glee was short-lived however, as Jesmyn took him down with a shot to the gut.

Over on the right side of the field, Val gave the all-clear signal.

"Who's left?" Kara asked.

Dani counted the bodies in the dead zone. "Just Will."

"He must be protecting the flag," Jesmyn said. "You guys go get it."

"Ready, Sundance?" Kara asked.

"Ready, Butch."

When they made it to the boys' home base, Dani jumped around the wall and yelled, "Freeze!"

Will dropped his gun and raised his hands in surrender. "Babe, it's me, your husband-to-be…"

Before he could finish, Dani shot him full of paint. "All's fair in love and war, babe."

Dani gleefully grabbed the flag as her lesser half walked to the dead zone.

"Go, girl. Take it back to base!" Kara whacked her butt.

Dani held the flag high and raced the entire length of the field, proudly waving the flag from side to side.

It was all square, one game apiece. It would come down to the rubber match, one game to determine the winner of two expensive dinners at the Met Grill—along with copious amounts of desserts.

The boys trudged back to base, shoulders sagging, their fate sealed the moment Jesmyn the sharpshooter stepped foot on the playing field. The third game was a formality. When the whistle blew, they slid into position to await the inevitable.

Back at their base, the girls strategized.

Zoey raised a hand. "Boss, I need to be up-front. I gotta bag a Lannister."

"Zoe, he's twelve," Jen reminded her.

"I'm just gonna fill him with paint."

Jen sighed and loaded her hopper with new ammo. "I want in on the action. I wanna shoot some shit."

Dani leaned into Zoey's ear. "That sounds a bit aggressive."

"She still has her period."

"I thought she had it last week."

Zoey lowered her voice. "We are currently experiencing the period from hell. It's like shark week."

Suddenly Jen was in front of them. "Are you talking about me?"

"No!" Dani blurted out. Already down a nip, she couldn't afford to lose any other body parts.

* * *

The whistle blew, and the ladies sprang into action.

Kara and Dani stayed behind, and the rest took off.

Dani leaned her elbows on the split rail fence in front of their base and Kara watched her for just a moment before joining her. They had a good view of the field from this vantage point.

"Well, Butch, it's not as exciting back here." Dani turned and smiled.

She was beautiful despite the myriad colors covering her body. The smile that Kara never thought she'd see was an added bonus. "I guess we had to share the fun. Although we made quite a pair, Sundance."

"We do make quite a pair."

A warmth bloomed in Kara's chest at the tense of Dani's verb.

The paintball battle unfolded in front of them.

"Oops, Will bit the dust," Kara said as Jen emptied her hopper all over him. Excessive force came to mind.

Dani shielded her eyes from the sun. "Yikes, Jolie's down. Joffrey got her."

"Well, might as well relax. Nobody's getting past Val and Jesmyn." Kara leaned her gun against the fence. "Whoa!"

"What?"

"I swear I just saw a blue bunny."

Dani gulped and turned in the other direction. "You must be mistaken. Why would a bunny be blue? I mean gray, yes, white, maybe, brown, of course. But blue? There's no such thing. Unless you're Alice in Wonderland..." Dani's voice trailed off.

"Dani?"

"Yes?"

"What did you do?"

"I shot him earlier. In my *Chariots of Fire* moment."

"Uh-huh."

"He's not hurt. I mean, he was hopping. And I'm sure it'll provide excellent cover if he runs through a field of bluebells."

Kara tried to appear stern, but Dani's comical rationalizations made her giggle. "You are such a bad shot." Kara turned her attention back to the field. "Uh-oh. There's Joff and Zoey."

Dani squinted. "What is she doing, throwing popcorn at him?"

"I guess she's out of ammo. And here comes Jen," Kara said. "Well, she nailed Joff. Oh...and she shot Zoey."

"And now she's got the grenade launcher."

Kara craned her neck. "She's taking aim at their base."

"Is that Murphy running out with his hands up, surrendering?" Dani asked.

"Hand up. The other one is holding his junk."

"Yikes, she shot him anyway. Well, 'never fuck with a woman who's had her period for eight days' is what I always say."

Kara's mouth twitched with humor. "Is that what you always say?"

"Yes, that's what I always say." Dani butted a hip into Kara's. "I may not be a good shot, but I'm good at other things."

Kara butted her back. "Oh, yeah? Such as?"

"Sayings. Clever sayings. And I'm a good cook."

Kara widened her eyes in surprise. "Really?"

Dani nudged her whole body into Kara. "Don't act so shocked. I'm an excellent cook."

"Excellent?" With each touch from Dani, Kara swore a piece of her soul caught fire.

Dani nodded. "Come over sometime, and I'll make you the best dinner you've ever had."

"I dated a woman once who was the chef at Andaluca in the Mayflower Park Hotel. She was pretty damn good."

"Is that a dare?"

Kara was quick to reply. "No, it wasn't a dare—"

"Cause if you're daring me, I'll take that dare." Dani's eyes turned a steely blue.

Kara shuddered at the sudden image of Dani standing over her, demanding a taste test of whatever she whipped up. She emphatically shook her head from side to side. "I didn't dare you—"

"It would be a challenge. That I would win, of course."

"I have no doubt you would win that dare." Kara turned her attention back to the field of play. "Well, most of the boys have been shot. And it looks like Jen is taking her mood out on Ethan."

Jen shot Ethan repeatedly at close range. He yelled at her as he walked over to the dead zone. At one point, Jen grabbed his paint gun and continued to shoot him as he walked away in surrender.

Kara chuckled. "He must have said something to piss her off."

"Holy shit," Dani said. "It's over."

At the opposite end of the field, Jen waved the boys' flag.

"We won!" Dani spread her arms wide for a celebratory hug, and Kara was in them instantly. They pulled apart when the hug lasted longer than standard friendship hug time.

Game, set, match. Jen strutted past the enemy combatants, jeering and gesturing and waving a fist. Zoey joined her, dropped her drawers, and mooned the dead.

Eventually they made their way to the large indoor auditorium, where free pizza would be served to all the contestants. Ethan waved the group over when he found an empty table, and everyone took their seats.

Aaron brought a stack of pizza boxes over to the table. "Okay. We've got plain, pepperoni, and veggie. Who wants what?"

When everyone had multiple slices, and beverages of choice, Jolie stood. "I'd like to thank everyone for coming. Every year this event is so much fun. The money we raise is used to buy computers and supplies for all the kids at the school, and a portion of it goes to a scholarship fund for disadvantaged students. So, thank you!"

They applauded, and Zoey stood next. "I'd just like to say, I'm looking forward to my ten desserts at the Met Grill."

"Ten?" Ethan's face contorted. "Now we're up to *ten*?"

"Shut it, Ethan." She raised a cup. "Drinks on Murphy!"

Murphy paled, cowered, and covered his head with his hands, expecting the worst as the table yelled, "Drinks on Murphy!"

Dani leaned into Kara's ear. "How did you become friends with Travis?" She took a bite of her pizza as she waited for Kara to answer.

"I met him at the school three years ago, and we hit it off." She shrugged. "I love kids."

"Do you want your own someday?"

"I do. A few. I don't wanna be the one to give birth, though." She laughed. "Hopefully my partner will. What about you?"

"Yeah, we both want them, but we're gonna wait until I'm done with my residency."

Kara knew Dani would be a wonderful mom. A stab of jealousy pierced her heart, because right then, she wanted to be the one to have babies with Dani. God, where did that come from? Friends don't have babies together. *Snap out of it. Don't be an idiot.* She was saved from further mental self-flagellation by the sound of Dani's laughter.

Dani poked her in the ribs and pointed at Zoey, who now had popcorn on her pizza, courtesy of Jesmyn. Kara grabbed Dani's finger to stop the prodding, and somehow their hands remained intertwined under the table.

After a few seconds, Dani shyly pulled her hand away. "Zoey and her popcorn." She leaned in close again, her breath caressing Kara's ear. "I figured out the Kardi thing, by the way."

Dani pulled back, a mischievous smile lighting up her face, and Kara knew then. She was a goner. Was there an exact moment when you knew you were in love with someone? Or was it a slow, steady progression of feelings until all at once your heart was full and your brain was on overload? And you didn't see it coming. And now you were lost. Because the person who stole your heart was someone you couldn't have.

Totally, unequivocally…fucked.

CHAPTER TWENTY-SEVEN

Today was Oliver's first training lesson. Dani stared at the clothes in her closet, clad only in blue panties. She'd been staring for fifteen minutes. Which was ridiculous. It was just a dog lesson.

Her favorite kitty perched on the dresser.

"What do you think, Jinx? Not bad, right?" Glancing at her reflection, she sucked in her tummy and patted it. Even with her hectic schedule, she'd put on a few pounds this year. One too many slices of pizza. Oh well. She cocked her head to the side. Would Kara find her body attractive? Her light-blue bra sat on the small chair next to her. Of course she would wear that. It was Kara's favorite. *Stop it. You're just friends.*

Oliver wandered in and leaned against her.

Dani smooched him on the head. "Hey, buddy, how was your walk with Daddy?"

After studying the three shirts on the bed, she chose the blue one, to match the bra and panties, and because the color would make her eyes pop. Jesus Christ. *Enough.* The only thing popping should be Zoey's popcorn.

Dani touched the base of her throat as her eyes focused into the middle distance. This would be the first time she and Kara would be alone since their last kiss. A kiss so soft and full of promise. It seemed like a lifetime ago, but it'd been only a few weeks. There were moments, mostly at night, when she would lie quietly in bed and ache to be kissed again. Or she would lie awake and recall how Kara's eyes sparkled when she teased her. How the corners of her mouth would lift when she tried to hold back a smile. How it felt to be wrapped in her embrace. And then the guilt would assault her, and she would roll over and punch her pillow in frustration. Frustration over not being able to control these wayward thoughts.

When would these feelings fade? Sometimes she swore they had only gotten stronger. Maybe enough time hadn't passed yet.

She pulled on jeans, tugged the blue shirt over her head, and finished the look off with a black pendant necklace. A spritz of perfume was the final addition. With hands on hips, she stood in front of the mirror.

Jinx meowed his approval and jogged from the room.

"Is that all you have to say? Am I boring you?"

Will came into the bedroom to change his shirt and gave her a questioning look. "Did you put perfume on? It's just a dog lesson, right?"

Her gut clenched. Shit. He'd caught her primping. Primping for someone who was supposed to be just a friend. "I always put perfume on," was her weak-ass defense.

His eyebrows rose, but before they could continue, the doorbell rang. "I'll get it."

A few seconds later, he called, "Kara's here. I'm heading out to get a quick nine holes in."

"Okay, I'll be right down." With one last glance in the mirror, she nodded at her reflection.

When she made it downstairs, she found Jinx sashaying along the back of the couch, stalking his prey. The prey being Kara. The color drained from her face when he climbed aboard her shoulders.

Dani snickered. "You look scared to death."

"Is he gonna kill me?"

"Don't be such a baby. He's saying hello." Dani scratched under Jinx's chin. "Good boy."

Jinx sniffed Kara's earlobe and took a taste.

"He's starting to eat me."

"It's a love nibble."

Jinx continued violating Kara's ear, all the while digging into her shoulder to anchor himself as he attempted to achieve the proper balance.

"Ouch. He's ripping my shoulder apart."

"He's kneading."

"Well, he *needs* to get off." Kara's body remained rigid and unmoving. "I think he's drawing blood."

"He's nesting."

"In my blood."

Jinx finished his meal and now perched precariously on Kara's right shoulder.

"He hates me."

"He loves you. Listen, he's purring."

Jinx took this opportunity to lick Kara's jawline.

"Your cat licked me."

"He must taste before he devours," Dani said with some saucy sass.

"Very funny."

Jinx eventually grew bored and jumped down, but not before ripping into Kara's shoulder on the dismount.

"Ow!"

He trotted from the room, tail held high, in search of a more interesting activity, like chasing stink bugs in the sunroom.

Kara reached under her shirt to assess the damage. A small amount of blood clung to her fingers. "I told you I was bleeding."

"Oh, shit, you are. Lemme see." Dani lifted Kara's black T-shirt at the collar. "It's not bad. I'll get some peroxide."

She returned with a bottle of hydrogen peroxide and sat close to Kara. She almost said, *take your shirt off.* Instead, she tried to work under the shirt. "Here, let me try to—"

And before Dani could continue, Kara whipped the shirt off. "There. Might be easier."

Dani's thoughts flew into the gutter so fast she almost fainted from the g-force. The cotton ball froze in midair as her eyes wandered down to Kara's lavender sports bra, then to her toned belly, before coming to rest at their final destination, the top of Kara's jeans. So easy to slip a finger in the waistband. She drew in an erratic breath. *This is why you don't ask an attractive woman to take her shirt off.*

Kara cleared her throat. "Are you gonna…" Her voice trailed off as their eyes met.

"Oh, yeah sorry. Just making sure…ah…there weren't any more cuts…anywhere else." She shut up before the sexual hole she was digging got any deeper.

"He sat on my shoulder," Kara teased. "He never made it down to my lap." A wry grin settled on her lips.

"I know that. I was just…admiring your belt."

Kara's smirk continued. "I don't have a belt on."

Dani had no retort. Yes. She'd been caught checking Kara out. Best to pretend it never happened. She soaked the cotton in the peroxide and dabbed it on the small cuts. A dab here, a dab there, a glance here, a glance there. Dani's eyes had a mind of their own. All the dabbing and glancing, plus their proximity, caused a warm sensation in the pit of her stomach. Or, to be more precise, at the top of her thighs. She needed a distraction from the heat spreading throughout her body. "How are my kittens?"

Kara turned and Dani held her breath. They were so close, not even a foot apart. So many urges assaulted her at once, the urge to lean in and kiss, the urge to trace her jawline, the urge to pull her closer. This friendship plan, that had seemed like such a brilliant idea at the time, threatened to jump the rails.

"They're good. I didn't give them away. Yet."

"Oh, please, you'll never give them away now." Dani bit her lip, hard, hoping the pain would make her forget she wanted to kiss the spot behind Kara's ear. "What did you end up naming them again?"

"I'll never tell."

"Oh, c'mon."

"Next time you stop by, I'll introduce you."

"Well, I'm stopping by then. All set. Minor cuts have been tended."

"Thank you, Dr. Clark. Although it was the least you could do, considering your cat tried to kill me."

"Well, maybe we should get to this dog training thing, before he comes back and finishes the job."

They took Oliver into the backyard, and Kara armed Dani with a handful of treats and went over basic commands and hand signals, complete with demonstrations.

She chuckled as Dani tried to be pack leader, Oliver totally not on board with it. "Dani, remember, you have to be Alpha. Act like you're in charge!"

"I'm trying."

Every time Dani told Oliver to stay, he would simply run off and get a toy. "Why doesn't he listen to me like he listens to you?"

After fifteen minutes of doggie disobedience, she collapsed onto the lawn with arms spread wide. "Aaahhhh. I suck at this."

Kara took a seat next to her. "You need to tame him."

"Tame him? What is he? A lion?"

Kara laughed. "No. Did you ever read *The Little Prince*?"

"No."

"It follows the adventures of this little prince. At one point, he meets a fox. And he wants to play with the fox, but the fox says the prince has to tame him first."

Dani sat up. "How did the prince tame him?"

"The fox told the prince to sit in the grass near him. And every day he could sit closer. To build up trust. And eventually the prince would tame the fox. And through the taming, they'd begin to need each other."

"Sounds more like falling in love than dog training."

"Well, it's about trust. But, yeah, I guess it could be about love too. To be tamed is to fall in love. Totally and completely."

"So I'm falling in love. With a dog."

"That's not what I meant. You'll gain his trust, little by little. Every day, you get closer and closer—"

"So, this could take years."

"It's not gonna take years. I'm—"

"Kara."

"What?" Kara asked, exasperated.

"I read the book." Dani laughed. "I'm teasing you. You should've seen your face."

"I'm gonna hurt you."

"I don't think so. I'm stronger than I look."

"Oh, yeah?" Kara pushed Dani onto the ground and straddled her, catching her by surprise. She pinned her shoulders down. "You will pay for your transgressions, Dr. Clark. Are you ticklish?"

"Oh, fuck, don't you dare." Dani was ticklish as shit. She raised her hands to defend herself. Half-heartedly, of course, because tickling meant Kara was touching her.

"Aha! We are ticklish." Kara grabbed Dani's sides as she squealed and writhed beneath her, trying to escape.

Dani gasped for breath. "Stop, stop! You better stop!"

Kara lost her leverage and collapsed on top of Dani.

The giggling and smiling ceased. Suddenly things weren't nearly as funny as they were a moment ago. What started out as lighthearted became heavy in a matter of seconds. Dani's chest heaved with every breath.

Kara's glance strayed to Dani's lips.

The world fell away, and it was just the two of them.

Dani whispered, "Have you ever been tamed?"

Kara hesitated, and the silence seemed to stretch across the universe. Finally, with a voice thick with emotion, she said, "Yes."

Dani, powerless to resist the pull between them, lifted her mouth to Kara's. Nirvana was seconds away, and she'd deal with the consequences later. Another inch or two and she'd satisfy this agonizing ache inside.

The ringtone of Dani's phone blared from the back pocket of her jeans, startling them both.

And just like that, the moment was ruined. Thankfully. Dani had no idea what could have happened after the kiss.

Kara rolled off and walked away to give Dani some space.

"Hey, Will."

"I forgot my wallet. Any chance you can run it over to the club?"

"Okay. See you in a bit." Dani hung up. "He forgot his wallet. I have to take it to him." Her chest constricted at what almost happened. *You're engaged!* "Um, I guess I have homework with my dog."

Kara smiled. "Yes. Next time, I'm giving you a test."

"When's our next time?" Dani cringed. Did that sound too eager?

"Whenever you say. Call me."

They walked through the house to the front door. Dani pulled Kara in for an awkward, quick hug.

This time there was no lingering. They had almost crossed an imaginary line a few moments ago, and she needed to get back on solid ground.

CHAPTER TWENTY-EIGHT

The Saturday after the dog lesson, Dani was at the grocery store, meandering up and down the aisles with her cart. She woke up with a hangover. The evening before, she and Will had dinner with Ethan and his wife, and they'd consumed too much wine. To top it off, when they came home, they'd had sex. Dani had been determined to chase Kara from her mind. Having sex with Will seemed like the perfect antidote, but that's not what happened. Her traitorous mind felt like she was cheating on Kara. Which was ridiculous. They were just friends. But clearly the physical pull was alive and well. Trying to deny it was like swimming against a riptide.

The jury was still out on this friendship plan of hers.

She took a ticket at the deli counter and waited her turn. Tonight was Will's work dinner. It'd been on the calendar for months. She wanted to beg out of it, but he wanted her there. It was the least she could do, considering the way she'd been acting.

As she placed her order, her phone buzzed. It was a voice mail from Ethan. Pressing the phone against her ear, she tried to understand his message. A siren blared in the background and the line was full of static. His voice cut in and out, making the message garbled.

"Dani, it's Ethan...wanted...Kara was in...accident...really bad. We're on our way...UWMC now. She...unconscious..."

The message cut off.

Dani stopped breathing and stared at her phone. Kara was in an accident? And it was bad? Her hands shook as she called him back. It went straight to voice mail. "Damn it!" Her heart slammed against her rib cage. It had to be a motorcycle accident. And he said it was really bad.

Motorcycle accidents could be deadly. What if she was seriously injured? Dani's world tilted upside down. She pushed the cart to the side and ran through the store. When she got into her car, she floored it out of the parking lot.

She pounded the steering wheel at every red light. Tears slipped from her eyes as she thought of Kara lying in the hospital, possibly dying. *She can't die, she just can't.*

This was punishment for Dani caring so deeply about her. For Dani cheating on Will with the kisses and sexual thoughts and dreams. For wanting to touch her constantly. For wanting to be friends and so much more. For being...

Dani stopped breathing. She was locked in traffic at a red light when her mind completed the thought. In love. She was in love. Oh God. She rested her forehead against the steering wheel. She was in love. And it wasn't with Will. It was supposed to be with Will. That was her destiny. It's what everybody wanted. But she was in love with Kara. And now she was probably losing her before they even had a chance.

Dani pulled into the hospital parking lot, not even bothering to park in a spot. She frantically ran through the doors leading to the emergency room, past the startled guard, and headed for the front desk.

The nurse on duty recognized her. "Dr. Clark, are you okay?"

Dani gulped in some much-needed air. "Kara Britton, accident, she was brought in a while ago?"

The nurse sensed the urgency. "Let me check. She was admitted twenty minutes ago. They put her in nine."

Dani ran down the corridor. When she arrived at room nine, she pulled back the curtain and was greeted by an empty bed with bloodstains on the pillow. She put a fist in her mouth, biting back a scream. Was she too late? Silent tears tracked down her face. She was one second away from collapsing onto the mattress sobbing when someone walked into the room.

"Hey, Dani, when did you get here?"

She turned and found Ethan with a smile on his face, eating a protein bar. She wiped her eyes and grabbed his arm. "Am I too late?"

"Too late for what?" He covered her hand. "Are you okay?"

"Is she...gone?" She bit her trembling lip.

"She's gone for a CT scan, if that's what you mean."

"What?"

"They took her down for a CT scan."

"She's alive?"

"Of course she's alive. The scan is precautionary. You know the drill."

She punched him because she didn't know what else to do. "You said it was really bad in your message!"

"Ow." He grabbed his arm. "I said I didn't think it was really too bad. She hit her head against the window, and it knocked her out for a few minutes. I guess they'll keep her overnight since she lost consciousness."

Dani punched him again. "I thought she died!" Emotions welled up inside, and try as she might, she couldn't stop the new flow of tears. Tears of relief. Tears of joy.

"It's okay." He embraced her.

She clung to him, sobbing.

"She's gonna be fine. She'll be back any second." He stroked her hair.

After a couple of minutes, Dani pulled back and wiped her face. "What happened?"

"Guy ran a red light and plowed into the front end of her van. Could've been a lot worse. She was lucky. Another couple of feet and they would have hit her square in the driver's side door. Then we'd be having a different conversation."

Dani thanked every deity she knew for those couple of feet that kept the damage to a minimum. She took a tissue from the box on the table next to the bed and blew her nose. She took another one and wiped at her eyes. "I'm gonna go to the bathroom and clean myself up. Thanks for calling me."

"No problem. I didn't know who else to call, and I wanted someone to be here for her. I'm heading out. You sure you're okay?"

Her lips quivered into a small smile. "I am now."

Dani ran into ladies' room down the hall. Turning the cold water on, she splashed her face repeatedly and patted it dry with paper towels. Another glance and she looked almost back to normal. She leaned on the sink and breathed. Breathed glorious air into her lungs. Her pulse slowed.

Kara was alive. She was *alive*. The anguish of the past half hour had drained her. She took one more deep breath, held it, and blew it out. She was in love. And now her life became a lot more complicated. Pushing all troubling thoughts aside, she left the restroom. She needed to see Kara now. She'd worry about these newly revealed feelings later.

When she arrived at room nine, Kara was back and talking on the phone.

"Val, I'm fine. No, stay there, we have a lot of kennel dogs right now. Call the insurance company for the van…okay…I'll talk to you later."

When the conversation ended, Dani pulled aside the curtain.

Kara glanced up, surprised. "Dani?"

"Hey." She walked over and touched the bandage on Kara's left temple.

"What are you doing here?"

"Ethan called me. How do you feel?" Dani grabbed Kara's wrist and took her pulse. She needed to keep touching her.

"I have a headache, but I'll live. The van is totaled, though. Thank God I didn't have any dogs in it."

Dani was satisfied with Kara's heart rate and perused her chart. "You have a concussion. Does anything else hurt?"

"My shoulder's sore. I guess I'll feel more tomorrow."

"Well, I'm gonna stay with you for a couple hours."

"I'm sure you have better things to do on a Saturday than hang in a hospital with a cranky patient."

"I don't, so you're stuck with me. And if I didn't have a dinner thing with Will, I'd stay all night to make sure you're okay."

"That would've been sweet, but totally unnecessary. I'm gonna be fine. But are *you* okay? You look like you've been crying."

"I thought you died." Dani tried to hide the small tremor in her voice. And failed.

"Why'd you think I died?"

"Ethan's message was muddled, and it sounded like you were hurt really bad, and I thought you were on your motorcycle—"

"Oh, the killing machine."

"Yes! I thought you were dead." Even saying it hypothetically cut her to the bone and made her heart ache.

"And you cried?"

Dani leaned her elbows on the side rails of the hospital bed and rested her chin on her hands. "Shut up. You would've done the same."

Kara cocked a playful eyebrow. "I don't know. I mean, it would've saved me five training lessons."

Dani smirked. "I'm gonna hurt you."

"You can't. It goes against your Hippocratic oath or something."

The nurses came in to move Kara to a room on the third floor. She signed admittance paperwork and they wheeled her away, Dani by her side the whole time. When they had her settled, Kara closed her eyes and groaned.

"What?" Dani pulled a chair over to the bedside.

"I've never liked hospitals."

"Because of your mom?"

"Yeah."

"You've never been admitted before?"

"Once when I was six. I had my tonsils out."

Dani's brows creased. "You had your tonsils removed when you were six?"

Before their conversation could continue, a nurse came back in to check her pulse and blood pressure.

After she left, Kara yawned. "God. I'm tired."

"Hey, close your eyes," Dani said. "I'll be right here if you need me."

As Kara nodded off, Dani settled in the chair next to her. Soon, she was sound asleep. Dani caressed every inch of her with her eyes. She slipped a hand into Kara's and fought the urge to lean down and kiss her. Instead, she pulled her legs into her chest and left her hand entwined with Kara's.

Her thoughts wandered to Will, and a nervous knot twisted in her belly. It was time to come clean with him. She had to find the strength to tell him how she felt, because no matter what would become of her feelings for Kara, and whether those feelings were reciprocated, she wasn't in love with him, and he needed to know that. She fought to keep a fresh set of tears from falling. It was going to be an awful conversation, but it had to be done. She'd do it after dinner.

* * *

When they got home from the dinner, Dani headed straight to the kitchen to get a glass of water. She needed to wash down the lump of anxiety that had formed in her throat on the drive home. Her feelings for Kara had simmered below the surface all evening, threatening to erupt. It took all she had to smile and make small talk with Will's colleagues. And now it was time to pay the piper.

After letting Oliver outside, Will took off his suit coat and turned on the TV to catch up on the day's sports.

Dani gulped down the water and placed the glass in the sink. She grabbed the countertop and took a few deep breaths. When she felt strong enough, she wandered into the living room and sat next to Will. "I need to talk to you."

"What's up?"

Dani rubbed at the cushion, trying to come up with the right words. "Can you turn off the TV?"

Will punched the power button on the remote and leaned forward, his elbows on his knees. "What's wrong?"

"I have to tell you something. And it's not easy."

He grabbed her hands. "What is it?"

She had a hard time meeting his eyes, knowing what she was about to say would cause him so much pain.

"Hey. Please tell me what's wrong," he pleaded.

When she finally had the strength to meet his gaze, the words came out in a rush. "I can't marry you."

His mouth dropped open and a few seconds of silence ensued. "What? What do you mean?"

Dani repeated the words, only this time they came out more measured. "I can't marry you."

He dropped her hands and stood. In a daze, he paced around in small circles. "I don't understand. I know you've been distant lately. For months. Hell, maybe for the past year. But…I thought it was the pressure from work." He sank to his knees in front of her. "Don't you love me?" His voice cracked from emotion.

A queasiness took hold in her gut. She did love him. She just wasn't *in* love with him. "Of course I love you." *Tell him!* Her voice was low and tinged with sadness. "I'm not…*in* love with you."

Will sank back onto his heels. He ran a shaky hand through his hair. "You're not…in love with me anymore?"

Time to rip the Band-Aid off. "I don't know if I ever was." Once those words escaped, somewhere deep inside was relief. A weight was lifted.

He took a seat on the couch while his eyes filled with tears. "How can you say that? We're great together. Everyone thinks we're great together. Harry and Sally. Best friends."

"Yes, we're best friends." She took a deep breath and rubbed at the sudden pain in her temples. "Sometimes, I feel it's all we've ever been. We've never had an all-consuming passion for each other. And if you marry someone, you have to be consumed by them." Dani paused and thought of Kara. "You have to tame them," she whispered.

Will wiped at the moisture in his eyes. "I love you. And I know I'm not perfect, but I thought…we were perfect together."

Dani tried desperately to make him understand. "Do I make you happy? Are you truly happy?"

When he didn't answer, she reached for his hand. "Will." He pulled away from her, pain etched on his face.

His lips set in a hard line. "Is there someone else?"

Dani opened her mouth, but no sound came out. She couldn't find her voice, and her silence screamed complicity.

Finally, a tear escaped, trickling down his cheek. "It's Kara, isn't it?"

His question caught her off-guard. "What?"

"I saw the way you looked at her at paintball. And the dog lesson the other day, you never just put perfume on."

His accusations hit the mark, and Dani flinched. She reached out again. "Will, I—"

"No, don't." He backed away.

He was defeated. Beaten down. Wounded. The look of betrayal in his eyes was devastating. She'd known him since high school. He'd been a part of her life for almost fifteen years, and this ripped her apart, inflicting so much pain upon him. Part of her wanted him to yell and scream, but he just stood there. Maybe the yelling would come later. Maybe the anger would be there tomorrow.

He shot off the couch and grabbed his car keys. "I gotta get out of here." He opened the door and walked out, leaving her alone to wrestle with her guilty conscience.

CHAPTER TWENTY-NINE

"We broke up." Dani brushed by a stationary Zoey in the doorway. The emotional upheaval from the previous evening had kept her up all night and she was exhausted. Six in the morning was an ungodly hour for a visit, but she knew her besties would forgive her.

Zoey turned slowly, shutting the door. "Oh, shit." She walked to the bottom of the staircase. "Babe! Downstairs, now!" She went to Dani and embraced her. "Are you okay?"

"I don't know. I don't know."

A sleepy Jen joined them in the kitchen, and Dani recounted the events of the previous day. She left out the part about being in love. It was something she wanted to keep to herself for now.

"What are you gonna do?" Jen asked.

That was the question of the day, wasn't it? What the hell would she do now? "I don't know."

"Is Kara okay?" Zoey asked.

"Yeah. She's going home today."

"Are you gonna go check on her?"

Dani chewed on her bottom lip. "Should I?"

"You were there with her yesterday. Might be nice if you checked on her."

Jen agreed.

"I guess I could head over there this afternoon." Dani gazed off into the distance. "What a shitty night." She covered her face with her hands, trying not to relive every awful moment. But she couldn't. It was on a constant loop in her brain.

Jen patted Dani's arm. "Hang with us this morning. We can watch movies and snuggle on the couch."

* * *

Val picked Kara up from the hospital and delivered her back to the farmhouse. They walked through the front door and were surprised to find a welcoming committee consisting of Jolie, Travis, and Jesmyn.

Jolie jumped to her feet and hugged her. "My God, how are you feeling?"

"Ouch. Sore ribs."

"Sorry." Jolie petted Kara's arm in sympathy.

Travis fist-bumped her and waved a video game. *We'll play.*

Jesmyn shook her head. "You're lucky it's just sore ribs and a concussion."

"Thanks for being here, guys," Kara said.

"I made some meals for you and put them in the fridge," Mother Hen Jolie said.

"Thanks. Sorry, I'm sure I look like hell." Kara self-consciously patted her hair.

Jolie continued clucking over her. "You're fine. Nobody expects you to look your best after a night in the hospital."

"You were just in a car accident, we don't expect you to look fresh as a daisy," Val said.

"Yeah, you ain't Wonder Woman, lady," Jesmyn said. "You can look as bad as you want for a few days. We won't judge you."

Kara hoped she would be back to normal sooner than a few days. She could use a shower, but her energy level was low.

Just relaxing on the couch was the only thing on her mind. And hanging with her close friends.

They fussed over her, and she relished the attention. The kittens made themselves comfortable on her lap, purring and kneading. Closing her eyes, she sighed with contentment, feeling loved.

There was a telltale buzz of an incoming text. After a few seconds, someone cleared their throat and a hand touched Kara's shoulder. She opened her eyes to find Jolie leaning over her.

"Um, Kara?"

Kara smiled, feeling relaxed and unmotivated. "Yeah?"

"Why don't I comb your hair for you? Maybe you'd feel better if I combed your hair."

Kara knitted her brows. "Why do I need my hair combed? I'm not going anywhere. I'm supposed to take it easy, right?"

Val poked at Kara's head. "Don't be silly. You need your hair combed. I'm having trouble even looking at you right now."

Her poking snagged a tangle. "Ouch." Kara rubbed her scalp.

Travis pinched his nose, then signed, *You smell. Take shower.*

"Shower? You all just told me I was fine."

"Well, that was before we smelled you." Jesmyn shushed the kittens away and dragged her from the couch.

"Why do I need to shower?"

"You look awful." Val joined Jesmyn in ushering Kara to the bathroom. "C'mon, let's get you showered."

"But I just came home from the hospital."

Val shook her head. "That's no excuse for poor hygiene. Next thing you know, you'll be sleeping under some bridge in the city."

They pulled her into the bathroom while Jolie looked on anxiously from the hallway.

Val turned on the water as Jesmyn started removing Kara's clothes. They had her naked and in the shower in record time.

"Do you need me to wash your hair?" Val asked.

"Can't I just rinse off? I don't feel like doing my hair," Kara called from behind the curtain. "Where's my shower cap?" She blindly waved at the hook by the shower. When she came up empty, she pulled back the curtain and saw Val toss the cap to Jesmyn, who snapped it rubber-band style across the bedroom to Jolie, who caught it and passed it to Travis, who ran back into the living room. "Hey. Gimme that back."

"No. Wash your hair. It smells."

What the hell is this all about? With a shake of her head, she closed the curtain. Now that her hair was wet, she may as well wash it.

Val yanked the shower curtain open and threw Kara's toothbrush at her, hitting her square in the chest. "Ow."

"Brush your teeth!" The shower curtain was yanked back into place.

Was her breath really that bad? "I need the—" Before she could finish, a tube of Colgate was tossed in. She had no clue what had gotten into everyone. She thought it was in her best interest to just brush her damn teeth, wash her damn hair, and get the hell out of the shower before she sustained another injury.

When Kara was done, Jolie pulled her toward the bed. "Which outfit do you like?"

"I just wanna put my sweatpants on. I don't feel like getting dressed."

"Don't be a slob," Val said. "You've got company."

"What happened to, 'You're lucky to be alive, Kara, just relax, Kara, nobody cares what you look like, Kara.'? What happened to that?"

After much arguing back and forth, Kara ended up in one of her nicer pairs of sweatpants and a green hoodie. She shuffled back to the living room and plopped on the couch, exhausted from the added exertion.

Travis burst through the front door and made googly eyes at Jolie.

Kara still had no clue what had gotten into everyone, but she was thankful for the company, even if they were all acting like whack jobs. "Maybe we could all eat some of the stuff that Jolie brought over." When she was met with silence, she glanced around.

"Can't, sorry. Got a go." Jesmyn put her jacket on.

"We gotta thing," Val added. "Later!"

"A thing?" Kara asked. "What thing?" But they were already gone.

Jolie bustled Travis toward the door. "Travis has a soccer game."

"I thought his season was over?"

"No, this is…another season. Summer league."

"He never played summer league before. Send me the schedule so I can see some games."

"It's only one game." Jolie grabbed her purse and yanked Travis out the door.

"What kind of league only has one game?"

"We're late. I'll talk to you later."

And before she knew it, Kara was alone. She found it hard to believe how quickly they all deserted her. Her bottom lip jutted out in a pout. Sitting by herself seemed unappealing and lonely. As she wallowed in a shallow pool of self-pity, the doorbell rang.

The dogs whined and barked.

Maybe Val and Jesmyn came back to keep her company. When she opened the door, her heart jumped into her throat.

"Hi. I wanted to check on you, so I thought I'd stop by," Dani said. "The gang seemed to be in a rush to get out of here. What happened? Are you grumpy?" she asked with hands on hips.

"No, I'm not grumpy. They all just got up and left."

Dani walked past her and stood in the foyer as the dogs demanded her attention. "Hi, boys. You guys missed me, didn't you? Good boys." She squatted down and hugged them both, and promptly got pushed to the ground by their exuberance.

"Hey, boys, that's enough," Kara scolded. "Calm down."

"They can't help it if they love me."

Kara gave her a hand up off the floor, and Dani pulled her in for a hug. Kara melted into her, ignoring the pain in her ribs for this small bit of intimacy, holding the hug way past standard hug time. She was obviously in a weakened state, what with the concussion and all. And Dani was comfortable.

Dani stepped out of the hug and Kara missed her immediately.

"Okay, where are those kittens? I see one, and there's the other one, and oh, what's he got in his mouth? Is that a shower cap?" Dani pried it out of the kitten's mouth and held it up. "Is this yours?"

Kara's eyes swept to the left, hiding her embarrassment. "Maybe?"

"It has ducks on it."

"So?" Kara grabbed the cap and shoved it in her pocket.

Dani giggled. "Nice shower cap."

"You're my doctor. You're not supposed to make fun of me."

"True. I apologize. It just kinda quacked me up."

Kara tried hard not to laugh. "Is that supposed to be funny?" She secretly loved goofy Dani.

Dani kept a straight face. "Yes, Karen. It was supposed to be funny."

The Karen comment cracked them both up.

"Okay, enough," Dani said. "Let's get quacking. Come here, kittens, let me see how big you got." She picked up the closest one, kissing him on the cheek and getting a paw to the face for her trouble. "Kara, please introduce me."

Kara bit her lip and put a hand behind her neck to rub at an imaginary crick. "That's, um, Thumper."

"You named him Thumper? You used my favorite name!" She hugged the kitten tighter and got another swat on the nose.

"Well, he likes to thump you, so it fits."

Dani released Thumper and snatched the other one. "And who's this handsome fellow?"

"Tigger." Kara felt her cheeks grow warm with a blush.

"Tigger? You used both of my favorite names!"

She held the kitten to her cheek, and Kara swore Dani's eyes filled up. She must be hallucinating. Surely the kittens' names wouldn't have such an effect on Dani's tear ducts.

"I feel honored you used those names." After greeting all the animals, she turned her attention back to Kara. "How you doing?"

"I have a headache, my ribs are sore, and my neck hurts. Other than that, I'm good."

"Did you take anything for the headache?"

"They gave me some Motrin before I left the hospital, but it's not working. I feel tired, and the light hurts my eyes."

"That's a by-product of your concussion. It might take a while for those symptoms to go away."

"I feel like lying on the couch and not getting up, to be honest."

"Well, go ahead, lie down. Better yet, here. I know some pressure points for headaches." Dani sat on the couch and patted the empty space next to her. "Lie down and put your head in my lap."

Kara tried to comprehend what Dani asked her to do. Does one hear things while concussed also? Because lying with her head in Dani's lap, while incredibly, unbelievably appealing, seemed like crossing the imaginary friendship line.

Dani was having none of it. "Come on. Lie down. I don't bite."

Kara weighed her options. Should she? Surely, refusing would be rude. Dani was trying to help. Dani was her doctor, at least she was last night. That must've carried over into today. "Okay, if you think it'll help."

"It might. C'mon."

Kara sat on the couch, situated herself properly, and slowly put her head into Dani's lap.

"Close your eyes."

Kara did as she was told. Dani's fingers danced gently over her face, and Kara sighed. The touch was so tender it was almost heartbreaking because it was what a lover would do. And Dani was not her lover. Would probably never be her lover.

Now Dani's fingertips were pressing under her eyebrows, and Kara felt relief from the pain in her head. Those magic fingers moved to her temple and applied the same pressure, and Kara felt her body relaxing into the touch. A sense of peace and comfort settled over her. Could she lie here forever? She wanted to. Her mind slowly drifted off, all thoughts evaporating, save for one. She was in heaven, and Dani was her angel.

Kara's eyes slowly blinked open, her body feeling warm and cozy. When she realized where she was, she gave a start.

"You're okay. I've got you." Dani stroked Kara's back.

"How long was I asleep?"

"An hour."

"Sorry. That must've been uncomfortable." She struggled to get up, but Dani was adamant, pushing her gently back down.

"Relax. How's your head feel?"

Kara gave up the ghost and collapsed back into Dani's lap. Who was she to argue with an attractive woman? Especially one Dani Clark, haunter of dreams and thief of hearts. She turned toward the TV. "It feels better, thank you. What are we watching? Is that *Butch Cassidy and the Sundance Kid*?"

Dani grinned. "Can you believe it? I had to watch it."

"Of course you did." Kara turned her attention back to the TV. Dani rubbed a hand up and down Kara's arm. She was taken aback by Dani's affection. Perhaps she treated all her patients like this. In her current condition, Kara was not about to complain. It felt so comforting, so right.

"This was my gram's favorite movie."

"Really?" Kara stared into blue eyes full of tenderness. She fought the urge to pull Dani down to her lips. She was probably just seeing things again, things that weren't there, things she would never see.

Dani's phone rang and she made no move to look at it as it lay on the coffee table. The call went to voice mail.

"Do you need to get that?"

Dani sighed. "I guess." She grabbed the phone. Her mom's voice was loud and agitated.

"Dani, where are you? Will's mom called and said you two broke up, what's going on? Why haven't you called us? The wedding is coming up soon, you probably just have cold feet. Everyone has been working so hard planning this, you can't just call it off. Now get back to me immediately so we can fix this."

Kara jolted upright and moved to the other side of the couch. With knees pulled tight to her chest, she stammered, "You…you broke up?"

Dani's body stiffened and she took a moment to answer. "Yeah."

"When?"

"Last night."

"Were you gonna tell me?"

"I was…I needed a little time."

Kara bit her bottom lip and nodded. She wouldn't be too keen to shout out she was breaking off a three-year engagement either. A tiny voice in her head whispered, *Dani is available*. And then, somewhere inside, a sprig of hope. A small seed planted deep in her heart. Would she have a chance with Dani now? And if not now, someday?

Dani's mouth pinched with worry. "I think I have to deal with this."

"Yeah. You gotta talk to her."

Dani rose from the couch, and Kara followed her to the door. She said goodbye to each animal, bestowing a kiss on each one. When it was Kara's turn for a goodbye, she hugged her. "Make sure you get plenty of rest. I need time to process all this. So, if you don't hear from me, I'm not purposefully ignoring you or anything like that, okay?" She pulled back to gauge Kara's reaction.

"Sure. I understand. I'll be here if you need to talk."

With eyes full of warm emotion, Dani gently cupped her face. "I know where to find you."

Kara watched her walk to the car. She leaned against the doorjamb, staring down the empty driveway long after Dani had left. The seed in her heart? Just sprouted.

CHAPTER THIRTY

Over the next few days, Kara's headaches subsided. Her sensitivity to light stayed, so she limited her driving.

Kara found she spent time with Oliver when he was at day care because it was a tenuous connection to Dani, whom she hadn't heard from since the day she left. Countless texts were written and never sent, just stared at and deleted.

The first week she remained hopeful. Hopeful Dani would find her way back.

As the next couple of weeks slipped by, she began doubting the signals she saw that day, the look in Dani's eyes, the touch goodbye, the affection. A decision was made. It was in her best interest to stop obsessing over it, best to save herself the pain and heartache. If Dani wanted her, Dani knew where to find her. So she took the seedling in her heart, tucked it away in a dark place, and shut the door.

* * *

A few weeks later, Kara sat on the couch, glasses on, laptop perched on her lap. One kitten snuggled in her lap, and the other pawed at her hands on the keyboard. The dogs whined and ran to the front door.

"What's up, buddies?"

Milo pawed at the door while Ziggy barked.

She walked over. A shadowy figure stood off to the side, so she threw open the door. Her heart completely stopped beating. It was Dani, standing with hands in the back pockets of her jeans, looking sexy and beautiful. All the hard work of trying to put Dani on the back burner flew out the window. The seedling in her heart moved into the light. And she may have watered it. "Dani."

"Hey."

The dogs twisted around her in joy. "I see my dogs still love me."

Kara wanted to shout that they weren't the only ones. "C'mon in."

"Where are my kittens?" Both padded over, rubbing against her legs and purring. She scratched under their chins, laughing when they rolled over onto their backs at the same time.

Kara couldn't quite read the vibe Dani gave off, but something was different. Did she get back together with Will?

"I love those glasses on you." Dani continued to pet the kittens. "They're very sexy."

Kara quietly accepted the compliment. She waited patiently for her to say more, feeling certain she didn't drive all the way here to tell her she looked sexy in glasses. Although that would've been kind of romantic. Dani's perfume wafted around the room, and Kara felt *weak*.

Dani wandered to the fireplace, inspecting the pictures on the mantel. "I tried," she said softly.

Kara had to strain to hear her. She waited for more, but the silence continued. "Tried what?"

"I tried to stay away."

"Stay away from what?" Kara held her breath.

"You." She turned, and their eyes finally met. "I tried to stay away from you." She walked over to the window and stared outside, her back to Kara. "I know Will and I broke up a few weeks ago. And I should take some time to be alone."

Kara continued to hold her breath.

"And I know I shouldn't drag you into this mess of a life I have right now. But..." She sighed. "I got in my car today. I wanted to drive, somewhere, anywhere, just to get away. It was like I blacked out until I was at your door." Dani faced Kara again, her eyes full of emotion. "I get it, if it's too much to handle, me showing up like this, so feel free to tell me to leave."

Kara exhaled. Her heart pounded. The first thought was that Dani came back. Dani couldn't stay away. She tried to tamp down the joy growing exponentially in her heart. She tried to play it cool, but the way Dani looked right now, eyes soft and vulnerable, ripped at her insides. Now Kara was the one who couldn't stay away, and she slowly walked over to her. When she was close enough, she rested her forehead against Dani's. A slight tilt of her head and her nose brushed Dani's. "I'm glad you're here," she murmured.

"I missed you." It was Dani's turn to brush their noses, her mouth slightly open. "I tried not to miss you." Her mouth remained open and moved dangerously close to Kara's lips. "So, just to summarize," she said slowly. "I tried to stay away, and I tried not to miss you. And failed miserably."

With Dani's lips so tantalizingly close, Kara's chest tightened, making it hard to breathe. "I should have dared you to come back." Her mouth ached to move closer. Was it possible to be this close and not touching? "I should have said, 'Dani Clark, I dare you to come see me.'"

"Ah." Dani's mouth quivered. "This is all your fault, then." Her bottom lip jutted out, brushing against Kara's.

Kara never wanted anybody as much as she wanted Dani. The hunger consumed her. She needed this now. Right fucking now. "I dare you to kiss me."

The tiny space between their mouths disappeared as Dani pressed moist lips to Kara's. Both exhaled into the other's mouth, groaning with pleasure. Their lips moved in tandem, opening at the same time as tongues explored and entwined. For the first time there was no rush, no worry of interruptions. No guilt. The pace was leisurely, each content to explore. Lips and tongues melded perfectly together as they teased and searched, reacquainting themselves with each other's rhythm.

Kara's hands wandered down Dani's back and pulled her close. Dani's leg slipped between hers and Kara ground against it to soothe the sweet ache at the top of her thighs. Her mouth trailed down Dani's neck, teeth nipping and tongue soothing.

Dani pulled back. With seductive eyes, she pulled off her jacket, dropping it on the chair. She walked toward the bedroom, stopping long enough to remove her shoes. Next came the sweater, leaving her in a tank top and jeans. She crooked a finger at Kara to encourage pursuit.

Kara almost fainted. Because this was a dream come to life, Dani beckoning her, stripping down, and leading her to the promised land. She may have whimpered. A pathetic sound she hoped Dani didn't hear. Throwing her glasses on the table, she took off, her stocking feet slipping on the wood flooring. She righted herself and grabbed Dani's outstretched hand at the entrance to the bedroom. Kicking back with her leg, she shut the door.

Dani jammed her against the closed door and brought her mouth to Kara's for another knee-knocking kiss. She broke it off and continued leading her by the hand toward the bed. "Let me warn you, I'm pretty good at this."

Kara had no clue how she managed to put one foot in front of the other. "Well, we did establish you're a good kisser."

She leaned into Kara's ear. "I'm not talking about kissing."

Kara's brows shot up and a shiver traveled along her spine. A sly smile made its way to her lips. "Well. I'm pretty good too."

Dani leered. "I guess we're about to find out"—she moved in to kiss her again—"who's better."

It sounded like a win-win to Kara. She put her hands behind Dani's head to bring her closer. "I accept that challenge." She gave Dani a featherlight kiss. Anticipation flowed through her veins, pumping out in every direction. Kara's chest heaved and the ache low in her belly threatened to unhinge her. The thought of finally touching Dani was almost too much to bear.

Dani's arms encircled her neck as she pulled Kara in for another passionate, furious kiss. When they broke apart, Dani whipped Kara's hoodie off, tossing it aside. She ran a hand over the soft red T-shirt underneath, her breath hitching when she discovered Kara was braless. The T-shirt hit the ground seconds later.

Dani stepped back. "You're so beautiful." She cupped Kara's breasts as her mouth found its way back to Kara's. While she busied herself with Kara's luscious bottom lip, her thumbs rolled over Kara's nipples, tweaking and circling.

Kara moaned, and her hands slipped under Dani's shirt to wander over bare skin. The heat between her legs was like an inferno, her underwear unbearably wet. She resisted the urge to put Dani's hand down her pants, so Dani could feel what she was doing to her. All in due time. But she did need everything off soon or she'd die from sexual frustration.

Thankfully, Dani was on the same page, as her hands left Kara's nipples and trailed down her belly, coming to a stop at the button of her jeans, which came open with the flick of a finger. Dani began kissing and lightly sucking on Kara's neck as her hand continued downward, slipping under cotton undies, heading straight down to the motherlode. The sounds that came out of their mouths were animal-like.

Dani pulled at the zipper of Kara's jeans.

Kara's breathing became ragged. "Oh God." Her legs were ready to give out. Before she fell into a heap on the floor, she needed Dani in some state of undress, so she pulled off the tank. And there was the light-blue bra. Kara's eyes glazed over, and her hands instinctively went to Dani's breasts, cupping them and caressing them through the lacy fabric, the nipples already peaking and stiff. She recalled in vivid detail all the dreams that haunted her these past few months.

"These really are spectacular." Kara wished she could've made that sound sexier, but she needed to verbalize her appreciation, and her mind was too clouded with lust to come up with something better.

It was time for the unveiling. She held her breath, and with a shaky hand lifted a strap and slowly slid it down Dani's shoulder. The other one soon followed.

Dani shrugged out of the bra and tossed it on the floor.

Here they were, in all their glory, ripe and oh so lush, begging for attention. Kara wanted to pinch herself to make sure she wasn't dreaming. Instead, she pinched an already engorged nipple, rolling it between her thumb and forefinger while Dani hissed with pleasure. Her other hand went to the other breast, not wanting it to feel left out, and she repeated the same motion, rolling, pinching, pulling. It still wasn't enough for Kara, so she bent her head down, and her mouth latched onto one, then the other, her lips sucking and her tongue flicking.

Dani brought Kara's lips back to hers. Her mouth was hungry, taking all Kara had to give, while her hands grabbed Kara's jeans and hiked them down. Kara removed her socks and ruined panties.

Dani quickly shed her own pants and underwear and they both stood close, each devouring the other with their eyes. Dani stepped forward, nudging Kara down onto the bed.

Kara collapsed onto the mattress and watched as Dani crawled over her, laying her body completely on top of Kara, nipples brushing nipples. Dani kissed her again, sending Kara's senses into a tailspin. She was ready to burst, so she tried to slow her breathing down and prolong the pleasure, not wanting to come undone so soon like some teenage boy.

"How am I doing so far?" Dani's lips made their way down Kara's neck, her tongue gliding over her pulse point.

Kara's heart pumped violently against her ribs as Dani sucked greedily at the base of her throat. "Not bad," Kara said breathlessly, not ready to crown a winner just yet.

By the time Dani made it down to her breasts, Kara was adrift, her body floating. *Oh God*s slipped repeatedly from her lips and Dani's tongue on her nipples drove her completely insane. It wouldn't take much more to send her spiraling over the edge.

Dani's hand reached between her legs and a loud groan escaped Kara's lips. She fought for control, because God help her, she wanted to feel Dani's mouth on her. Her legs fell apart invitingly, and she pleaded, "I'm so close, please—"

She was cut off by the sensation of Dani's mouth licking and sucking its way across her belly and finally traveling south. Kara gasped as Dani's finger circled her opening, and she was not ashamed to raise her hips, encouraging Dani to slip that finger inside.

Dani was only too happy to oblige. Her finger plunged inside. Soon her tongue found Kara's clit, and she stroked it. A second finger slipped inside, and Kara bucked her hips in time with Dani's fingers, meeting each thrust with her own.

Kara panted quiet expletives, finding it hard to take a deep breath. A few more seconds and she would completely lose it. "Oh fuck, fuck." Suddenly, she was free-falling. Bright lights exploded behind her closed eyes as the orgasm ricocheted through her body. She called out Dani's name with each pulsating wave. It stretched on forever with an astounding intensity. Kara felt like she was breaking apart at the seams. Finally, the last wave subsided, and the jackhammering of her heart slowed.

Her hands tangled in red hair while she tried to catch her breath. But Dani had other ideas. Her tongue continued to swirl, and she coaxed another from her, this one sharper and shorter but just as satisfying. When the throbbing inside finally stopped, Kara melted into the sheets. Her eyes stared at the ceiling. She couldn't move any of her limbs but did manage a slight nod of her head. Yep, Dani was damn good at this.

Dani slowly made her way back to Kara's mouth, kissing across her stomach, over her breasts, across her collarbone, covering areas she missed on the way down. One last deep kiss and she slid off to the side, lying full length against Kara's body. She put her head in her hand and lightly trailed a finger across Kara's chest, circling her nipple playfully. "You okay?"

Kara smiled and traced a finger along Dani's lips. "Yeah." She wanted to declare her feelings, wanted to tell the whole world. But she didn't. It was only their first time together, and she didn't want to be that person who shouted out their love while in the throes of passion. There would be plenty of time for declarations.

* * *

Dani nibbled on Kara's earlobe. "Has anybody ever told you that you have adorable ears." She sucked it into her mouth and thrilled at the tiny squeak of pleasure that fell from Kara's lips.

"It's usually the first thing I hear." Kara began kissing Dani's jawline. "Many women have complimented me on my ears."

"Is that so? Many women?" Dani pinched a nipple.

Kara flinched and chuckled. "Now, these." She fondled Dani's breasts. "They've starred in many of my dreams."

"Mm-hmm." Dani's eyes squeezed shut. "How often did you dream about me?"

"Every fucking night. At least it felt like every night." Her tongue teased Dani's rose-colored nipples.

She gasped and ran her hands through Kara's hair. "We may have to re-create all our dreams."

"That could take all week."

"Sounds good to me." Dani rolled on top of Kara, pushing her onto her back. "So, tell me, Miss Britton, how was I?" She lightly kissed her neck.

Kara became pensive. "I've had better."

Dani pulled back in a panic. "What?"

She was met by teasing green eyes and pursed lips. "I've had better."

Dani cocked a brow and one corner of her mouth lifted, as she played along. "I can do better." She nodded. "I know I can do better."

They laughed, remembering that fateful day in the bathroom at the golf course, each trying to best the other, each wanting to be crowned "top kisser."

Dani shook her head. "All I wanted to do was hate you. And it was impossible."

"Well, I'm impossible to hate. It's the ears." Kara rolled Dani over onto her back. "You were so sexy in your golf outfit." She kissed Dani's throat. "You were in my lap and your panties were soaked and I was dying I wanted you so bad."

Dani was amazed at how quickly aroused she became with Kara. These past few years sex had been uninteresting, more like a chore. But this, this was how sex was supposed to be. Passionate, consuming, life-altering…fucking mind-blowing. She cried out in pleasure when Kara's mouth tugged on an erect nipple. Dani's voice quivered with need. "Oh…that feels so good." Her hips had a mind of their own, pressing against Kara, begging for friction to ease the throbbing between her legs.

Kara's mouth was suddenly covering hers, and the kiss was so deep it made her toes curl. A hand traced down her stomach and teased at the top of her legs. The ache became unbearable, and she grabbed Kara's hand and pushed it lower. "I'm gonna scream if you don't touch me."

Fingers dove between Dani's legs, and she almost passed out with pleasure. She couldn't even kiss Kara back, she was too busy trying to breathe.

Kara's mouth left hers and she kissed her way down Dani's body, nipping at the soft skin under her breast, biting at the flesh around her hip bone. When she positioned herself between Dani's legs, Dani held her breath, desperate to feel Kara's tongue. And when it happened, she moaned, a primal sound emitting from deep inside her chest. She wasn't usually vocal during sex, but the sensations shooting through her body called for it.

Soon, her belly coiled into a tight ball and she shouted out her pleasure. Kara was gonna win this competition, and she didn't give a flying fuck. She was about to come. "Oh, my, fucking…yes!" Those elegant, beautiful fingers stroked inside, and Dani shattered into a million pieces.

CHAPTER THIRTY-ONE

Kara opened the door to the bathroom and leaned against the doorjamb. "Your dream come true, good doctor." She was barefoot and braless, hair hanging down around her shoulders, wearing jeans and a white see-through tank top.

Dani sank lower in the claw-foot tub. "Why don't you come over here?" She licked her lips.

Kara sauntered over to the edge of the tub.

With hungry eyes, Dani threaded a finger through a belt loop and gave a not-so-gentle tug. She was about to pull her zipper down when Kara splashed into the tub, fully clothed. A wave of water and bubbles cascaded onto the tile floor. Dani's laughter filled the room. "No, that wasn't the dream!"

"You said I got into the tub with you?" Kara pulled Dani toward her.

Dani cackled at the absurdity of Kara's actions. "I'm supposed to undress you."

"Why didn't you say so?" Kara was all smiles as she tugged Dani onto her lap and nibbled on her throat. Her hands kneaded Dani's ass.

With eyes closed in ecstasy, Dani sighed and melted into Kara. "I thought I did."

"I don't think so, Sundance. Nice hat, by the way."

Dani touched the duck-covered shower cap. "What? This old thing? You like it?"

"It's superhot, and it's making me super horny."

"I always say, nothing says sex like a duck-covered shower cap."

"Hmm, is that another one of your famous sayings?" Kara cupped Dani's face and kissed her, all dreams and hats soon forgotten. Their kisses were deep and wet, tongues probing and pressing. Their thirst for each other was unquenchable as their bodies writhed together in messy harmony.

"It's a shame you have so many clothes on, Butch." Dani began to grind into Kara's lap, trying to get herself off.

Kara groaned in exasperation. "I guess I didn't think this through." The sight of Dani grinding her hips, head thrown back in determination, made Kara's already wet jeans even wetter. Only Dani could look this hot in a duck-covered shower cap.

Her hand slipped between them, finding Dani's slicked-up opening.

Dani cried out while her hips jerked as she got closer to an orgasm. "I love those fingers of yours," she moaned. "First thing I noticed about you."

"Really?" Kara rubbed her forehead on Dani's chest to wipe away the perspiration. "Seems an odd thing to notice."

Dani moaned, finding just the right spot on Kara's jeans. "I have a thing for hands. Oh God…"

"Interesting." Kara ignored the cramp in her wrist as she continued to pleasure Dani. She floated on cloud nine. Or twelve. If there was a cloud twelve, she was on it now. Salty perspiration dotted between Dani's breasts, and she licked along her collarbone. Wrapping a free arm around Dani's waist, Kara held her tightly through her climax.

Dani's hands reached for Kara's shoulders as her body shuddered before collapsing onto Kara, spent. She inhaled deeply as her body came down off its high. "So good, so good…" she kept whispering.

Kara held her for a few minutes before dipping her hands into the tub and rinsing the sweat from Dani's back.

"That was good." Dani placed a chaste kiss on her lips.

Kara grinned. "I'm glad you enjoyed it. Meanwhile, I'm about to burst."

"That'll teach you to wear clothes in the bathtub."

"Dani…" she pleaded.

"What, baby? Are we a little frustrated?" She nipped Kara's ear, then ran her tongue behind it.

"I want you," Kara whispered. "Please."

"Take your pants off."

* * *

Later, Kara rested her head on Dani's shoulder, as tiny sparks of pleasure continued to ripple along her nerve endings.

With a deep, satisfied sigh, she contemplated her life up until this point. Was she even living before Dani? Before Dani, everything was in black and white, and now her world was in Technicolor, all blues and greens, reds and golds.

She buried her nose in Dani's hair, breathing in the fresh scent of her shampoo. "You're staying the night, right?"

"If you want me to."

"Yes, please." The thought of waking up next to Dani made her positively giddy. "What time do you have to leave tomorrow?"

"My shift starts at noon."

Kara's arms tightened around her. "Call in sick."

"Ugh. I can't."

Her hands began massaging Dani's breasts. She wanted to make love to her as many times as possible before she left. More water splashed on the floor as they eagerly reached for each other. Their journey just beginning.

* * *

Dani's eyes slowly opened to the moonlight leaking in from the edges of the curtains. It took a moment for the clock to come into focus. It was almost four a.m. Soon she'd have to find the strength to disentangle herself from this incredible woman wrapped in her arms right now. She placed a soft kiss on Kara's shoulder. What a night. The word spectacular didn't even do it justice. Epic, otherworldly, fantabulous. It was, without a doubt, the best sex of her life. The physical nature of her relationship with Will was not even close. Not even in the same stratosphere. Her heart and mind were so full of love, she almost cried.

Of course, a small dollop of dread existed somewhere in the pit of her stomach when she thought of telling her parents. Telling them about Kara.

Their reaction to the news of her first girlfriend in college was still fresh in her mind, even after all these years. On the day she graduated, Dani had declared she was moving to New York to be with Suzanne. At first her parents were in shock, then came the anger, the threats of cutting her off. Then came the pleading, telling her it was a phase. They used Gram Evelyn and her battle with Alzheimer's as an emotional bludgeon. Repeating how much her gram needed her, and how Dani had to stay in Seattle to be close with her. Eventually they wore Dani down. She'd enrolled in med school in Seattle and tried to carry on a long-distance relationship with Suzanne. It didn't end well.

She couldn't wait to lay this one on them. What a dreaded conversation that would be. It gave her a headache just thinking about it. And a tummy ache. She rubbed her belly, suddenly feeling queasy.

Dani crept from bed and into the hall bath where the queasiness turned into full-blown nausea. Staggering to the ground, she gripped the sides of the toilet and retched into the bowl.

When her stomach calmed down, she splashed water on her face. Fishing around under the sink, she found a new toothbrush and a tube of toothpaste and brushed her teeth. This was probably from all the stress of the last month, all the texts from her parents saying how she was ruining her life by not marrying Will.

At four thirty, she snuggled back against Kara.

* * *

When Dani woke again, it was eight a.m. Her mouth was dry, so she pulled on one of Kara's University of Oregon T-shirts and headed to the kitchen, four furry bodyguards hot on her heels. She stopped short, so short in fact that Ziggy banged into Milo, who banged into the back of Dani's legs, making her stumble forward. A frightened Tigger Halloween-kittied across the room, hissing. Thumper tangled in her legs and down she went, right onto her backside, T-shirt hiked up past her hips, lady bits on full display. She grabbed at the hem and yanked it down, trying in vain to maintain some semblance of dignity in front of an unexpected audience.

Val and Jesmyn sat at the kitchen table.

Dani quickly jumped to her feet, a hot flush creeping into her cheeks. "Uh, hi?"

Val's spoon was frozen somewhere in the middle between her mouth and the bowl. "Hey?"

Jesmyn folded the corner of the newspaper down and peeked around it, her expression giving away nothing.

Dani was at a loss for words as she gave another tug to the bottom of the shirt, trying desperately to drag it farther down her body. "Uh, I um...slept over. It was late. So, I slept over." She slowly backed up, embarrassed by the whole situation. "I'll just...head back." Her thirst could wait.

Their hushed voices followed her down the hallway.

"I thought I smelled sex," Jesmyn said.

"Kara's right. She does have a nice ass."

Dani slipped into the bedroom with the pet parade in tow. Pulling the shirt off, she crawled back into bed. Kara was on her stomach, lying diagonally across the bed, the sheet lying low across her hips, leaving her upper torso bare.

"You're actually here," Kara said with a sleepy smile. "I thought it was another dream."

Dani bent down and kissed her back. "Nope." She rolled onto her side, resting her head in her hand while leaning on her elbow, and traced a finger around the butterfly tattoo on Kara's back. "You never told me you had a tattoo. Does it have some sort of significance?"

"My mom loved butterflies."

Dani hopped from the bed and ran into Kara's bathroom. She was back in a flash with a tube of lipstick.

"What are you doing?"

"I'm drawing another one." She rolled the lipstick up and began to draw. Tigger jumped on the bed and pawed at Dani's hand, making a mess of the picture. "Oops. Tigger's helping."

"I can't see it."

"Hold on." Dani headed back to the bathroom and returned with a hand mirror.

Kara's brows rose. "I thought you said you could draw?"

"Tigger messed it up. Here, I'll show you how good an artist I am." She put the mirror down and continued to draw. When she was finished, she held the mirror up again to show two stick figures holding hands. "A portrait of us."

"That is quite possibly the worst portrait I've ever seen."

Dani pretended to be offended. "Hey! I won awards with this talent."

"When you were two?"

Dani giggled and placed the mirror on the nightstand. "You're very funny." She began kissing Kara's back again.

"What can I say? I'm funny, *and* I have cute ears."

"Someday I'll draw a proper portrait of you." Dani rested her head on Kara's back. "In charcoal. I used to love sketching in charcoal." She nibbled on the back of her neck. "Jesmyn and Val are here, by the way. I may have mooned them."

"I'm sure they enjoyed it. You do have a nice ass."

"Oh, they saw more than my ass, trust me. It was like an episode of 'Twat's That.'"

Kara burst out laughing. "Or 'Twat's My Line?'"

"Suffice to say, I was sufficiently humiliated. I told them we just had a sleepover."

Kara slowly shook her head. "That will not pass muster with Jesmyn. She's a super cop, in case you've forgotten."

"How could I forget?"

"Why do I fear the jig is up and the whole crew knows we had sex?"

"Ugh, you're probably right. I can hear the popcorn popping from here."

Kara rolled on top of Dani and kissed her neck while her hand wandered downward.

"What about Jesmyn and Val?" Dani asked.

"Shh." Her mouth began a slow exploration of Dani's breasts, tongue swirling around an already erect nipple.

"Won't they know what we're doing?"

"Of course. It's Jes." Her hand made its way down between Dani's legs.

"Oh, fuck," Dani said breathlessly.

Kara's lips hesitated. "Should I stop?"

Dani threw an arm over her eyes, blocking out everything to concentrate on the sensations coursing through her body. Would her hunger for this woman ever be satisfied? "Never."

* * *

Barking dogs and slamming car doors interrupted them an hour later.

"I better get up." Kara stared at Dani, and it took every ounce of self-control to not kiss her again. "God, you're beautiful." She tucked an errant curl behind Dani's ear.

Dani caressed Kara's cheek. "Funny, I was thinking the same thing."

"When will I see you again?"

"I have nightmare shifts this week. But I'll make it happen. I promise."

Kara kissed her softly, then buried her face in Dani's neck. She would hold her to that promise because the thought of being away from her for even one second was painful, let alone a full week.

* * *

Kara finally made an appearance in the store an hour later.

"Did you have a nice evening?" Val asked.

She grinned. "You could say that."

"So, when did all this happen?"

"She showed up yesterday." Kara jammed her hands into the pockets of her jeans.

"You look happy, so it must've been good."

"Good? I might say fantastic, but good works." With a happy sigh, she leaned against the wall. "I think she's the one."

"The *one*?"

Kara nodded. "Yeah. It feels like fate. Like we were meant for each other."

"Where is she now?"

"Taking a shower. She's gotta go to work."

"I've got things covered here if you wanna go say a proper goodbye."

Kara wandered back into the house and found Dani showered and dressed. Her hair was in a messy bun on top of her head. A pair of Kara's sweatpants hung low on her hips and the same T-shirt from earlier completed the ensemble. She took Kara's breath away.

"I hope you don't mind, I borrowed some of your clothes." Dani wrapped her arms around Kara's waist and placed a light kiss on her lips.

"No, I don't mind."

"I gotta go. I'll talk to you later." Dani placed one last kiss on Kara's lips.

Kara followed her and waved as Dani pulled out of the driveway. She was ecstatic. On top of the world. Being in love and having the best sex of your life could do that to a person.

She headed back inside for a cup of coffee to give her a jolt of energy. When she passed by the kitchen table, an envelope with her name scrawled across the front in red lipstick caught her eye. Opening it, she slid out a sheet of notebook paper with jagged edges. A wide grin split her face. It was a pencil sketch of Kara leaning against her motorcycle. "Holy shit, this is good."

Underneath the picture was Dani's handwriting. *I drew this after our first ride. Guess you were on my mind.* A smiley face ended the sentence.

Dani was right; she was a damn good artist. She had signed the picture with a flourish. *By Danielle Clark.* Kara ran a thumb over the cursive script. Why did it seem familiar? She puzzled over it for a bit, then chalked it up to déjà vu. Again.

* * *

While in the car, Dani's phone rang. The caller ID picture was a big bag of popcorn. Because nothing said Zoey like a ginormous bag of popcorn. "Yes?"

"So how was it?"

"How did you find out?"

"Does it matter? You need to stop being so sensitive. We're all curious about what's happening in your life. It should make you feel important. Now, how was it?"

"It was great, and that's all I'm gonna say."

"When's the wedding? Sorry, let me clarify. When's the gay wedding?"

"You're ridiculous. Nobody's getting married. I gotta go, bye." She hung up before Zoey could go off on a wild tangent.

When Dani rushed into the surgeon's lounge, she was pleasantly surprised to find Kyle relaxing on the couch with his laptop. Dani had been confiding in him for the last couple of weeks, sharing her interactions with her family and Will, because he was her no-judgment zone. "Hey." She placed her backpack on the table and shoved a Keurig cup into the machine.

"You on call today?" he asked.

"Yeah. Anything exciting happening?"

"Nope. Your mom was looking for you earlier."

"Oh, shit. I'm not in the mood for the lecture today. Not today!" With a smile, she reached for a clean mug from the cabinet.

"It's good to see you smiling again."

"Thanks." While waiting for her coffee, she prowled around with restless energy. Spotting the Nerf basketball, she grabbed it, tossing it toward the net. And for once, for the very first time, Dani Clark hit nothing but net.

Her jaw dropped. "Did you see that?"

"Nothing but net!"

"Yes!" Dani squealed.

"Today must be your lucky day, buddy."

"Must be." When her coffee was done, she poured some French Vanilla creamer into the mug. She inhaled the aromatic smell of a good cup of Joe and her insides twisted. "Oh, crap."

A look of concern crossed Kyle's face. "What's the matter?"

"I'm gonna throw up." Dani shot into the restroom, slamming the door shut behind her.

When she came back out, her face felt clammy. She wandered over to the couch and sat down next to Kyle. "Shit. That's twice today."

"Twice?"

"I threw up this morning." Dani blew out a breath. Her eyes narrowed as the wheels started turning inside her brain. "I felt nauseous Friday, too, but I didn't throw up." She counted the days in her head. Her cycle was like clockwork. It never varied. Never. Twenty-six days. On the dot. Shit. She was a couple of weeks late. How the fuck did she not notice? Emotional distress. Too many other things on her mind. "Shit." Her eyes widened. "I skipped a month."

"You don't think you're…no. You've been under a huge amount of stress. That might cause you to skip a month. Let me run down to Obstetrics and get a test. I'll be right back."

Dani was in full-blown panic mode. She counted back to the last time she and Will had sex, which was the night before Kara's accident, about six weeks ago.

She bit her lip and prayed. Prayed with all her heart. *No, it can't be. It can't be!* She made deals with every deity and every devil. *Not now, please.* She took a couple of deep breaths and pressed her hands to her temples. *It's stress. Stress can wreak havoc on your body.*

Her phone buzzed with a text. Kara sent a pic of all the animals moping around. *Everyone misses you.*

Her heart clenched, and suddenly she couldn't breathe.

Another message came through, this time from her mom. *Why don't you and Will come over for dinner this week and we can all talk?*

Dani hurled the phone across the room.

It took Kyle exactly ten minutes to come back. The longest ten minutes of Dani's life. She went into the bathroom. After flushing and washing her hands, she took a seat on the closed lid of the toilet. With bated breath and shaking hands, she waited. When the result showed, tears filled her eyes...and the bottom of her world fell out.

CHAPTER THIRTY-TWO

"Maybe it's a false positive," Kyle said.

"I did it twice." Dani sighed.

They sat in companionable silence for a minute or two.

"What am I gonna do?" she asked.

"Do you want the baby?"

She bit her lip, taking a few seconds to answer. "Of course, I do. It's just…the timing is awful. It couldn't be much worse. I didn't think I'd have a child until my career was on track. I certainly didn't want one while I'm still in my residency. Ugh." She covered her face with her hands. "Unbelievable."

"Are you gonna tell Will?"

"Of course. He has a right to know."

"How will he react?"

"He'll be ecstatic. It's all he's ever talked about, having kids." Dani's arms flopped back down on the couch.

"Will you get back together with him?"

She took a moment to ponder the question. Was that an option? Kara's face suddenly swam before her eyes, and her heart skipped a beat. Dani quickly pushed the image from her brain, not ready to deal with it right now. She didn't want to remember the happiness that was there a mere hour ago. "I don't know," was the only answer she could give at the moment.

* * *

Dani moved like a zombie all through her shift at the hospital. Everything was different now. The world had changed in the last couple of hours. How naive she was, thinking life was complicated before. Thinking that breaking up a three-year engagement was complicated. That bucking her parent's wishes for the first time was complicated. Ha! Child's play. *Now* life was complicated. *Now* there was nowhere to run or hide. The decisions she would make in the next couple of days would have a lasting effect, not just on her, but on other people. But she wasn't making them now. They could wait, at least until she was off the clock.

Pushing all thoughts aside, she immersed herself in work. With a strength Dani didn't know she possessed, she shut down her mind and went through her routines. There was comfort in routines. Comfort in doing the same things you'd been doing, day after day. A normalcy. At exactly three, she had a cup of coffee. At five, it was off to the cafeteria to get something to eat. Even though the meal was unappetizing, even though the food ended up getting pushed around the plate, this was what she did. At seven, with no emergencies looming, she cleared up paperwork from the week before. Because that's what she normally did when it was slow.

Since the breakup, she'd been crashing at Zoey and Jen's while looking for an apartment that allowed pets. She'd talked with Will a few times. At first it had been awkward, but eventually they'd established an uneasy truce. Dani would pop in every day to spend time with Jinx and Oliver. Most times he wasn't home, but when he was, he would ask about her day, and she would ask about his, both acting like nothing had changed.

Maybe this was his routine, his normalcy. His way of coping.

* * *

Will was expecting her, so she twisted the key in the lock and pushed open the door. Oliver was the first to greet her. "Hey, Ollie. How's my boy?" Leaning over, she gave him a hug and a kiss on the nose, smiling when he answered in kind. Jinx was next, weaving between her legs and twitching his tail. Will sat on the couch, watching TV, and she took a seat next to him.

He looked at her questioningly, seeming to sense that something was different. "Are you okay?"

She was amazed after all that had happened in the past six weeks he could still show so much concern for her. Still be so in tune to her feelings and moods. Years of knowing someone could do that. "We have to talk."

"What's wrong?"

She forced a sad smile. "I'm pregnant."

At first, Will's reply was a blank stare. Then a chain reaction of emotions played across his face. First came confusion, then comprehension, then disbelief, then a tiny bit of controlled joy. "What?"

"I'm pregnant."

"When...?"

"After dinner at Ethan's?"

His eyes widened. "Oh, right." Jumping to his feet, he rubbed the back of his neck. "When did you find out?"

"Today."

"What are you gonna do?" he asked with knitted brows.

"I'm having it."

His face relaxed and he sank onto the couch next to Dani. "That's good. Right?"

"I guess. Timing sucks."

After a few moments of silence, Will took her hand. "Let's raise our baby together."

Dani's heart constricted at the hopefulness in his eyes. "I don't know..." He would be a terrific dad. How many times did he say if they had a boy, he was going to teach him to play baseball? If they had a daughter, he would teach her to play softball.

"We'll start fresh. Leave the past in the past. It'll be a new beginning."

Dani slowly disengaged her hands from his. "I have to think about it. I need time to sort it all out."

"Of course. I'm sorry. Think about it. But I'm here for you. Whatever you need, okay?"

"Thanks. I'm gonna head out. We'll talk later."

Dani went straight to her room when she arrived at Zoey's. They were out with friends tonight, thankfully. Tomorrow she would tell them, but tonight she didn't have the strength. All she wanted was to fall asleep, to have some peace and forget everything.

Sleep was elusive, however. She tossed and turned for hours while an inner dialogue ran rampant in her brain. *Our baby.* They had created a tiny life together.

Dani rested a hand on her abdomen, already feeling the connection. This child was now the most important thing in Dani's life. Everything else paled in comparison. This baby's happiness would come before all else, would come before Dani's happiness, before Dani's needs. This is what she did best. Others before self. She'd been doing it for over thirty years and was used to it. She had to make the right decision as far as their futures were concerned.

At one point she was so restless, she rose and walked around the room, continuing to try and sort through what was going on in her head.

Her thoughts drifted to Kara. Kara, who made her smile and laugh. Whose touch was so tender it was almost heartbreaking. Dani ran a hand over the T-shirt on the bureau. Kara's T-shirt. She brought it to her nose and inhaled the scent of her. If she closed her eyes, she could feel Kara's arms around her. For the first time in her life, Dani had been free. Free to love, free from expectations. Free from pleasing other people.

Taking off her nightshirt, Dani slipped the T-shirt on instead and was wrapped in instant warmth as she continued to pace around the room. How could she possibly ask Kara to take this on? They met barely four months ago. Four months! They had spent most of those four months butting heads, and when they'd called their truce, her breakup with Will happened, which meant more time apart. So, really, they'd been friends for

244 Lori G. Matthews

no time at all when she thought about it. She couldn't ask. It was too much.

Crawling back into bed, she pulled her knees into her chest, sighing. They had spent a wonderful weekend together. Well, it wasn't even a full weekend. Hell, it wasn't even a full day. Just an incredible eighteen hours. Yes, the sex was fantastic. Intense and hot. But what if in a few months the sex wasn't as intense and Kara started feeling stuck—stuck with Dani and a baby that wasn't hers? Trapped. How could she do such a thing to Kara? Having a baby wasn't like moving in together or buying a house together. Having a baby was a lifetime commitment. You don't dump this kind of thing on someone you haven't even known for long. Right? Of course you don't.

Yes, Dani was crazy about Kara. But now, everything was different. There was someone else to consider. And maybe Kara wasn't in love. She'd never declared any feelings.

By the time Dani was done talking to Dani, it was five in the morning and she was convinced a couple-week friendship turned sexual relationship could not withstand a baby. Every rational bone in her body told her it was too much. It was crazy. It was unheard of.

Maybe she and Kara could go back to being friends. Maybe friendship had a chance now. Maybe having sex would have taken the edge off their physical attraction, and they could still be in each other's lives.

Dani curled her body into a tight ball.

That was a lot of maybes.

CHAPTER THIRTY-THREE

Dani snuggled between her two besties. Three gloomy faces stared at nothing.

"Are you sure?" Zoey asked.

"As sure as you can be," Dani said.

"Maybe it was wrong. Tests are wrong all the time," Jen said.

"No, the chances are extremely slim, like barely possible. And I had morning sickness twice already. And I just know. I can't describe how, but I do."

Zoey was inconsolable. "But you just grew your lady balls. It was wrong. Take it again."

"Zoe, I took it twice."

"Maybe Kara will want to have the baby with you," Zoey said.

"You want me to ask a woman I've only known for four months to raise a baby with me?"

"Yes," Zoey stated, rather loudly. "That's what you should ask."

"Nobody has a baby with someone they barely know! It's not fair to ask her. Babies are a lifetime commitment." She took a breath before saying, "Maybe I should go back to Will."

"No!" Zoey wailed. "You don't love him."

"It doesn't matter. This baby matters." Dani excelled at two things: intricate surgery and putting someone else's needs above hers. She was fatally selfless. "Maybe Kara and I could go back to being friends." She looked to her friends for affirmation but was met with skepticism.

"I can't imagine that happening," Jen said. "At least not for a long time."

Zoey agreed, "No way."

Deep down, Dani knew they were right.

"Jesus Christ, this whole thing is like some cruel joke," Zoey said. Her head faded back against the cushions. "You and Kara were great together."

"We were only together one day. Not even a day. Just eighteen hours."

Zoey's voice was lifeless. "Can't you just say a day? It sounds better."

"I could. I guess. But it wasn't a full day."

"Dani, round it up," Zoey insisted.

In the interest of making Zoey feel better, Dani relented. "Okay. We spent one day together." It did sound better.

"Are you in love with her?" Zoey asked.

Dani opened her mouth to answer, then thought better of it. Maybe if she didn't say it out loud, she could pretend it wasn't true.

"Dani, are you in love with Kara?"

Dani squeezed her eyes shut. "Please. This is hard enough."

"It's a simple question."

"Let it go, babe," Jen said.

"Okay." Zoey let out a big, heavy sigh. "Stay here. We'll all raise the kid. It'll have three moms."

"You don't like kids," Dani said.

Zoey shrugged. "I learned to love dogs. I can learn to love kids."

"I'm not sure I would trust you to babysit, let alone raise my child."

"How can you say that? I'd be a great babysitter." Zoey crossed her arms in defiance. "I'm gonna be this kid's favorite aunt. You'll see. Right, Jen?"

Jen's lip curled in doubt, and she ignored the question. "When are you gonna tell Kara?"

"Tonight after work." Dani hoped she could get through that visit without leaving jagged pieces of herself behind.

* * *

Dani fiddled with her phone as she sat in the surgeon's lounge in the hospital. The melancholy mood that engulfed her worsened by the minute as she scrolled through previous texts from Kara. She was saved from further torture when *Lunch with Mom* popped up in the calendar alerts.

When she arrived at the cafeteria, her mom was already seated in the corner at her favorite table. Dani bent down to peck her mom on the cheek before taking a seat. "Hey."

"How are you today?"

"I'm okay."

"Just okay? What's wrong? I ordered your lunch. The special today was your favorite, a tuna melt."

"Thanks." Dani stared down at the plate in front of her. Tuna melts could put a smile on anyone's face, but not today. She picked up a french fry and shoved it in her mouth. *There's never enough salt on these things.* She grabbed the saltshaker and liberally applied more.

"My goodness, that's a lot of salt."

Dani rolled her eyes, took another fry, rubbed more salt on it, and shoved it in her mouth.

Her mother shook her head. "Suit yourself. You are what you eat. If you choose to be unhealthy, then so be it."

The next fry froze in midair right before Dani's lips. She put it back down on the plate. *Shit.* She ate for two now. She needed to make healthier choices.

Her mother cocked an eyebrow before taking a bite of salad. "Since when do you listen to me about food?"

Dani shrugged.

Rebecca dabbed her mouth with a napkin. "How's Will? Are you two still talking? Relationships take work. It's not fun and games all the time. Sometimes things are hard, and you need to get through them together. It's all about communication."

Dani gritted her teeth at the relationship lecture. Which she'd been hearing nonstop since the breakup. "I know relationships take work. I didn't leave because things got hard."

Rebecca raised a hand, signaling the end to that part of the lecture. "Okay."

"I'm pregnant."

Rebecca's face paled. "Are you sure?"

"I took a blood test this morning."

"Is it Will's?"

"Of course it's Will's!"

"Well, how do I know? Your father and I thought maybe you found someone else."

Dani's heart stuttered at the mention of someone else. "No. It's his."

"What are you going to do?"

"I don't know yet."

Rebecca straightened in her chair, and a sparkle appeared in her eyes. "Well, we may be able to keep the same date for the wedding. I'll talk to the reverend."

"I didn't say we were getting married."

After a moment of silence, a muscle in her mom's jaw twitched. "Of course you're getting married. You cannot have a baby out of wedlock—"

"Mom," Dani said forcibly.

"What?"

"I haven't made any decisions yet. So please leave it be for now."

Her mom pursed her lips but didn't put up too much of a fight. "Whatever your decision, I'm happy for you both. You'll make excellent parents."

Dani listened to her mother drone on and on about how she was able to have a career and a baby, and Dani should have no trouble doing the same. A page to scrub in for an emergency saved her.

On the way to surgery, she crossed her mother off her list of difficult conversations to have sooner rather than later. However, her heart was still heavy because the worst conversation of the day was yet to come.

* * *

Kara puttered around the cottage, humming along with a tune on the radio. A smile had barely left her face for the past two days. She hadn't talked to Dani since Sunday, which seemed odd, but then again, doctors worked crazy long hours. Maybe she'd hear from her tonight, and if not, Kara would call. Hearing a knock at the door, she spun around. Her smile widened because Dani was visible through the window.

Hustling to the door, Kara pulled it open. All the pets rushed over. "I was just thinking about you. Well, actually not just. It's been pretty nonstop since you left." Kara paused. She wanted to kiss Dani, but something seemed off. "What's the matter?"

Dani petted the animals, then straightened. She bit her lip and stared at the ground. "I need to talk to you."

Kara's gut clenched. "What's wrong?" Dani refused to meet her gaze, and dread settled in the pit of Kara's stomach. "Dani?"

After wandering into the living room, Dani finally made eye contact. Tears dotted her lashes. "I'm pregnant."

Kara's mouth dropped open. "Holy shit." Her legs wobbled, and she staggered to the couch and collapsed. "When did you find out?" Dani chose to sit at the opposite end, and Kara's dread grew. The physical distance between them was only four feet, but it seemed like miles.

"After I left on Sunday. I was nauseous, and then I realized I skipped a period. So I took a test." She tossed her keys on the side table and stared out the window.

A silence descended as Kara's mind worked through this stunning development. "Is that why I haven't heard from you since Sunday?"

"Yeah. It's been a stressful couple of days." Dani closed her eyes and slumped against the back of the couch.

"Are you gonna have it?"

She gave a wordless nod.

"Okay."

"Ugh. I'm not ready for this. I…I don't know what I'm gonna do. I don't even have a place to live."

Kara nibbled on her bottom lip. What she was about to say would probably sound crazy. But hell, love made you do and say crazy things. *Go big or go home, right?* "Why don't you move in here?"

Dani's eyes snapped toward her. "What?"

"Move in here. We'll turn the second bedroom into a nursery. If we need more room, we'll add on a bedroom suite. With a nice big soaking tub. I mean, we both love tubs, right?" Her heart rate ramped into high gear. *This could work.* "I know a contractor, and he owes me, so maybe we can get a discount or something." To Kara, this was the perfect solution.

Dani's facial expression suggested otherwise. Her brows creased into a frown and her mouth hung open. Kara felt as though she'd grown three heads.

"I…I can't move in here," Dani stammered.

"Why not?"

"We've only known each other a few months. And most of that time we spent yelling at each other."

Kara held up a hand in surrender. "Okay. You're right. It was a crazy suggestion."

They sat in silence for a few moments.

"We didn't yell this past weekend, and it was fantastic," Kara said.

"True. It was."

"We can still see each other. We'll date!"

"What about the baby?"

"I love kids. Travis and I are great together."

"He's a teenager, not an infant. Babies don't play baseball and video games."

"They will eventually." Kara gave Dani a wide toothy grin, hoping to pull a smile from those lips she loved so much. The smile she sought was not forthcoming. "Okay. I admit I've never taken care of a baby, but that doesn't mean I can't learn."

"Having a baby and working is gonna be hard. I'm not gonna have a lot of free time."

"I don't care. I'll do whatever it takes to make it work."

"I have to consider Will in all this. It's his child."

At the mention of Will, the muscles in Kara's stomach tightened. "You're not thinking of getting back together with him, I hope."

"I don't know what I'm gonna do yet."

"You can't go back to him." Kara's voice rose as she tried to make her point. "You don't love him!"

The kittens sensed the tension in the room and skittered down the hallway.

Despite Kara's outburst, Dani remained calm. "Please understand. It doesn't matter what I feel or what I want. This child is now the most important thing in my life. And I have to put his or her needs above everything else."

"Your needs are important too!" Kara needed more time to convince Dani. "Let me make you dinner. We'll hang out and talk, or we'll just watch TV."

A flicker of interest appeared in Dani's eyes, but then she shook her head. "I should go home. I need some space, some time to think. Rain check?"

"Okay." A rain check was good. It was promising.

"I'm gonna head out." Dani grabbed her keys and Kara followed her to the door. Before she walked outside, she turned back. "I'll talk to you soon."

Kara squeezed her hands into fists. She ached to kiss Dani goodbye but wasn't sure if the kiss would be rebuffed. *To kiss? Or not to kiss?* She was frozen with uncertainty.

Dani came to the rescue and her lips lightly brushed Kara's cheek. "Bye."

Kara stood in the open doorway, her eyes never leaving Dani. Suddenly, the dogs barreled past her, and she had to grab the doorjamb to stay upright. "Boys!"

As Dani walked toward her car, she had no idea her fan club was in hot pursuit. When the car door opened, both dogs jumped in before she could stop them. Milo settled into the passenger seat and hung his head out of the open window, and Ziggy jumped into the back. Both wore the typical pittie smile, mouth open, tongue lolling, lips curled up at the back.

"Milo! Ziggy!" Kara hustled over to pull the dogs from the car. She gave Dani a sheepish grin. "Obviously, I haven't learned to control my dogs yet."

The corner of Dani's lips twitched up. "Maybe I need to give *you* a lesson."

Kara smiled. "Maybe you do."

When she made it back inside, she slid down to the floor in front of the couch. Both dogs settled in next to her, probably sensing her mood. She scratched Milo behind the ears. "She'll come back. She just needs some time. Right?"

She received a slobbery kiss on the cheek.

"I'll take that as a yes."

CHAPTER THIRTY-FOUR

As Dani drove to Jen and Zoey's after her shift was over on Friday, she thought back to her dream from the previous night. She was with Kara at the park, and they had two young children: one little girl with devilish green eyes, and a happy-go-lucky boy with curly hair and an infectious laugh. They were so happy.

When she'd woken, the joy was still in her heart, but soon the dream had faded and so did the joy. In its wake was a feeling of loss and loneliness.

She turned into the driveway and hoped her two roomies were home. Working late hours meant she hadn't seen them since their talk on Monday night. And after that dream, she desperately needed some F-bombing and bonding with her besties.

She turned the key in the lock and pushed the door open. "Anybody home?" The smell of something delectable wafted around her. The slice of pizza she'd eaten at lunch was long digested and her stomach felt distinctly empty. Roscoe and Rocky pranced around begging for some attention.

"In the kitchen!" Jen called.

"Whatever you're cooking smells delicious." Dani hugged her. "Where's Zoe?"

"She's upstairs. I'm making chicken teriyaki. I hope you're hungry."

"I'm starving. I haven't seen you guys all week."

"I know. How's work been?"

"Awful. I barely had time to pee."

"Dans!" Zoey puttered into the room wearing a backpack on her front and big fluffy slippers on her feet. "How you feeling?"

"Good. When I'm not puking."

"Ew. How long will that last?"

Dani pulled some plates down from the cabinets. "Weeks. Why do you have a backpack on backward?"

"Well. I'm glad you asked. After our discussion on Monday. I was very hurt that you thought you couldn't trust me with your baby—"

"I was kinda kidding."

"I don't think you were. Anyway, instead of pouting about it, I decided to learn how to baby."

"Learn how to what?"

"I'm gonna learn how to fucking baby."

Dani sought out Jen, who smirked. "She's gonna learn how to baby."

"Huh. I'm curious. How exactly does wearing a backpack backward constitute learning how to baby."

"It's not a backpack," Zoey said as she helped set the table. "It's a baby pack. Well, this is actually a pooch pouch for dogs. But it's the same concept."

Dani craned her neck to get a better look at the pooch pouch baby pack. "And you got something in there I see. Is it a pooch?"

"Ha, ha. No. It's my baby."

"It looks like a stuffed giraffe."

"It was all I had. I made do."

"Okay, MacGyver. Babies weigh more than stuffed animals, by the way. You might wanna add a dumbbell or something in there. Is he allowed out?"

Zoey pulled the giraffe from his confines and propped him up on the table with a proud smile.

"Is that a diaper?" Dani asked.

"It's Jen's bandana." Zoey adjusted said bandana to better cover the giraffe's privates.

Jen scowled. "What the hell? I was looking for that. Gross. He better not poop on it."

"Very funny, babe."

After the table was set, they all took a seat and placed their napkins in their laps.

Dani inhaled and her eyes rolled skyward. "Smells delicious. I haven't had a good meal all week." After taking a healthy bite of chicken and humming her satisfaction, Dani asked, "So, where do you take your baby?"

Zoey filled everyone's glass with water. "Everywhere. Right, babe?"

Jen nodded. "Yep. And it's hysterical when people go to coo over it and realize it's a stuffed animal."

"And you carry this baby all the time?" Dani asked.

"Mostly. Sometimes I put him down."

"Oh, it's a he?"

"Jeff."

"Jeff. I see. And have you ever left Jeff anywhere?"

Zoey stopped eating and narrowed her eyes. "Why do you ask that?"

"Cause I know you. Answer the question."

Zoey paused. "Maybe."

"And where have you left him?"

Jen snickered. "Where hasn't she left him."

Zoey glared at her. "It happened one time. I was going to the bathroom at Whole Foods, and I left him in the stall."

"You left the baby in the *stall*?"

"I can't pee with this thing on, so I hung it on the hook on the back of the door. And then I forgot him."

"When, pray tell, did you realize he was gone?" Dani asked.

"It didn't take long. What, like a day, babe?"

"Sounds about right," Jen said.

"I went back to the store, and he was in the lost and found box."

Dani suppressed a giggle. "Somebody put your baby in the lost and found box?"

"Yeah. Thank God, right?"

The giggle bubbled forth and morphed into a belly laugh, and soon Jen and Zoey joined in. When they caught their breath, Dani threw an arm around Zoey's shoulders and squeezed. "I love you, Z. I don't know why, but I do."

"You love me cause your mom hates me. It's your way of sticking it to her."

"She doesn't hate you."

"She's never approved of me from day one."

Dani pretended to get dreamy. "Ah, I can still remember that fateful first day in our college dorm room. It was the first time we'd met." She pointed her fork at Zoey. "You should've locked the door."

"I didn't know you were going to show up a day early. Besides, I'm the one who should've been pissed. I was on the verge of an orgasm when you all walked in. Talk about coitus interruptus."

Dani smiled at the memory. "First time I saw my mom speechless. She was in a state of shock for days."

Jen laughed. "Seeing a girl's head in another girl's cooch can do that to someone."

"Especially my conservative family. Whew. They didn't know what hit them. My mom wanted to march right into the Dean's office and demand he give me a new roommate. I was like, no way. I think I like this girl." They all chuckled again, and Dani basked in this short happy moment with her friends. "Oh, those were the good old days. Everything was simple back then." Suddenly, the memory of last weekend in the claw-foot tub washed over Dani, and the weight of the past week's stress descended on her. Her body and mind sagged.

Jen touched her arm. "Are you all right?"

"Sorry. Sometimes I get overwhelmed."

"Have you talked to Kara since the other day?"

"We've texted a couple times. I told her I needed time to think."

All three fell silent. Zoey pushed the chicken around her plate. "Have you made any decisions yet?"

"No. Sometimes I think I should just get back together with Will." With a big sigh, she sat back in her chair. Her hunger had evaporated, and she fiddled with her fork. "I've known Will for years. He knows me. I was settled before I met Kara. My life was simple. Uncomplicated. And then I met her, and everything… changed."

"It changed for the better," Zoey said.

"No, it didn't." Dani's eyes filled up. "It felt like I had no control anymore. I questioned everything in my life. It was scary. It *is* scary."

Jen grasped her hand. "The unknown is always scary. But scary doesn't mean bad."

"I know. Maybe I'm just gutless. Maybe I'm too afraid to try with Kara."

"You're not gutless," Jen said. "Listen. This is the biggest decision of your life, and it doesn't have to be made in a week, or a month, or a few months."

Dani's mood lifted slightly. Nothing definitive needed to happen right now. She managed a small smile. "You're right. I want to make the right decision, so I'm gonna take my time."

"Absolutely," Zoey said. "Just maybe, you should make a decision before the kid is ready for preschool."

Dani's smile widened. "Yeah. Preschool choices can be overwhelming, and I'll need someone else's input." The knot of anxiety in her belly loosened, and her appetite came back. The conversation shifted to Jen's workday and her *Adventures in Babysitting* with Jon-Jon and the kids, and Dani managed to place her troubles on the back burner for a few hours.

CHAPTER THIRTY-FIVE

On Sunday morning, Kara slid into the booth across from Zoey and Jen. They were at Barjot's for breakfast, and Kara had an inkling that they wanted to pepper her with questions about Dani. Kara pointed to the backpack hanging on Zoey's chest. "What's that?"

"My baby. Dani said she'd never let me babysit. So I'm learning how to baby."

"Oh." Kara pulled down the flap. "Whatcha got in here?" A stuffed animal stared back at her. "That is one long-necked baby."

"It's all I could come up with on such short notice," Zoey said. "I have some ankle weights in here to simulate baby weight."

Kara sighed. "Maybe I need one too. Then I can prove to Dani I can handle a baby."

"Well. Funny you should say that." Zoey reached down and plopped another backpack on the table. "I took some initiative. On the off chance you were interested in furthering your education."

"Oh. Is this for me?"

"Yep."

Kara peeked inside. An adorable stuffed otter was nestled in a fleece blanket. "Well, hello, cutie."

"I got it at the Seattle Aquarium last year. So don't lose it."

"I won't lose my baby." She put the bag on her lap. "Does he have a name?"

Zoey glared. "Of course he has a name. Who doesn't name their stuffed animals?"

Kara exchanged a look with Jen, who shrugged. "She's thirty-three and names her stuffed animals."

Kara fingered the plush ears of the otter and made a mental note to keep it away from the dogs. Milo especially liked soft, furry things. "I don't have any stuffed animals. I will treasure him forever."

With a sharp intake of breath, Zoey went bug-eyed. "You're not keeping him."

"Oh. Okay."

"He's just a loaner."

Kara pressed her lips together to hide her smile. Zoey's seriousness cracked her up. It was like the otter was a living, breathing, beloved family pet. "What's his name?" Kara asked.

"Oscar Otter."

A chuckle gurgled in her throat. "Well. That's a good name."

"Is this funny?" Zoey asked.

Kara slowly shook her head. "No." But of course it was, and both she and Jen chuckled.

When the laughter stopped, Zoey asked, "Are you done?"

Properly admonished, both settled down.

"I'm going with Jen to her nanny job on Wednesday so I can be around Jon-Jon," Zoey said. "You should come. We both can use the practice."

"How old is he?" Kara asked.

"Seven months," Jen answered.

Kara mulled over Zoey's suggestion. Maybe this was a good idea. Maybe this would help convince Dani that Kara was serious. And she could sure use the practice. "Okay. I'll go to baby class too."

The waitress came over with coffee and they placed their orders.

"So what's going on with you and Dani?" Jen asked.

The question depressed Kara, and the lightness of the stuffed otter conversation vanished. "Nothing much. She's so stubborn. I don't know why she won't give us chance."

"Don't give up," Zoey said. "We'll work on her. Operation Popcorn is still on." And to prove her point, she pulled a bag of popcorn from her baby pouch and passed it around.

* * *

Kara knelt on the floor with Zoey and Jen in baby Jon-Jon's room. She'd taken the day off and left Val in charge back at the farm. Today would put her one step closer to Dani. At least, she hoped it would.

Jen placed her hands on her knees. "I'd like to welcome you both to How to Baby 101. Today, we'll learn the fine art of diapering and feeding a very small human being."

Seven-month-old Jon-Jon lay on his changing pad on the floor, gurgling, smiling, and flopping all his tiny limbs. His wispy blond hair stuck out in different directions and his big brown eyes twinkled.

Jen continued, pointing to the items on the ground. "We have diapers, wipes, and ointment. We'll practice on this doll first, then move on to Jon-Jon. Let's begin." Jen readied the doll. "Now, when diapering, you will gently grasp his ankles, raise him up like so, and slide out the dirty diaper. Wipe away any residue—"

"You mean poop," Zoey said.

"Poop or urine, doesn't matter, wipe the entire area with the cleansing wipes. Then you place the new diaper, like so"—she held up a fresh diaper and showed the proper orientation—"and slide it under his bottom. Before you close the diaper, rub some ointment around, and then close the tabs. Done. Easy!"

Zoey and Kara took a turn diapering the doll.

Jen nodded with a look of satisfaction. "Very good, ladies. Shall we try it on a live baby?"

Zoey crinkled her nose. "What's that smell?"

They sniffed the air.

Jen gave them her best uh-oh face. "You're about to get a really good lesson in diaper changing."

Zoey pointed to Jon-Jon. "Is that smell coming from him?"

"Highly likely." Jen forced a smile. "Who wants to go first?"

Zoey's lip curled and she pointed to Kara.

With a shrug, Kara said, "I'll try." She loosened the tabs on Jon-Jon's diaper. When she pulled down the front, her nostrils were assaulted by a heinous odor, and she quickly closed the diaper.

"Oh my God!" Zoey screeched. "What the hell was that? What did you feed this kid?"

Jen became thoughtful. "Probably the peas from yesterday."

While breathing through her mouth, Kara pulled down the diaper again. The substance was now on full display. It was greenish brown and gooey. It was Marcie's brownies incarnate. She stared, unsure of how to proceed, and her hesitation cost her. A stream of urine hit her in the chest. "Oh, shit!"

Jon-Jon's wee-wee wiggled all around, like an unmoored hose, sending tiny spurts around the room.

"Jesus Christ!" Zoey shielded herself with a clean diaper. "First the dog, now a kid? Strap that thing down!"

Jen quickly covered Jon-Jon's privates with a towel and handed another one to Kara. "Sorry. Forgot to warn you. When you change boys, you gotta keep that little pee-pee covered."

"Seems like a big thing to forget," Zoey muttered.

Jon-Jon giggled and squirmed with delight.

Kara tapped his nose with her finger and cooed, "You think that's funny, do you?"

He grabbed her finger and squeezed. She smiled.

"You're lucky you're adorable."

After the massive clean-up in aisle three, they each took turns practicing on a very patient Jon-Jon.

On Kara's last try, she threw her hands in the air. "Done!"

Zoey checked her phone. "Not bad, fifteen seconds."

"I beat you. I win."

Jen rolled her eyes. "This isn't a rodeo. Nobody gets a prize for fastest diapering."

"Well, they should," Kara said.

"She's right. I owe you a beer," Zoey said.

The rest of the day was spent tending to Jon-Jon. He was bathed, fed, and burped multiple times. By late afternoon, Kara was exhausted. Babying was hard work. She lay on the sectional couch in the living room with a sleeping Jon-Jon curled in her arms. Jen sat nearby, with Zoey curled up in *her* arms sound asleep. A bit of green goop stuck to Zoey's hair. Kara hoped it was the peas from lunch and not the poop.

"You're a natural," Jen said.

Kara smiled. "It feels…right somehow."

Jen took a photo with her phone. "My A student."

CHAPTER THIRTY-SIX

Kara sat at the kitchen table, chin in hand, staring at nothing. She had no idea what time it was. Hell, she didn't even know what day it was. The calendar on the fridge said Sunday. Dani had left two weeks ago.

Thumper jumped onto the table. One paw found its way into her coffee mug. *I wonder where that paw's been? Probably in the litter box.* She shrugged and brought the mug to her lips anyway.

The gray Seattle weather was not helping her mood, as the persistent drizzle of the last few days made her extra morose. She could barely stand to be in the cottage. Everything reminded her of Dani. She kept the guest bathroom door shut, not being able to stomach looking at the claw-foot tub every time she walked down the hallway.

The first time Kara had taken a shower and reached for the duck-covered shower cap, her hand had frozen and the muscles in her stomach had clenched. With shaky legs, she'd sunk down to the shower floor. The cap was now residing in the drawer next to the sink. If Dani came back—no, *when* Dani came back—she would hang it back up. But not now. Not with every memory so fresh in her mind. She fiddled with her phone, reading the last text message Dani had sent. She'd said she needed time, but she hadn't told her to stop texting, so Kara snapped a picture of the dogs who lay at her feet, and sent it off. *The boys are pining for you.*

The reply was instant. *Oh, my boys. Give them a kiss for me.*

The kittens perched close by, so she sent a picture of them also. *They miss you too.*

I miss everyone. A heart emoji followed.

Kara stared at the phone and held her breath. Was the emoji meant for her too? Did the heart mean love? When no more text bubbles appeared, she expelled the breath from her lungs, packed up Oscar and the laptop, and headed to the store.

Val and Jesmyn sat behind the cash register eating lunch.

"Hey, buddy," Val said with a look of pity. "You okay?"

"I'm fine."

"What's in the backpack?" Jesmyn asked.

"Oscar Otter. Zoey loaned him to me. We're both learning how to baby."

Val placed a sandwich on a paper plate with some potato chips and slid it in front of Kara. "Here, turkey and Swiss on rye."

"Thanks." Kara inhaled and pushed out a shaky breath, thankful she didn't need to keep up some false facade of happiness around her friends. "Weather sucks."

"Sun's coming out tomorrow," Val said.

Jesmyn handed her a bottle of water. "So, what's with the otter and the baby thing?"

"I've been taking care of Oscar here, and I went with Jen to her nanny job to hang out with a seven-month-old. I'm gonna prove to Dani that I can be a mother."

"Good for you."

"Why don't you come over for dinner tonight?" Val asked. "Might do you good to get yourself out of the house."

Jesmyn nodded. "Rachel asked about you the other night. She's adopting one of our foster dogs."

"The dog's a wild one, maybe you could help her with it," Val said.

Kara munched on a potato chip. "I have zero interest in dating her again."

"I don't mean date her. Jesus, I would never suggest that. I mean hang out again. It'll give you something to do other than stare at your claw-foot tub."

Kara glared at Val. "I don't stare at my claw-foot tub."

"You open the door and look at it sometimes. I don't know what the hell you're doing."

"I'm thinking of repainting, that's all."

Val held a hand up. "Okay, if you say so."

"Have you heard from her?" Jesmyn asked.

"We've texted. Just superficial stuff."

"Give it some time. It's all gonna work out. Now, I gotta go, duty calls." She leaned in to Val and kissed her. "See you tonight."

"Jes is right. It's gonna work out," Val said.

Kara broke off a small piece of her sandwich. "When?"

"Patience."

"It's hard to be patient. I just wanna talk to her and convince her to give us a chance."

"Listen. A child changes your life. I can't even imagine what the hell's going on in her head right now."

"You're right. I'll give her some space." Kara buried her face in her hands. "I should've told her I loved her. I wonder if it would've made a difference?"

"You'll get a chance to tell her." She touched her hand. "Hey, if Jes says it'll work out, it'll work out. She's rarely wrong."

Kara sat back and nodded as her anxiety abated. Of course Jes was right.

She was a super cop, after all.

CHAPTER THIRTY-SEVEN

It was a beautiful afternoon, so Dani had taken a quick lunch break from work and met Zoey at the park where they now relaxed on a bench. Work had again been crazy the past week, and she'd barely been home.

"Where's Jeff?" she asked. "It's been, what? Three weeks? Are we losing interest in babying already?"

"No. He's home napping."

"Alone?"

"The dogs are there."

"You know you can't leave a baby alone in a house, right?"

Zoey's eyes rolled skyward. "I know that. And I'm still babying. I spent a day with Jon-Jon last week."

"How'd that go?"

"Great. I diapered. I fed. I burped." She pointed at Dani's belly. "I'm gonna babysit the shit out of this kid."

Dani placed an arm around Zoey. "You really are going all out, aren't you?" Staring off into the distance, she spotted a familiar figure. Her heart jumped into her throat when she recognized Kara.

"What?" Zoey asked.

Dani couldn't speak. Kara wasn't alone; Rachel was with her. A dog was on a leash, and she could tell Kara was trying to teach Rachel how to handle the dog.

Zoey finally spied what held Dani's gaze. "Oh. It's Kara. And Rachel."

Dani felt a stab of disappointment, and something else. Was she forgotten already? Anger flooded through her chest. "Great. I've been gone less than a month, and she's back with Rachel. Obviously, she's not too broken up over me. See? I was right. What was between us was just physical, nothing else. I don't know why I've wasted my time even thinking about her. Because she's not thinking about me!" She scowled and crossed her arms.

"Jealous much?"

"I am not jealous! I am merely stating a fact that she has thrown me to the curb."

"Calm the fuck down. They didn't get back together."

"How do you know?"

"Because I talk to her, and I know for a fact that she's helping Rachel with her crazy dog. That's exactly what's going on over there."

Dani refused to believe her own eyes. Kara and Rachel looked like nothing more than friends. There was no touching, or hugging, or kissing. Nothing nefarious was going on. But tell that to her hormones. "It's no big deal. She's back with Rachel."

"They're not back together."

"It's fine. We weren't even a couple. I mean, we only spent one day together."

"Eighteen hours, wasn't it?" Zoey said.

Dani puffed out her chest with false swagger despite her friend humoring her. "Exactly. It wasn't even a full day."

"Nope, not even a full day. Barely half a day."

Dani's bluster evaporated quickly. "It was more than half a day." Her bottom lip wobbled. "It was really closer to a whole day." Images of making love with Kara flooded her brain like an unstoppable high tide, and another stab of jealousy assaulted her. She couldn't stand the sight of Kara with someone else.

"Jesus Christ. Will you just get back together with her?" Zoey reached into a pocket and pulled out a sandwich baggie.

"Is that popcorn?"

"Yes. Want some?"

"No!" She knew what the popcorn represented. However, her stomach rumbled, and her resolve wavered. She'd forgotten to eat lunch. *Maybe just a few kernels.* "Well, I am a little hungry. But this means nothing!"

Zoey poured some popcorn into Dani's fist and chuckled. "Sure, it doesn't."

CHAPTER THIRTY-EIGHT

Kara's alarm trilled at six a.m. She rolled over and gazed longingly at the other side of the bed, remembering that one special weekend, waking up next to Dani, feeling such happiness and love. It had been over a month, and with each passing week, she grew more frustrated.

After showering and making herself somewhat presentable, she headed to the kitchen. The dogs barked to be let out, and she opened the door, happy to oblige. After turning the coffeepot on, she stood in front of the fridge, staring at the contents. Everything was unappealing. The kittens twisted between her legs, begging for breakfast. Tigger sank his claws into Kara's slipper, and she dragged him around the room. It was their thing in the morning.

Thank heaven for the pets. The menial tasks of taking care of their needs kept her somewhat sane. It was nice to be needed.

Later in the day, she wandered over to the barn and found Val going through some boxes near the loft. "Hey."

"Hey." Papers lay scattered around Val's feet. "We have to move some of the old business files to the loft. I need more room in the filing cabinets."

"Okay."

"I found these boxes. They're from your mom's house. Do you wanna go through them?"

"Sure." Kara opened the first box. She smiled as she pulled out old photo albums. "Holy crap. My old baby pictures. I thought she threw this stuff out."

Val peered over her shoulder. "You were a cute kid."

"Here's Mom." Kara touched the picture in front of her; nostalgia and melancholy washed over her in waves. It was the one time they had gone to a beach, and they'd spent hours building sandcastles that day, only to watch the high tide eviscerate them. "I miss her." Tears misted in her eyes.

Val pushed another box in her direction. "This has some old toys and books in it."

"Toys? I'll probably donate those."

"You going to the flea market today?"

Kara sighed. Travis's school was hosting a large indoor flea market. Jolie had asked if she wanted to man one of the refreshment stands with her and Aaron, but Kara declined because Zoey, Jen, and Dani would all be there, and Kara thought it best to not put Dani in an awkward position in case they ran into each other. "No. Dani's gonna be there."

"Oh. Okay. I'm gonna go check on the kennel dogs."

Kara sank to the ground and sifted through the box, pulling out old puzzles and toys she would take to Seattle Children's Hospital. The last things in the box were all her cherished children's books. She paged through the first one. Reading the words took her back to when she was small and her mom would read to her every night before bed.

Kara was ready to put the box aside when she spotted one more book at the bottom. She hesitated. A sudden chill tickled her spine, and goose bumps pimpled her arms. Odd. It was hot and stuffy in the barn. The haunting déjà vu sensation came back with a vengeance. The clouded memory that had been dancing on the edge of her consciousness for the last half a year reappeared, only this time the tendrils of fog started swirling away.

"Oh. My. God."

* * *

Kara spent half an hour weaving in and out of the slow-moving Saturday morning traffic, almost getting creamed twice. At one point she blew a red light, and flashing lights appeared in the rearview mirror. "Fuck me. Goddamn it!"

For a fleeting moment, Kara thought about gunning it, consequences be damned. But she didn't need to get arrested, so she pulled over. Christ. This was going to be an expensive ticket. But instead of stopping behind her, the unmarked car pulled alongside with a familiar face behind the wheel. Kara's mood brightened.

"Hey, hot stuff. You late for something?" Jesmyn asked.

Relief and excitement coursed through her body. "I need to get to that flea market at Travis's school. I've gotta find Dani right away."

"Follow me." She pulled in front, and Kara followed the police escort all the way to the school.

When they arrived, Kara puttered up and down the aisles in the parking lot. *Jesus. This place is packed.* Jesmyn was on a reconnaissance mission in the next row and beeped her horn. She'd found an empty spot.

Kara headed over and parked, grabbing the book before locking her car.

"Good luck," Jes called.

Kara pointed in her direction. "I owe you!" She raced toward the entrance of the school and pushed through the glass front doors. The flea market was in the gymnasium at the back of the building, and when she entered the gym, she skidded to a stop. It was packed with people. She fired off a text to Zoey. *Are you still at the flea market?*

Yeah, why?

Is Dani with you? Need to find her asap.
She wandered off. We'll look for her!

Kara found a vacant metal folding chair and stood on it, hoping for a better view. She scanned the crowd, her eyes landing on every redhead, only to be disappointed when an unfamiliar face was revealed. She ignored the smells surrounding her. Burgers, fries, hot dogs. And even though she'd barely eaten, she wasn't hungry. This was not the time to eat.

* * *

Dani wandered aimlessly up and down the aisles, stopping at one table filled with cat toys. She smiled, her mind immediately going to Kara and the kittens. She fingered them and bit her lip. Without hesitation, she handed over five dollars for the catnip-filled mice. Thumper and Tigger would have a field day with these.

Her belly rumbled from lack of food. Breakfast had been a power bar, not enough sustenance for her and the baby. Maybe she could grab a quick snack before she headed out, since dinner wasn't until later tonight.

A wave of dread washed over her. *Dinner. Ugh. Should be fun.* Will was going to be there, along with both sets of parents. They'd be pressing for a decision and kicking up a fuss when Dani would say there was no decision yet. Although they wouldn't make too much of a fuss. One didn't make a scene at Altura, one of the most expensive restaurants in Seattle.

She continued walking and stopped at the end of the aisle. Groups of students, sporting their school hoodies, played hacky sack. She smiled. Was hacky sack still a thing? The kids showed off some mad skills. There were five or six kids per circle, four circles total. Travis was in one of the groups, and when he spotted her he lost his concentration, and the hacky hit him in the chest and dropped to the ground. There was much gesturing and signing, and Dani assumed he was getting some serious shit for letting the sack hit the ground. With a sheepish grin and pinkened cheeks, he waved.

Dani signed, *You look good,* and his grin widened while signing a response, but her ASL was still very limited and she had no clue what he was saying. She tried to convey that fact to him by shaking her head and lifting her shoulders, all of which just made him laugh. A boy next to him gave him a playful shove and his attention turned back to the game.

What a great kid. Dani's hand went to her belly. Would she have a rough-and-tumble boy? Or a little girl, full of sass and spunk. *Sass and spunk.* Kara probably was full of sass and spunk growing up. She took out her phone and pulled up the picture Jen had sent: Kara smiling while tiny Jon-Jon slept on her chest. Tears welled into her eyes. Kara had learned how to baby. For her. To prove herself to Dani.

A rush of love overwhelmed her, so much so that she nearly toppled over. Images of their time together played like a movie in her head. The motorcycle rides. The golf outing. The paintball. The kisses. Making love in the bathtub. All of them assaulted her senses and snatched her breath away. She hungered for Kara's kisses. She ached to hold her in her arms. Nobody had ever affected Dani this way. Nobody.

What in God's name am I doing? All these weeks of torturing herself over "the decision." There was no decision to make. It was a done deal. She was in love. She wanted to be with Kara, and goddamn it, that's what she would do. It was time to grow those lady balls Zoey always talked about. Consequences be damned.

She'd go to the farm now and beg Kara to forgive her. Forgive her for being so foolish. Forgive her for not believing in them. Her heart pounded with excitement at the thought of being with her again.

But first, she needed break the news to Will and her parents. She took out her phone and headed to a nearby hallway. Tucking herself into a quiet alcove, she inhaled before punching in Will's number.

He answered on the second ring. "Everything okay?"

A small sigh escaped her lips. "I'm not coming to dinner."

"Are you sick?"

"No, I'm fine." She took a moment to gather her thoughts. "Listen. You know this last month has been a struggle for me, trying to decide what to do."

"I know."

"Well, I've decided." She crouched down and leaned against the wall. The muscles in her stomach tensed. "I'm in love with Kara, and I wanna be with her."

"Uh…oh."

"I'm so sorry. I know you probably hate me."

She was met with silence, and she blinked her eyes to keep the tears at bay. Somehow, his hating her would be too much to bear.

His soft voice finally echoed over the phone. "I could never hate you." He took a breath before continuing, "I've been doing a lot of thinking also. I keep going back to what you said that day, that you loved me but you weren't in love with me. And at first, I was devastated. But the more I thought about it, the more I could see what you meant. We were such good friends, and when we started dating, everyone said we were the perfect couple. Our parents were ecstatic and pushed us to get married. And I think we both got caught up in being perfect and making everyone happy. We got along so well, so being together was easy. But…we both deserve to be in love, and to be with someone who's in love with us."

"We do. You do." The tension in her body eased. They were going to be okay. "I hope you're still excited about the baby because I want you to be a big part of his or her life."

"I'm super excited, and I can't wait."

After hanging up with Will, Dani stared at her mother's number. The tension that had eased a few minutes ago came roaring back. Did she have the strength to do this? Did she have the lady balls?

But then something happened. Confidence took root and grew. It swelled inside her chest, blooming like a rose on the vine. It was time to live her own life. It was time to find her own happiness. She tapped the call button.

"Hello?"

"Hey, Mom."

"Is something wrong?"

"No. Well, yes. I'm not coming to dinner." She waited for the explosion.

"Why? Are you not feeling well?"

"No, I'm feeling great. I'm just not coming to dinner. I made other plans." Other plans that hopefully included a certain claw-foot tub. And with that thought, Dani's resolve became stronger.

"We made reservations. The Kincaids are coming."

"I know. I'm sorry. I talked to Will. He's not coming either."

With each response, her mom's voice rose in volume. "What…what is going on? I'm putting you on speaker so your father can hear this."

Dani slid to the floor and stretched her legs out. "Hi, Dad."

"Dani? Why is your mother upset?"

"Because I'm not coming to dinner," she stated matter-of-factly. Her newfound confidence was awesome. And sort of fun. "I'm in love. And it's not with Will. It's with Kara." *That felt good.*

"Who is Kara?" her mom demanded.

"She's my girlfriend." *Oh, that felt really good.*

"What about the baby?"

Dani flicked a piece of lint off her jeans. "For now, I'll be a single mom."

"This is ridiculous. You need to marry Will," her mom demanded.

"No, I don't. This is my life. And I'm gonna start living it. I gotta go. I'll talk to you guys later." She disconnected the call and rested her head against the wall. A small smile tickled her lips. A soft chuckle followed.

"'Bout time, girl," she announced to no one in particular.

* * *

Kara kept texting everyone. Evidently, Dani had disappeared into thin air. She wanted to hurl her phone into the cosmos but tucked it into her back pocket instead. With clenched fists, she growled in frustration.

Her back pocket vibrated, and she yanked her phone back out.

She's over by the outdoor exit.

Kara's heart jumped into her throat. *Thank God!* She began pushing her way through the throngs of people, cursing every time she had to stop. She strained her neck and caught sight of Dani, who was headed for the door. *Shit!* At least forty yards still separated them. "Dani!" Her bellow bounced off the walls of the gym, and Dani twirled around.

"Kara?"

The crowd stopped moving and everyone stared.

"Don't move. Stay there!"

Perhaps sensing Kara's anxiousness, the throng of onlookers parted like the Red Sea, and an alley opened up between her and Dani. She rushed forward and stood in front of the woman she loved.

"What are you doing here?" Dani asked.

Kara's confidence wavered. An eerie silence had descended. The crowd hadn't dispersed; in fact it was growing. Zoey and Jen appeared, popcorn in hand, and Travis and his friends had formed a circle around them. With deft hands, he gave the kids a blow-by-blow of the situation.

Kara hadn't prepared to give her speech in front of this many people, and her mind went blank. She licked her lips nervously. Sweat trickled down her back. Travis beamed a smile in her direction, and she steadied herself. *Your happiness depends on this moment, so get it together!* "I found this book. You made it for me when we were six years old."

"What?" Dani inched closer.

Kara showed her the book. It was obvious a child had drawn the picture on the front. It was a woman with long hair in a lab coat with a stethoscope hanging around her neck. "You brought this to me when I was in the hospital. I was getting my tonsils out. You stayed with me to make me feel better. We ate ice cream and chocolate pudding and you said we'd be together forever. You wrote that in the book. I found it today in a box of old stuff, and…it was like a sign or something." Kara was rambling and probably not making any sense, but she needed to convince Dani to give them a chance. And most of all, she had to tell Dani how much she loved her.

Dani reached for the book.

Travis signed away, and the kids shifted and smiled. Some elbowed each other and giggled. Others' mouths just hung open as they took it all in.

Kara stood next to her while Dani opened the book. On page one was a picture of the doctor from the cover and a young girl with big green eyes and a bandage around her throat. The caption said, *Dr. Becca sees Kari*. As Dani flipped the pages, her eyes filled with tears. "I remember making this. You're my Kari?"

"Yes." Tears leaked from both their eyes.

Dani cupped Kara's cheek. "I never could get your name right."

"I know. And it's really not that difficult."

"But it's kinda charming, right?"

"It's very charming."

"I always say, it's better to be charming than right."

"Is that what you say?"

"Yes, Kari. That's what I say." Dani chuckled. "I can't believe you kept it all this time." She continued to page through the book. "Here's our farm, with all the puppies and kittens." She gently bumped her shoulder into Kara's. "You loved puppies."

Kara bumped her back. "You loved kittens. And you insisted they'd all get along."

"Well, they would've."

"You stole chocolate puddings from the lunch cart."

"It was good pudding." Dani turned to the last page and placed a hand at the base of her throat. "I remember drawing this." On the page, in big blocky red letters inside a heart, were the words, *Danielle and Kari Forever.*

Kara moved in front of Dani and placed her hands on Dani's forearms. "Come with me. Right now. Take a chance on us. Please. I've been practicing with Jon-Jon. I can do this. I know I can handle it. And I swear, I'll make you and the baby happy." Kara paused and gazed into her favorite pair of blue eyes. "You've tamed me, Dani Clark. I'm in love with you. I'm *so* in love with you." Her voice strengthened. "And I dare you to love me back."

A serious expression settled on Dani's features, and she glanced down at the book.

Kara held her breath. *Oh God, she doesn't love me. She's not taking the dare!*

With her head still bowed, Dani said, "Well. Truth be told, I was headed out to the farm right now." When she looked up, her eyes sparkled. "You see, I don't have to take your dare." She leaned in and placed a soft kiss on Kara's lips. "I'm already in love with you."

All of Kara's anguish from the last month drifted away and was replaced with infinite joy. And rightness. She wrapped her arms around Dani and gave her a twirl. When she set her down, she returned the kiss—not quite as passionately as she would have liked because they had a G-rated audience. But she did add a touch of drama and dipped Dani low before bringing her back up.

Zoey whooped while the kids clapped and laughed. The adults in the crowd dispersed now that the ending no longer hung in the balance.

Kara rested her forehead against Dani's. "So, you had already decided to come back."

"Yeah."

"I didn't have to make a speech in front of a thousand people?"

"No. Probably not."

"You just let me go on and on."

"You seemed to be on a roll. I didn't wanna interrupt."

Kara tried to look stern. "I feel like you've done this before."

"I have…Karen."

Kara chuckled at the familiar moniker. "I've missed you so much."

Dani wrapped her arms around Kara's neck and whispered into her ear, "I've been dying without you. I'm so sorry. I need to make it up to you somehow."

Kara pulled back and wiggled her eyebrows. "I can think of a few ways for you to do that."

Dani grinned at the innuendo. "Let's get the hell outta here."

"Did you drive?"

"No, I Ubered over with Zoe and Jen."

They walked hand and hand out to the parking lot. Every few feet they came together to share a kiss. It was slow going, but neither was in a rush.

As they crawled along with the traffic on Meridian Avenue, a car pulled next to them and they both glanced at the occupants. The Walkers laughed and waved.

"Hi, guys!" Jolie snapped a photo with her phone.

Kara waved back. "Hi, Walkers."

You drive slow, Travis signed.

"I know, buddy. I've got precious cargo." She winked and nodded her head at Dani.

"You both need to come over for dinner next week," Aaron called from the driver's side of the car.

"Sure. What can we bring?" Kara asked.

"I hope you're making brownies," Dani implored.

"Brownies would be great," Jolie agreed. "Text me and we'll pick a day."

The Walkers moved on.

A small toot of a horn alerted them to another car pulling alongside.

Zoey hung from the back window like a Labrador retriever. "Jesus Christ, I could run faster than you're going." They'd hitched a ride with Jesmyn and were cozied up in the back of her squad car.

"You finally getting arrested for something, I hope?" Dani asked.

Zoey made a face. "Very funny." She rested an elbow on the door and put her chin in her hand. "When you guys take a break from having sex, give us a call. Here." Zoey tossed a baggie through the open back window.

"Oh, shit, popcorn." Dani laughed and opened the bag. She fed Kara one kernel at a time.

Jesmyn pulled away, with Zoey and Jen screaming, "Kardi forever!"

* * *

Three hours later, they relaxed in the claw-foot tub.

"I love this tub." Dani sank low in the water. Bubbles danced along the tops of her breasts.

Kara admired the view from the opposite end. "Mm-hmm. I love you in this tub."

Dani giggled. Her mind was clear and quiet. All the pain and indecision from the last month was long forgotten. She was where she belonged. In Kara's arms.

They'd made love as soon as they fell through the front door. And it was as spectacular as before. Dani leaned forward and kissed her. "Hey, where's my cap?"

"Oh, shit, hold on." Kara rose from the tub and took a naked, dripping romp through the house in search of one duck-covered shower cap. Returning quickly, she splashed back in and affixed the cap to Dani's head.

"Where was it?"

"In the drawer in the other bathroom. I had to put it away. It reminded me too much of you." Kara situated herself behind Dani, and her hands wandered aimlessly over her body. They were sated and sleepy.

Dani closed her eyes and sighed. "I missed you so much. I couldn't breathe without you," she whispered. "I saw you with Rachel. And I was so jealous."

"Nothing happened with Rachel, silly."

"I know. I was an idiot." Dani placed a soft kiss on Kara's lips. "When Ethan called me that day to tell me you were in an accident, I almost died thinking something happened to you. I knew then. I knew I was in love with you. But then I found out I was pregnant. I had this tiny being inside who needed me, and I was confused and scared."

Kara tightened her embrace. "It's okay. I can't even imagine what you were going through."

"I'm sorry."

"No more apologies, baby. New rule."

"Can you forgive me for doubting us?"

"I've already forgiven you."

Dani turned in Kara's arms and melded herself closer. "Okay."

"Have you talked to Will?"

Kara's hands stroked her back and she quietly moaned before answering. "I talked to Will before you found me at the fair. I told him everything. He sounded relieved, in a way."

"What about your parents?"

Wandering hands brushed the sides of her breasts and her breath hitched. "I talked to them also."

The hands stopped and Dani felt Kara's body tense. "And?"

Dani shrugged. "They weren't happy. But I guess if they wanna see their grandchild, they'll accept my decision. And they'll accept you." She kissed Kara again, and as it was with most of their kisses, things became heated in an instant. Dani took Kara's hand and placed it between her legs.

Before long, her cries of pleasure echoed around the room and her body quaked, sending water over the side of the tub. Dani collapsed against Kara's body. "Uhhh…fuck. I love sex in this tub." She sighed in pleasure, her words slow and languorous. "You're good at this."

"Am I champion again?"

"Yes. You're champion. I relinquish my previously claimed title. That I stole from you an hour ago."

"Just so you know, you can try and steal it back. *Try* being the operative word. Cause I'm not sure you can."

Dani raised her brows. "Is that a dare?"

Kara chuckled. "Yes. I dare you to steal it back."

Dani perked up at the challenge. This particular dare promised to be the sweetest of all. She maneuvered herself into Kara's lap, purring, "I'll take that dare…"

They were both ready for a lifetime of dares.

Bella Books, Inc.

Women. Books. Even Better Together.

P.O. Box 10543
Tallahassee, FL 32302

Phone: 800-729-4992
www.bellabooks.com